MW00577701

Hit The Road, Jake!

The Lindsey Lark Series

Book Three

Cricket Rohman

Cricket Rohman

Cover design & interior formatting by
Sweet 'N Spicy Designs

Author photos by Curtis Ryan

ISBN: 9780989697170

Novels by
Cricket Rohman

THE LINDSEY LARK SERIES
Wanted: An Honest Man, Book 1
Letters, Lovers, & Lies, Book 2
Hit the Road, Jake!, Book 3

For my modern day Jeremiah

Acknowledgments

I would like to thank:

My feedback readers: Pat Vreeland, Carol Anfinson, Sharon Campbell, and Diane Rayburn.

Designer, Jaycee DeLorenzo for her creativity, technical knowledge, speed, and patience.

The town of Estes Park, Colorado and the Rocky Mountain National Park just for being there. I couldn't have asked for a better place to grow up and gather magnificent memories.

PROLOGUE

No one could deny the young woman's ambitious nature. She knew exactly what she wanted and, more often than not, she got it. Her latest meticulous, foolproof plan had been in development for over a year, not because she possessed the virtue of patience, but rather she fixated on perfection and refused to settle for anything less.

Heads turned as she walked down the city street with the gait and poise of a runway model. Deep in thought, she barely noticed those looks of appreciation. Unable to push today's surprising predicament from her thoughts, her pace slowed, then stopped. This disruption proved to be as sickening as the smell of singed hair and burned flesh on a young cow's hide. Breathe. Breathe. She desperately needed to breathe.

With a deliberate intake of fresh air she refocused on the big picture, determined to keep this mere hiccup, this untimely detour, from destroying her self-made destiny. No. Too many years of hard work would not go to waste. She'd let nothing prevent the fulfillment of her lifelong ambition. Nothing. And especially . . . not this.

Thirty-eight years later . . .

NORTHERN ARIZONA:

THE FIRST STOP

ONE

Lindsey

This time, no one would be left behind.

The house was closed up tight. Jake double-checked all the windows and doors as I looked over the items we'd packed in the RV. We'd be on the road and residing in our home-on-wheels for almost six weeks and I wanted everything to be perfect. Perfect for Jake, my husband of eighteen months, who was also my best friend, my novella writer, my PhD, my detective, my pet daddy, the man who made me smile, even laugh . . . my everything.

After a year of working for Elisabeth Meriwether and her educational corporation as a consultant and keynote speaker, I was now doing my own thing, self-employed, with Jake as my partner, my partner in crime. Hopefully, *crime* was too strong of a word, but we'd definitely be a team working together to solve educational mini-mysteries. No more separation, not even from the pets—Wendell, our giant-sized tan mastiff and Malcolm, our little white cockatiel. They'd be right here with us every step of the way.

"I think the property is secure. How are we doing in here? Come on, Ms. List Lady. You must have a checklist for the RV's readiness."

"Is it that obvious?"

I detected a hint of that boyish grin I loved so much. "Well, you are the most organized woman I know."

"But I write on Post-its. A pile of Post-its is not a list." We often teased each other, bantering back and forth, adding fun to our already playful lives.

"I love you, Lindsey. Post-its and all."

Subtly, I glanced down at my stack of little paper squares: dog food, check; bird food, check; phones, computers, notepads and folders, four checks. I removed the Flagstaff school's folder from the plastic file box so we could review and discuss its information during the drive north.

Malcolm sat happily in his cage, which was snugly attached to the side bench with a seatbelt. Wendell sat ready to ride shotgun as if he'd done that before. Hmm. I was fairly sure that my eyes flashed a stealthy teacher look at Jake who innocently shrugged his shoulders and motioned for the dog to move. And, off we drove, leaving Tucson and the saguaro cacti behind. Our road trip, our new adventure, had officially begun.

The interior of the RV was calm and quiet except for the occasional chirp followed by a soft woof. How does a dog that big make such a tiny little sound as if he were whispering? Sometimes, when I observed the two of them together, they seemed to converse in a unique language comprehensible only to each other. Or, possibly, I just had a great imagination.

Once through the Phoenix traffic, I took a serious look at the Flagstaff folder. We'd selected this specific location and school for several reasons: it was relatively close to home and the requester's needs seemed simple, almost too easy, in fact. But 'easy' was a good starting place. After all, we were new at this.

This. What was *this*? Jake and I had attempted to define it, name it, to no avail. Our lack of a decent definition wasn't all that surprising though, because we were creating *this* as we went along.

We knew that a problem beyond the boundaries of everyday education, a mystery of sorts, existed at each site. The person or persons wanting solutions also wanted to avoid police or media involvement that could lead to bad publicity for their schools or districts. And, they didn't wish to alarm others—students, families, teachers, staff, or the local community—unnecessarily. That was where Jake came in. He was the mystery man, the fact finder, the problem solver.

To give our presence a legitimate purpose, I would work with teachers, staff, or students in an educational consulting capacity—workshops, meetings, instructional observations—that the requester had chosen from my menu of topics. Jake liked to call that our 'cover.' We would each contribute our expertise while in the midst of doing what we loved: teaching, solving problems and mysteries, and being together. It was perfect.

"The more I look at Mr. Farley's application, Jake, the more I think we've booked too much time for him and his problem. And now I'm wondering why we book him at all."

"The way I see it, that's a plus. More time for us to play, to hike in the forest, to . . . well, you know."

I nodded. I did know. We were so much in love. And in spite of the threats, the danger, the trauma we'd endured in the past, now, with this wonderful adventure ahead of us, we felt like newlyweds once again.

"I suspect our Mr. Farley is quite a character or perhaps he's getting up there in age. He's the only potential client who filled out his application by hand and sent it via snail mail."

Jake nodded, keeping his eyes on the road, letting me know that he agreed with my reasoning. A good amount of time and creative energy had gone into the design of our user-friendly, online form; it required a minimal amount of input and could be returned with the click of a key. I continued to peruse the application.

"He selected 'Setting Up Writing Centers' from the menu of topics, and his only non-educational issue is the theft of some bricks, some plants, and some files. Seems too simple."

"That's why we selected it. Remember? We wanted *easy* this first time out."

"You're right, but still, I find it odd that he'd call us in to help with a minor theft."

We drove the RV into the campground and around the three loops of sites that it offered. Just a little over five hours from Tucson and yet it felt like another world—a cool, green, forested world.

"Hey, how about over there, Linds? That looks like a good spot."

They all looked good to me, but Jake knew that our state-of-the-art, sizeable RV wouldn't fit in just any campsite, and because he'd only driven this vehicle a few times, I think he wanted a site where he could pull straight in without needing to use any tricky maneuvers. I appreciated his caution and I also hoped to keep our magnificent RV dent-free.

TWO

Jake

Today was our first official workday. Within an hour, we'd be face to face with our first client and his school theft problems.

After waking from a restful night's sleep with my woman still in my arms, I'd slid out of bed quietly, turned on the coffee machine, and went outside to unhook the Jeep Liberty we'd towed behind the RV. Before completing that task, Lindsey was at my side with a steaming cup of coffee. We took Wendell for a short walk, then headed into the town of Flagstaff to the Denny's restaurant where our first meeting with Mr. Farley would take place.

A stocky man I presumed to be in his sixties moved stiffly toward us with an outstretched hand and said, "Bud Farley, here." Then, with a wink he added, "If it isn't Sherlock Holmes and Dr. Watson."

Before we could lower our raised eyebrows, I whispered in Lindsey's ear, "We will discuss that later."

With steaming hot coffee all creamed and sugared before us, I began.

"So, late last March some bricks disappeared; late in April some plants and bushes turned up missing; and at the end of May, you think someone stole student files. Do I have that correct?"

"Yep. That's what happened," confirmed Mr. Farley.

"So, you'd like us to track down this petty thief?"

"Yes, indeedy! But you've got to know that when the thief brought his petty crimes into the building, it got more serious and not so petty. I called the school safety department soon after the files went missing and they came out right away, but they considered it a minor act of vandalism and did next to nothing. Just wrote a report. They didn't get it; stealing student files—the ones we have to keep locked up—is a problem. And . . . it would not look good on any principal's evaluation."

Lindsey sat, quietly listening, obviously thinking before speaking up. "He's right, Jake. That is big. And it's odd."

"Why?" When it came to understanding elementary school issues, procedures, and even mysteries, Lindsey was the expert.

"Think about it. Who would be interested in or want to take every student's elementary school data? A disgruntled parent might want their child's file, but they could have that information any time. All they'd have to do is request a copy."

Mr. Farley began to sweat. A few beads formed on his forehead, and those armpits? *Whoa!* The telltale damp darkness on his pale blue shirt was expanding quicker than an oil spill on a calm body of water. Was he feeling anxious? Was he lying about something? Hmm. Interesting.

"Here's the thing. I found a file in the principal's desk and—"

Lindsey interrupted his statement. "I'm sorry. You just lost me. You're the principal, right?"

"No. Not exactly. I'm just filling in till he comes back." His eyes seemed fixed upon his own index fingers that tapped the table as he spoke.

"So you were not the principal when this all began?" This new fact was a small thing, but in my experience I've learned that little things can, ultimately, be highly significant.

"You got that right. I was retired, playing golf when I got the call." He must not play that often. No trace of a golf-tan on his puffy, pale skin. And wouldn't that big beer belly interfere with his swing? If Lindsey had heard my unkind thoughts, she'd be giving me a little kick under the table. To me, they were just . . . observations.

"The principal took some sort of medical leave. I was only supposed to be here for a few weeks in May. Being the end of the school year and all, I was going to let it go, move on, just hold down the fort, ya know? But when the files turned up missing on my watch and the school safety guys did nothing, and then that follow-up note arrived, well, I started nosing around for some help and found you guys. So, here we are."

A follow-up note? Perhaps there was more to this small mystery than we'd anticipated. No doubt the plot was thickening like turkey drippings receiving another spoonful of flour. Lindsey and I looked at each other with questioning eyes, wondering what could or should be done. For now, without the opportunity to confer beyond our non-verbal communication, I began an altered line of questioning.

"Has anything new or unusual occurred since you received that follow-up note?"

"Yes. But before I go on, there is something you need to know. When I filled out your application form, I thought this would be a piece of cake for you guys and that you might not mind if I didn't have a "donation" for your, you know, your snooping around stuff, because I don't—"

"That's all right, Mr. Farley," Lindsey jumped in. "Don't worry about that. My fee for working with your teachers will be sufficient."

A huge smile spread across the man's pudgy, dimpled face. "But I was able to get the district to pay $400 a day for you instead of your rate of $350." He was obviously delighted with this financial deal he had orchestrated. We smiled right back at him.

"Please go on with your new information, Mr. Farley."

"Aw, hey. Call me Bud, you guys. Got another note a couple of weeks ago. Not a follow-up, though. It was more like an advanced warning. If it's true, this guy intends to destroy our computer lab soon. That would be awful. The teachers and the students use it regularly. And the computers are only a year old. Things are escalating. I really want to get this son of a bitch!"

We attempted to make a list of possible suspects based upon my questions and Bud's replies. I learned that he had no personal enemies except that one of his golf buddies was often mad at him because Bud always won, plus the guy hated being referred to as one of Bud's buddies. His complete answer to my simple question was much longer and resembled an unrelated story with far too much information. I'd work on clarifying the facts and speeding things up.

"Any upset staff members that you know of?"

"Ppfff. We have an all-female teaching staff and you know how women are. So sure, at least one or more has a beef about something, but it's always trivial stuff." I could see it in her face, her disapproval regarding his sexist statement, and I'd hoped she'd suppress it for now. Luckily, Bud continued before I needed to send an under the table, non-verbal message of my own.

"Some are just grumpy people. Most are great. I can't imagine anyone here stooping so low, hurting their own school, and in such a strange way. It's not like teachers have much free time on their hands."

Okay. So much for speeding things up. "Who has keys to the building?"

Shrugging his shoulders, Bud replied, "Almost everyone has a front entrance key."

"What about the locked filing cabinets that house the confidential student files?"

"Just me and the office manager. You're gonna like her. She's a real sweetie."

Okay. We were on a roll now, picking up speed. "And the computer lab. Who has access to that?"

"Just the custodian; he's a guy. Seems to be a good guy. At least he does his job. I think there is another lab key in the lockbox inside of the vault. But, heck, anyone with a strong arm and a crow bar could probably break into the lab *sans* a key."

Bud paused, waiting for our reaction. When one did not come, he informed us, quite proudly, that *sans* meant 'without.' Pretty sure he'd just recently added a new and foreign word to his vocabulary.

"Last question. The building is alarmed, right?" The positive nod I'd assumed would come, did. "Who knows how to operate that system, how to turn it on and off?"

"Just the office manager, the custodian, and the district's school safety staff. That's about it. I used to know, but that's not the kind of thing a retired guy like me remembers, if you get my drift?"

I didn't, but proceeded to stand up anyway preparing for our get away. Ooops, I meant departure. Bud handed Lindsey a rather thick file folder, which she peeked into while we walked toward the restaurant's exit. I informed him that we'd study the folder's contents over the weekend and put together an initial plan by Monday morning. *So much for a list of suspects—if I could put one together, it would fit on one of Lindsey's Post-its. One of the tiny ones.* Since no specific individuals stood out yet, everyone was a suspect, even Bud. No need to write the word *everyone* down.

"Please remember to keep this investigation off the grid. For now, all your staff members need to know is that we are here so Lindsey can work with your teachers setting up writing centers. Only those topics will be discussed on school grounds. Okay? And, you need to learn how to set the school's alarm system ... today!"

"Oh, Bud?" asked Lindsey as we stood in the parking lot. "Was the regular principal's name Jack by any chance?" Her question was so out in left field. I'd hoped my face wasn't too contorted.

"No. Not Jack. Homer. His name is Homer."

What did she know that I didn't know?

THREE

Jake

I was all set to get my kicks on Route 66. So, after driving around the school's perimeter a few times, scoping out the lay of the land, we donned our tourist hats and explored Flagstaff. Some of our exploration was on foot, but most of the sights were viewed from the car. Lindsey couldn't get enough of the fresh pine scent that permeated the air and I found it fun to be driving almost side by side with a train. We were easily amused.

"We should get back," Lindsey reminded me. "There's no doggie door on the RV."

She was right, as usual. And, we were famished. Pulling up to the campsite we could see our dog's huge head peering out the side window, wearing his *welcome home* smile. The second we opened the RV's door, he over-powered us with his wagging tail, jumping body, and licking tongue. We laughed and leaped around like kids matching the energy of our wonderful dog.

"We missed you, too, Wendell."

Outside, I gathered some dried pine needles, twigs, and branches and proceeded to build a fire. Lindsey added a few bricks of charcoal just to make sure our fire was perfect for cooking the turkey dogs on skewers and the corn on the cob wrapped in foil. Does food cooked over a fire really taste better than food cooked in a kitchen? It seemed to. Or were we just in a better frame of mind out here in the forest? Didn't matter; it was all good.

"Our Mr. Farley sure is an odd fellow. Did you hear his Sherlock comment, Lindsey?"

"I certainly did, and I have but one comment of my own about that issue. Who's who?"

"Uh, that's more of a question than a comment, but since you asked, I am the doctor in the family, PhD and all, so shouldn't I be Dr. Watson?"

"Nope. A PhD does not qualify you for that. Besides, I called you Sherlock first, a long time ago. Remember?"

"Yeah. Maybe. But these additional names are just between us. There will be no *Sherlocking* me in public. Agreed?"

She hesitated and then slowly replied, "Sure." My Lindsey is a brilliant and humorous woman.

The sun dipped below the surrounding tree-covered hills and the temperature plummeted. Not yet ready to go inside, we put warm jackets on our bodies and another log on the fire. Then, wow! Déjà vu! Thoughts, memories of our time together two summers ago, in the Zuni Mountains, flooded in.

"Lindsey?"

"This feels familiar, doesn't it?" Her thoughts had traveled the same path as mine. We held hands and reminisced. "That's when we fell in love." She spoke with a dreamy, whispery, far away voice.

"That is when *you* fell in love; I'd already loved you for months."

15

She looked surprised. "Really?"

"Really."

"How many months?"

"Hmm. About eight or nine."

"But that would mean . . . "

"Yes. For me it was almost *love at first sight*. I could not get you out of my mind since that night I delivered Chinese food to your house . . . to you."

"Oh, my."

We sat in silence for a while, the only sound was the crackling of the fire. Then, glancing back at the RV she continued. "It does feel like that wonderful night in Zuni except that instead of sleeping in a distressed, old tent we've upgraded to a luxurious RV. Though with the presence of Wendell, Malcolm, and all of our stuff, it still feels . . . kind of cozy."

"And that, my dear woman, sounds like a song."

"Oh, Jake. I really wish I could sing or write music like a pro. Perhaps in another lifetime."

"In the meantime, we'll make do with the talents we've got."

I took her hand, led her into the RV, then back toward the bed, singing all the while. "Gonna get cozy . . . in the camper." Wendell mumbled, Malcolm chirped, and, if I'm not mistaken, Lindsey cringed.

"Sherlock becomes Johnny One Note before my very eyes. Or should I say ears? You do have more than one note in your repertoire, right?"

"Of course, I do. Just not when I'm singing." My smart-aleck side had surfaced and the look on her face told me I'd be wise to smother her with kisses before she could vocalize her own clever reply. Ah, sweet wisdom.

FOUR

Lindsey

Do I dare look? Yes! I checked the mirror in the tiny bathroom. Staring back at me was a mass of tousled hair and a very contented, glowing face thanks to Jake's never-ending love for me, and his continuing education when it came to bedroom techniques. Yes. I looked exactly the way I felt: happy as a lark and oh, so satisfied.

Jake aimed to please, not just in the bedroom, so when I requested that we put off any serious work for a couple of hours and take Wendell for a real hike, he was good with that. In fact, he loved the idea.

We threw a few dog biscuits and granola bars into the backpack, grabbed two canteens, one for the humans and the other for the dog, locked the RV, and walked toward a trailhead we'd spotted yesterday.

The trail was curvy and, so far, mostly uphill. We'd gone half a mile according to the trail marker, though it seemed like more, when Wendell turned around, facing downhill, and sat. Just sat. We coaxed him to keep

17

walking with us, which he did, but he repeated his 'turn around, sit down' behavior over and over. So we sat down with him for a while trying to figure out what was going on in our big dog's brain.

"Maybe he doesn't feel well. The altitude is a lot higher here than it is in Tucson, especially now that we've been walking up hill for an hour."

"Or, possibly, he's showing concern for Malcolm. We left him behind, alone."

Without any additional discussion, we all rose up and headed down the trail. No more sitting for Wendell. In fact, he moved so quickly, we could barely keep up with him.

Through the window we could see Malcolm perched peacefully in his cage. He was fine. But our dog, that was another matter. He couldn't settle down. "Oh, Wendell, I don't understand what's going on with you. During the hike all you wanted to do was sit, and now that we've returned and we want to sit, you're pacing back and forth like an expectant father."

"You're right, Lindsey. He is acting strange, almost anxious. Wendell, you are carrying on like you've got bees in your bonnet."

Well, that broke the tension. My jaw dropped, my head turned toward Jake as I attempted to speak through my laughter. "Where on earth did *that* come from? You just aged thirty years right before my eyes. Hmm. For an encore you could wear the cat's pajamas. I remember my dad saying that when I was a small child. I also remember him telling me that was an old-fashioned saying back then. So it must be ancient by now."

Jake remained speechless for a few seconds; the perfect comeback evaded him, so he said, "I'll get the dog a few biscuits. Food always helps. It will take his mind off . . . whatever."

My helpful Jake, always wanting to fix the problem at hand. He jumped up, skipping the bottom step at the RV's entrance. That's when I heard it. Snap! Crunch! Crash! Followed by stifled moans and groans of pain.

"Jake, are you all right?" He definitely did not sound all right.

The step had come apart, fallen to the ground, as Jake had put his weight on it. That made no sense to me. Jake was not a heavy man; in fact, fit and trim are the words that come to mind. And this was a state-of-the-art, practically new motor home.

"I'll get the snacks for Wendell and some ice for you."

"Grab some aspirin and a bottle of wine while you're at it," he requested as he hopped to the picnic table to sit and elevate his ankle. The swelling was already off to a good start.

On my second trip to and from the RV, I brought Bud's folder out along with Jake's laptop. He wanted to get to work. Said it would take his mind off the throbbing. I had my doubts about the effectiveness of his deductive reasoning considering the combination of his pain, the aspirin, and the wine. Oh, well. I had my project, and Jake had his. We each got down to work at our picnic table in the woods. What a life! Who could ask for more?

Before I could even open my own packet of materials, Jake spoke up. "Oh, now I get why you asked Bud if the principal's name was Jack. Did you get to read any of this?"

"Nope. Just glanced long enough to see that the rhyme 'The House that Jack Built' was mentioned."

"Lindsey, you've got to see this stuff. I am going to need your help."

Jake flipped back to the first page in the folder. The original principal—whose name was not Jack—had scribbled a hand-written note that said:

Third weekend in March our stack of bricks out back went missing. Value about $200. The parent gardening group was planning on building a brick path around the soon-to-be upgraded and planted garden area. I'll ask the PTO to replace the stolen bricks. HB

We went on to page 2, which was the follow-up note. There was no envelope, though. Jake jotted down (on one of my Post-its, a pink one) to check with Bud about the envelope or at least find out how the note had arrived at the school. Not many words appeared in this note, but the letters in those few words were enlarged so they filled up most of the page.

THIS WAS THE HOUSE THAT JACK FOOLISHLY BUILT

The note included a hand-written comment from HB, too. We both assumed the 'H' stood for Homer.

Because this arrived April 1, I'm thinking it is someone's idea of an April Fool's joke albeit a joke possibly involved with a theft on our school's campus. HB

"His assumption is a good one not only because of the timing but also because the root word 'fool' has been added to the first line of the rhyme."

Jake had his thinking face on. "So 'foolishly' is not in the original version?"

I shook my head and explained that it wasn't part of any version I knew of. We examined this tiny bit of evidence from every angle. Some bricks were stolen, then a rhyme about building a house appeared. Could that be a mere coincidence? It made sense, in a way, but provided no answers.

"Someone is giving their little adventure in petty thievery some thought. Some literary thought."

Jake, hand to his chin, appeared deep into his own thoughts. "Yes, indeed. And I like the way you think, Dr. Watson."

"Well, I have not lived with Sherlock for nothing, you know."

We were a great team whether making love, making jokes, or solving problems. Now our first case had a name. Jake named it The HJB Case. At first, not quite up to speed, I gave Jake a questioning look. To which he replied, "H for house; J for Jack; B for built."

"That works."

FIVE

Jake

Mondays were always okay with me, though I was well aware that not everyone felt that way. I recalled a singer who wailed, 'Just another manic Monday'. That was a downer. Oh, well. To each his own. My day, our day, would be just fine.

Lindsey and I were almost ready to head back to Denny's for our second meeting with Bud, so I took Wendell out for a mini-walk. He walked. I limped. That should have been a quick and simple task. Keywords: should have been. The dog ran toward the back of the RV and scratched at the ground as if he were digging up a previously buried bone. "What is the matter, big guy? You are just out of sorts here, aren't you?" I'd hoped that once he understood he'd be going with us today, he'd calm down.

My plan was to park the RV in the staff parking lot and work from there with my foot propped up, the pets happy to be with me, and Lindsey just a few feet away getting to know the teachers and setting up her workshops. If anyone saw me, and I assumed they would, I'd just be Lindsey's loving husband. I'd say helpful husband, but my ankle would need at least another day of rest before I could be considered helpful. Today I would be moral support just a stone's throw away.

We were nearing Denny's when the engine began to chug and jerk and, finally, stall. Long story a little bit shorter, we were out of gasoline. How could that be? Suddenly, I was the one wailing on a Monday. We'd just filled the tank before we'd arrived at the campground. Weird! Then we both looked at Wendell. He knew something and that's why he'd scratched at the ground.

"Wouldn't you have noticed a leak under the RV, where Wendell was digging? That much gasoline would have made a puddle, or at least dampened the ground, wouldn't it?" Lindsey asked.

"That sounds logical, but I'm not sure. This could be a case of evaporation . . . Or, maybe someone siphoned out the gas."

"Possibly. If someone was desperate for gas, but had no money, siphoning might have occurred. If that's the case, they needed the fuel more than we did."

No one accentuated the positive better than Lindsey, and though I appreciated her attempt to look at the bright side, I didn't buy her theory this time.

Fortunately, there was a gas station almost directly across the road. We'd only be a little late for our meeting.

Bud didn't get up this time; he just waved from the booth as he sipped from his coffee cup. "Good morning, you guys. Do I *detect* a limp, Mr. Lee?" He'd raised his arms and made the motion for quotation marks with his fingers as he spoke the word *detect,* which was quickly followed by a hearty laugh. This man was a riot. *Sarcasm. Using sarcasm there.*

"Good morning to you, too."

We got right to work since we had only an hour before Bud would be introducing Lindsey to the entire school population at their Monday Morning Assembly. Taking out the notes we'd accumulated over the weekend, I began by summarizing some of the current facts and asking a few more pertinent questions. I quickly skimmed over the events from March and moved ahead.

"Late in April, the principal noted that some potted plants and bushes that were to be planted in the new garden had been stolen, but he also wrote that one of the small almond trees had been chopped down to almost nothing. I'd like to see what's left of that tree."

"Sorry. No can do. The grounds team came and cut it down completely. Too many sharp edges there. A kid could get hurt . . . So far, Jake, you're not telling me anything I don't already know."

"Hang on. It's coming. In the second follow-up note that arrived May 1, the 'Jack' rhyme continued. Lindsey, please read that for us."

"Sure. It says:

THIS IS THE BASKET SO PERFECTLY MADE
THAT LAY AT THE DOOR
OF THE HOUSE THAT JACK FOOLISHLY BUILT
THESE ARE THE NUTS FROM THE TREE OUT
BACK
THAT FILLED UP THE BASKET SO PERFECTLY
MADE
THAT LAY AT THE DOOR
OF THE HOUSE THAT JACK FOOLISHLY BUILT"

I was fairly certain that Bud had read the note before—he must have—but I was also sure that he'd not given it much thought. But now, hearing it read rhythmically by Lindsey, he was definitely thinking.

"Was there a basket, Bud? Were there any nuts in that basket?"

With a mischievous gleam in his eye, Bud answered. "Oh, yeah! There were plenty of nuts . . . in the basket. You see, Homer discovered—"

"That's the principal, right? What's his full name?"

"I never met him, never knew him and most people referred to him as Mr. B I'd heard he used to get teased about his name, though. Anyway, he discovered a basket right at the front entrance. In fact, if the story is true, he almost stepped on it. I guess when the fire alarm began to honk and ring and flash, Homer, the staff, and the students all hurried out of the building. Doesn't the file tell you that?"

"No. We didn't find any comments from Mr. B on that follow-up note."

"You're right. Come to think of it, I didn't see any either when I made a clean copy of the note for you. It was so crumpled and torn . . . from being shoved into that basket, I guess. But back to Homer. Maybe he was a little embarrassed. The office manager said he was the first one out the door. Ran out in a panic. Everyone else assumed it was just another fire drill, but not Homer. He knew different because he's the one that schedules those drills and flips the switch. No drill was scheduled and he hadn't been anywhere near the switch. At least that's what I heard. Odd, huh?"

Lindsey jumped in. "There might be a connection between our thief, the rhyme, the chopped down nut trees and the basket. It's a long shot, for sure, but perhaps the basket was meant to represent May Day." She pulled out a sheet of paper and began to read her own research notes: "Folklore states that on May 1 baskets were filled with nuts, flowers, and sometimes cheese treats and left at the door of a friend, a special friend. The doorbell was rung and then the giver would dash away. Next step? The receiver tries to catch the giver and, if that happens, a kiss is exchanged."

As Lindsey and I thought out loud with our back and forth questions and comments, Bud listened attentively, his head turning like a trained seal as he tried to keep up with our ping-ponging ideas.

"So, our thief is not only using the House That Jack Built rhyme but also other folk traditions. Coincidence?" I wondered.

Lindsey added, "Maybe he or she was hoping to act out this little mini-scenario. That seems like a lot of trouble just to get a kiss, though. Who would normally exit that door first during a fire evacuation?"

Bud had an answer he was anxious to tell. "That would be our attendance tech, if she was still there; she's a half-time employee. She'd hold the door open for the kids that exit out that way. Oh, boy. She's a looker. I don't think anybody would mind a little peck on the cheek from her, if you get my drift." I didn't, but what did it matter?

Lindsey was truly in her element now, but, between Bud and his comments and all this folktale business, my patience was being tested. My own annoying habits surfaced: I tapped my pencil rhythmically on my notepad like it was a drumstick, my uninjured foot performed an anxious, unstoppable bounce that traveled all the way up my leg, and I scratched my head. Yes, I knew myself well.

Lindsey kept going. "So, maybe, *she* was supposed to find the basket. But whom would she run after to catch and to kiss? She'd need to know the folktale or be part of the plot."

I couldn't take this line of thinking any more. "Okay. Let's move on. Toward the end of May, someone got into the school and the students' locked files and removed those files. Correct?"

"That would be a lot to carry. They'd need a wheel barrow or something."

I'd wished that Lindsey had thought of that when we were back at the campsite discussing this yesterday. We learned from Bud that only the first and second grade files were missing. And those could have been carried out in several of those cloth grocery bags the residents in Flagstaff were supposed to be using when they shopped. We all concluded that just about anyone could have carried out those files once the file cabinet was unlocked. I began to feel like we weren't getting anywhere, just spinning our wheels and telling stories. As much as I didn't want to, we needed to go over the last follow-up note that Bud received early in June. It went like this:

THESE ARE THE HANDS THAT FLIPPED THE COIN
THAT CRACKED THE NUTS FROM THE TREE OUT
BACK
THAT FILLED UP THE BASKET SO PERFECTLY
MADE
THAT LAY AT THE DOOR
OF THE HOUSE THAT JACK FOOLISHLY BUILT

THIS IS THE RULER THAT TIED THE HANDS
THAT FLIPPED THE COIN
THAT CRACKED THE NUTS FROM THE TREE OUT
BACK
THAT FILLED UP THE BASKET SO PERFECTLY
MADE
THAT LAY AT THE DOOR
OF THE HOUSE THAT JACK FOOLISHLY BUILT

"Bud, is there anything, anything at all, that you can say about the meaning of these words?" I asked, knowing I was grasping at straws.

I could see his wheels spinning, searching for an answer. The man really did want to be helpful.

"They kind of rhyme?" *Did I just witness Lindsey rolling her eyes? That's a rare sight.* Bud went on. "I can see how the theft of the bricks has to do with building the house, and then there's the May Day basket. That kind of makes sense . . . but I haven't the slightest idea what the ruler, the hands, the coins is all about."

Straws, all straws, nothing but straws.

I had nothing to add either, but Lindsey did.

"I'm not sure of the relevance, Bud, but we do know the note arrived on June 1st and, according to some calendars, June 1st is Dare Day. You dare someone to do something. Some even refer to it as Double Dog Dare Day, in which case one person dares another to do something, but they must do it first."

Bud sat shaking his head—mine was shaking, too—while Lindsey added that June 1st was also Flip-a-Coin Day, which originated back in the day of Julius Caesar. It was written that he'd flip a coin to make a decision where the right choice was unclear. Good grief! This was not what I'd signed up for. I wanted to be deep into real detective work, not this nursery rhyme stuff.

"What the hell does that all mean?" Bud complained, holding his almost hairless head in his hands.

Frustrated and, without a doubt, out of his comfort zone, Bud began to drum all eight of his fingers on the veneer surface of the table adding to my leg bouncing and pencil tapping. We had a regular rhythm section performing in booth 22 at the Flagstaff Denny's.

"More coffee, anyone?" offered the cheerful waitress.

"Not for me," Lindsey answered quickly. "Jake, I'm going to go out and check on the pets. See you in a few minutes."

I sensed we were complicating this interim principal's life far beyond his tolerance for problems and details. Bud confided in me that he'd like us to forget about all the House That Jack Built "*crapola*" and concentrate only on the threat to vandalize the computer lab. As he put it, 'I didn't ask for any of this; I wish it would all go away.'

He was candid and comfortable when it came to Lindsey's participation at the school. Her expertise was welcomed and needed. He said, and I quote, "I can keep any ship a-float, but don't ask me about the common core curriculum or teaching strategies. That all came after my time." And now all I could think about was that Lindsey could do this guy's job in her sleep and do it a thousand times better.

SIX

Lindsey

I stood off to the side of the outdoor cement stage while a member of the student council led the other children in the pledge of allegiance and the singing of "America, the Beautiful." It brought back fond memories of my full-time teaching days. Eventually, I might return to the classroom; I missed the close relationships with my kindergarten students as well as their innocence and their insatiable appetites for learning.

Bud stepped up and began my introduction. "Boys and girls, I'd like you to meet a special lady. She not only teaches children, she teaches teachers. Let's give Ms. Lindsey a big welcome."

Oh, my. This group knew how to clap. I had to admit I enjoyed the applause.

"Good morning, everyone. I am very glad to be here. Before the week is over I hope to visit each and every classroom. So I will definitely see you again."

I stepped back and was about to walk away when I noticed dozens of hands going up. I looked at Bud. He just shrugged his shoulders, apparently leaving the next move up to me.

"We have time for a few questions. Let's see. In the second row by the bench . . . the young man wearing the colorful Angry Birds jacket. Tell me your name first, please."

"My name is Noah and I think you are pretty."

Oh, dear. The older students rolled their eyes and mumbled some put-downs at the small child and his words.

"Thank you for the compliment, Noah. I appreciate your statement. Do you have a question?"

"Oh, uh. Where do you live?"

"I spend most of my time in Tucson, Arizona. This year, however, I will be working here in Flagstaff, then in Albuquerque, and after that Estes Park, Colorado. One more quick question. Way in the back. Yes, you with the beautiful red hair. Tell me—"

She cut me off. And was ever so . . . confident. Raising both arms and palms in the air as if she could stop a train, she stated, "I *know* what to do." Then she placed her hands on her hips and continued. "My name is Harper and I want to know if you have any kids."

I knew right off the bat that this young girl marched to her own tune; she'd be fun to teach. "No. No children yet, but I do have a wonderful dog named Wendell and he is so big, he weighs more than I do." That information created a bit of a buzz. I walked off stage, smiling.

Back in Bud's office, we went over my schedule for the week. Because this was a small school, I'd be able to pop into all twelve classrooms for a quick fifteen-minute visit today with the intention of getting a feel for each teacher's style and the physical environment of the room. I left his office feeling excited about the work that lay ahead of me—I was back in my element—but another feeling floated over me like an errant aura; one I did not like and could not even name.

SEVEN

Jake

Rain plunked down on the roof of the RV. Smiling, Lindsey said that it reminded her of 10,000 tiny tap-dancing ants. I did not share her enthusiasm for this unexpected wet weather. With my frustration level on the rise, I required space to pace. The interior of our RV didn't quite fit the bill, especially now that it was occupied by all four of us.

I was no closer to solving this simple little mystery of petty theft and nursery rhymes. I'd dusted for prints around the garden area and the file cabinets; I even attempted to get prints from the follow-up notes. I struck out. Not a single print worthy of calling in a favor from any of my detective friends. Our thief must have worn gloves or had extremely clean hands.

"I've got nothing, Linds. Nothing. A big fat zero."

"Did you ever stop to think that maybe there is really nothing to get?"

I hadn't. I wasn't wired for *nothing*.

"Maybe someone, a staff member, a parent, a neighbor got angry and went off on a weird tangent of retribution and then got over it. Maybe there is nothing more to it and it's over."

It amazed me how my lady could go from tiny tap-dancing ants to a tangent of retribution in a minute's time, but that's Lindsey. Got to love her, and I do. I'd better pull myself together one way or another.

"We've got tomorrow and Friday to wrap this up in a neat little package. We don't want to be failures on our first case." I tried to sound upbeat, positive, though I'd classify my attempt as pitiful.

"I agree, Jake." She was so much better at being positive than I was. "So, let's rethink and rewrite a list of possible suspects."

I handed her a pad of Post-its. She smiled. She laughed. She wrote a few words on one of the pink squares and stuck it on the RV's fridge where I could easily read it. It said: Do Not Disturb! And she'd drawn a little arrow pointing toward the sleeping area. I think the rethinking was temporarily on pause.

Some nights our lovemaking did not begin until we were both in bed and under the covers. I knew right away that this was not one of those nights. Lindsey took hold of my belt buckle and coaxed me onto the couch where she proceeded to unbuckle the belt and unzip the khakis while gently biting me on the neck. Talk about multi-tasking!

I relaxed and enjoyed her sensual, teasing moves and let her run the event, the show. *Oh, that feels good.* Before long we were both down to our bare essentials. Lindsey in her little white tank top and matching panties—so cute and sexy—and me in my blue checkered boxers—so . . . functional.

After the frustrating day I'd had, the next surprising move soon became one of my favorites. My lady

34

straddled my middle (that alone would have been more than enough) and rubbed my aching head, my tired eyes, even my ears. *I've never had my ears rubbed before. What a treat!* It was heaven.

"Your turn, Lindsey. I want to do that for you."

"Okay. If you insist, but there is just one more part of you I want to rub first."

Oh, boy. What a woman. A woman with multiple surprises. She took one of my hands in hers and began to massage its palm, then worked on each finger individually, pulling, squeezing, tickling.

"Lindsey, my love, it would never have occurred to me to give a hand massage." That didn't come out quite right, but she knew what I meant. "How did you know that would feel so fantastic?"

"I didn't. That was sort of an experiment."

"Okay. Then how did you know what to do?"

"Jake, you are not the only one that conducts research on the Internet.

With the day's tension gone, no longer limiting my energy, I swept her up into my arms and carried her carefully down the narrow hallway to the bed. The prolonged anticipation was almost unbearable; my passion for her now obvious. The boxers were gone in a flash. I did that. Lindsey's tank top and panties were suddenly nowhere to be seen. I did not do that. A sense of urgency drove us both.

Slow and gentle was not the status quo tonight. No, we touched each other like hot and horny new lovers finally able to release their pent up passions. With no clothing left to strip from our tantalized bodies, we got right to it. My turn to do the straddling. What a view! My beautiful woman, naked and flush with desire . . . for me! The feeling was mutual. My hands roamed eagerly over her perky breasts and then skimmed downward on both sides of her body.

I had a few moves of my own. Backing up to free her legs from their tightly closed position, I kissed her toes and tickled them with my tongue. She miggled. (That is my own word to describe the combined sounds of moaning and giggling that is unique to Lindsey.) Then, raising one lovely leg at a time, I kissed and gently massaged each calf. She liked that, I could tell by the sultry sigh, her closed eyes, and a sweet smile forming on her pretty lips.

Next, I licked and sucked the sensitive area behind her knees before heading closer to the main event, the delicate prize. Lindsey let her knees fall to the side as she opened herself to me. The glorious view just got better; the heat, the urgency intensified. And now some of my best moves would have to wait. We were on a journey, the destination close at hand, and for me, time was of the essence.

Skin on skin and fully engaged, we became one in a downpour of 10,000 twinkling sparklers. The real world spun and careened on its axis. *Lately, we'd had enough of the real world anyway.* We needed this orbital change.

Neither of us smoked so we munched on microwave popcorn while we looked over our list of suspects. (Made up of three sticky squares of paper. Three!)

1. An upset parent or family member—Maybe, but no evidence

2. A disgruntled staff member—Maybe, again no evidence

3. The interim, Bud—just odd enough but couldn't pull off HJB rhyme

4. The absent Homer B—We know little and need to talk to him

5. Someone unknown to us—Needle in a haystack

We couldn't think of anyone else to add to our pitiful list. After agreeing to ban any more work talk until morning, I covered the bird, let Wendell out to pee, then popped a DVD into the player in the sleeping area and we watched *Jeremiah Johnson* for the ten millionth time, according to Lindsey.

EIGHT

Lindsey

Bud was an interesting man. Sometimes funny, sometimes confused. But I sensed his heart was in the right place. Today, he'd asked me to spend a little extra time with one of his teachers who'd been placed on a Plan for Improvement last semester. He wanted to know if, with a little more help, she was capable of good teaching or if she was one of those people not cut out for the profession. Fortunately, he had the foresight to realize he might not know the difference. Got to give him credit for that. Off I went to Ms. Judy Jillstrom's second grade classroom.

"Hello. Ms. Jillstrom. It looks like all your students have left for the day. You were expecting me, yes?" I was the only one smiling.

"Uh, huh. The buddy boy said you were coming. What do you need to do?"

"Let's just sit and talk and we'll see where our conversation leads us."

We sat down at one of the round tables and I passed out some of my best dark chocolate as my eyes took a second and, hopefully, subtle look around the room. I knew this was by no means a model classroom, but I didn't expect to be shocked by what I saw. There was absolutely no evidence of student work or student learning; no class rules or procedures posted; no instructional information or handy references to help students become independent learners. Nothing. Nothing that you'd expect to find in a typical second grade classroom was visible. *These poor kids.*

Only a few store-bought posters containing nursery rhyme text or excerpts from fairy tales decorated the room. One shelf held math and reading textbooks, and some gray wire baskets filled with plain and lined paper sat on the counter along the windowed wall. That was it. This lackluster environment was justification enough for dismissal, and my concern for the students intensified.

At least we had an inkling of common ground—fairy tales, nursery rhymes, and chocolate. That was a start.

"You certainly have a lot of colorful posters, Ms. Jillstrom. May I call you Judy?"

"No, but you can call me Jill. I like that better than Judy." Her tone was sullen and cold. She didn't try to mask her annoyance with my presence.

"Oh, all right. Tell me, Jill, do you use your posters during the day for instructional purposes?"

"I do! Every day."

"Great! Could you show me or give me an example of how you do that?"

A tentative smile adorned the teacher's face. "Sometimes I read them to the students." Then her smile grew to Cheshire cat proportions. "But mostly, I sing them!"

Her sudden off key, operatic version of "Twinkle, Twinkle Little Star" was . . . more than a little startling. "Oh, my goodness. You weren't kidding about the singing. Tell me. What do the students do when you are singing or reading the text from one of the posters?"

"They listen. Very well, I might add."

"Listening is one of the language arts skills for second grade students and . . ."

Before I could finish my sentence—apparently, this teacher would benefit from a little lesson in listening herself—Jill began to belt out a passionate version of "Jack and Jill." Fortunately, she stopped after the first verse. With lightning speed I suggested that we use that verse to create several activities suitable for the students to use in the writing center she would eventually create . . . or not.

"Of course, you'll want to use the highly successful *I DO, WE DO, YOU DO* approach as you introduce each new activity." As suspected, Jill's face displayed a vague look of confusion. "Basically, you want to begin by modeling what you want your students to do."

Oh, dear. Another vague look. So I modeled how to model and wondered all the while what this teacher had learned in college about the use of teaching strategies.

"Well, you get the idea. Yes?"

Jill's eyes squinted oddly as if she were thinking about her response. "Sure, I get it, but let's not lose our heads." Her words were followed by a giggle, not a cute giggle, but a . . . creepy one.

NINE

Jake

Bored and annoyed with the nursery rhyme aspect of this case and making no progress anyway, I was about to call it a day, even though it was barely midafternoon. Then I discovered several teacher evaluations from last semester among the stack of files Bud had left with me. Flipping through them sluggishly and only because I could think of nothing else to do, I noticed that the principal signed these forms with HJB rather than just the HB. That got me thinking. What does the 'J' stand for? I played around searching on Google for names that began with J for a few minutes before coming to my senses.

I picked up my cell phone and pressed the numbers for the office. "Hey, Shelley. This is Jake Lee, Lindsey's husband."

"Oh, hello, Jake. Lindsey is in a conference with a teacher right now. What can I do for you?"

"You wouldn't happen to know what Mr. B's middle initial stands for, would you?"

"Sure. That's easy. It's Jay."

"No. I know it's the letter J but what does that letter stand for?"

The office manager was laughing at me now. "The initial J stands for J A Y. His middle name is Jay."

"Oh. Got it. Thanks. One more question. How does Mr. B spell his last name?"

"B I L D A R."

Wendell stared at me, his head cocking from side to side, as I repeated the name and the initials over several times. Homer Jay Bildar. HJB. HJB. House Jack Built. Homer Jay Bildar. House/Hom-er . . . Jack/Jay . . .Built/Bild-ar. The last name was a problem, didn't quite fit my evolving pattern. Was I finally on to something, though, or off on a wild goose chase? Either way, I needed to speak with Principal Bildar. After all, this whole petty theft and follow-up note business started with him. It took less than a minute to find the address in Flagstaff for a Homer J. Bildar. With a name like that, it had to be him. Come on guys, we're going for a little drive.

Not sure what I'd expected a principal's wife to look like, but the woman that opened the door wasn't it. She definitely was not looking good today. Most folks have put on clothes and brushed their hair by three o'clock in the afternoon.

"Hello. Mrs. Bildar?" I said using the cheeriest tone I could muster.

She scowled. "It's *Bill-der*," she said correcting my pronunciation. I'd been saying his name as if it rhymed with *wilde*r. "I'm Linda Bildar. Who are you and what do you want?" No cheeriness there. Just animus.

"My name is Jake Lee and I'm working over at your husband's school this week. It would really help me to speak with him. Is he here?"

"No. He's not here. I threw the bastard out last June."
The door began to close. Instinctively, I placed my foot
between the door and the jam to keep it from closing all
the way. *Do real people make that move?* I wondered. *Or
is my reaction a mere imitation of a TV drama?*

Hmm. Wow. She was obviously still angry with him
for something. Poor guy. Marital *and* medical issues.
That's a tough combo. I took a deep breath and continued.
Maybe with some careful coaxing she would tell me
where he was.

"I see. Wasn't he having some medical problems?"

Mrs. Bildar opened the door wider. She had
something to say; something she wanted to say.

"Oh, yeah. He's sick all right. Real sick."

"You've obviously experienced some difficult times.
My apologies, but why would you turn him away when he
was ill and must have needed you? Didn't you repeat the
'in sickness and in health' wedding vows?" *Geez. Did I
really just say that?*

"Are you kidding me?" Her anger intensified to the
level of a mad hornet. "Why does any woman dump her
husband?"

"I am so sorry. I . . . I didn't mean to upset you. I'm
just trying to find him. It's important."

"Well, you won't find him here."

Slam! Bang! went the door, grateful my foot was no
longer in the way. She was not a happy camper. Our
conversation? Over. That woman served up one hefty
helping of hostility. However, by the time I was sitting in
the driver's seat of the RV (after Wendell moved from my
seat to the floor) I was able to smile. My cheerful,
wonderful wife loved alliteration. She would have
enjoyed all those H's.

We pulled up just as Lindsey was walking out the
front entrance of the school.

"Hey, where have you been? I got worried when I looked out and you weren't here. Busy day?"

The train whistle blew just then. I loved that sound—during the day, that is. "Hop on board, ma'am. This train is about to leave the station."

"I thought you quit ma'aming me a few years ago?" I could tell she was in a good mood. Must have had a good day, too.

"That was before I had a train." Not everyone understood me and my humor, but Lindsey did.

She listened to my *Mrs. Bildar* experience. It was short though not sweet and I was able to share a few of the woman's exact quotes.

"Can you believe it? She even said to me, 'Why does any woman dump her husband?'"

"Jake, that's a no-brainer. He must have been cheating on her, having an affair."

Oh! That made sense. And now the invisible, cartoon light bulb hovering over my head flickered, illuminating my thoughts.

"If she was this angry now, she must have been a real hell-cat back when she first learned of the affair."

Our ideas took shape faster than viewing a potter at his wheel on time-lapse photography.

Lindsey began with, "Maybe she wanted to ruin his career."

"And, she would have access to his keys."

"She must have known her way around the school, too."

"Motive and opportunity!" I concluded.

"Sounds like this woman, this woman scorned, might also enjoy making him look foolish in the eyes of his peers . . ."

Finally, we were on a roll. The more we talked, the more new ideas sprang forth. "Ah, ha! Foolish! The house that Jack *foolishly* built."

"But his name is Homer." Lindsey pouted her lips and squinted her eyes.

Okay, it wasn't a perfect scenario, but it was the best we had so far. And Mrs. Bildar did strike me as the type that would seek revenge. Her name would not only be included on the list of suspects now, it would get top billing.

TEN

Lindsey

No mercury needed to know that the evening temperature had dropped and that jackets would be worn, but the air was still and wonderfully fragrant, so we decided to cook our dinner over the fire. We had only two nights left at this lovely spot in the woods and we wanted to make the most of our time. I could wait until after we ate and relaxed a bit to tell my *Jill Jillstrom* story.

With the fire, our jackets, and the warmed snifters of Grand Marnier Jake had poured for us, we remained outside feeling relatively comfortable in spite of the cold air.

"Your turn, Linds. Tell me about your day."

"It's a long story; I will attempt to summarize. Jake, she is the oddest teacher I have ever met. I wouldn't want any child of mine to spend even one day in that classroom with her. Besides her unorthodox approach to teaching, if you could even call it teaching, she gave off a strange vibe, an aura, something difficult to put into words."

"Try, Lindsey. You could be on to something here."

I shared everything I could remember about my hour after school with Ms. Jillstrom: the posters; the lack of books, art materials, folders, and student work; the strange vibes . . . everything. So much for summarizing.

The classroom's physical environment was not as shocking to Jake as it was to me, but he'd never been an elementary teacher. I did sense a heightened interest emanating from him though and could almost see Sherlock emerging with questions.

"Did she tell you how long she'd been teaching?"

"No, but she did allude to the fact that she didn't attend college right out of high school, and she mentioned something about being bounced around from district to district, town to town."

"Is that significant?"

"Educationally speaking, maybe. It could mean that she hasn't been teaching very long . . . or very well. Schools go out of their way to keep good teachers."

A transformation occurred. This was no longer story telling or even a conversation. Jake, with his best detective hat on, seemed to be conducting an interrogation. That was all right with me. I loved his level of intensity. And we were running out of time.

"Did she talk about her life beyond the classroom's walls?"

Jake gave me a funny look when I said that Ms. Jillstrom's main contribution wasn't talking, it was singing.

"I did get the impression that she was a lonely woman. A lonely woman whose main interest in life was fairy tales and nursery rhymes and . . ."

"You, of all people, can't hold that against her, right?"

"You're correct about that, but her use of them, especially her obsession with 'Jack and Jill,' was way over the top. She even insisted that I call her Jill instead of Judy."

"Her last name is Jillstrom, so that could make sense. Hmm. Interesting. Jill . . . Jack and Jill . . . Of course. That's it!"

Here it comes. Jake's excellent logic was about to point out what should be obvious to me, but wasn't. "What's *it*? We may have a Jill, but we don't have a Jack."

"I think we might; I think we do! Lindsey, try to find out if Jill ever called Homer, Jack, and, if Homer ever used the name Jack as a nickname."

This second grade teacher just made our list of suspects, too, though not the top of the list, she was in the top three. Even if Homer was *Jack* and Judy was *Jill* that didn't prove anything other than they were two odd people, nor did it directly connect them with the theft, the threats, or the notes. We couldn't accuse anyone, just yet.

Though delighted with our findings, our day had left us mentally exhausted. We headed for bed a little earlier than usual.

"Jake, are you still awake?" I whispered.

"Sure am. How about some chamomile tea?"

Jake brewed the tea. We sat up and slowly sipped the warming, calming beverage that helped our minds unwind . . . and eventually, with our bodies gently entwined, we drifted off into a peaceful sleep.

ELEVEN

Jake

I awoke suddenly. The space around me was darker, blacker than usual. No moon tonight; clouds must have rolled in. The dimly glowing clock displayed the numerals 2:15. Why was I awake?

Then Wendell whimpered and I noticed he was not near the foot of our bed, his favorite place to sleep. He sat at attention near the front of the RV. Did he need to go out? Maybe, but that would be unusual. He didn't even look my way as I approached. Odd. Very odd. My skin prickled, my danger antennae thrashed about. Suspecting tonight's outdoor investigation might involve more than a roaming raccoon, I grabbed my handgun from the built-in drawer and tiptoed closer to the intently focused dog by the door.

His whimper became a deep growl just before the barking began. Opening the door, Wendell bounded out. That's when I heard the footsteps running away.

"Wendell, STOP! STAY!" I didn't want anything bad to happen to our dog.

"Jake, what's going on?"

"Wendell heard something. Someone was very close to the RV but ran away just as the dog jumped out of the door."

Lindsey handed me a flashlight and I circled the RV taking a cursory look. I'd need to check the area more thoroughly in the light of day. We went back to bed, but we couldn't sleep. We talked. Maybe there was a tie between our RV troubles and Bud Farley's little mystery. The broken step, the empty gas tank, and now . . . what? What was this?

We found footprints circling around the RV, but none of them was very clear or remarkable. Nothing appeared to be disturbed or tampered with. And there was no evidence that the person had kneeled down or backtracked. My worst-case conclusion? That someone had surveyed the vehicle for future theft opportunities or else it was just a curious kid . . . with big feet.

TWELVE

Lindsey

Coffee. This morning I needed coffee. Lots of it. We were both exhausted from our sleepless night, so Jake kept a pot going in the RV while I headed into the school. My final meeting with Bud would begin in a few minutes.

Good news was what I liked to give as well as receive. Today I had some great news for the interim principal. His teachers were wildly receptive to the concept, the set up, and the implementation of their classroom writing centers. I reminded him that this would be an on-going learning experience and that I'd be happy to keep in contact with the teachers. My comments about Ms. Jillstrom would not fall into the good news category.

"Bud, I have multiple concerns about Judy, I mean Jill. What do you call her?"

He gave me a strange look. "I haven't really had any one-on-one conversations with her. I think her first name is Judy, but I call all the teachers by their last names, so it would be Ms. Jillstrom, I suppose." No help there.

I recommended that he keep her Plan for Improvement in place and obtain some assistance from the district's language arts director . . . and have a chat with the legal department because I sensed trouble far deeper than her lack of instructional ability. I was about to make one last visit to the classrooms when Shelley knocked at the open door and proceeded to hand Bud a note.

He stared at the half-sheet of paper, his pasty white face lightening to translucent and beads of sweat began to form. "Let's get Jake in here. Talking about this can't wait for an off campus meeting."

The moment Jake walked in, we passed the office manager's written phone message around, each reading it silently. Then Bud asked, "Shelley, could you come back in here for just a minute?"

"Hey, I'm just the messenger, Mr. Farley. And you know what they say?"

"Yeah, Yeah. Don't shoot . . . something or other."

Jake began his questioning. He was a master of inquiry. "Shelley, who was the caller?"

"I have no idea, but she sounded kind of gravely, you know, witchy? It could have been a man or a woman really because the voice came across as . . . bad acting."

"What exactly did the caller say?"

"I don't do 'exact' but it was something like: Tell your buddy boy that Bildar's lab is going down just as soon as your meddlers use their peddlers. I believe that's what I wrote in the note."

"Okay. Thank you."

I studied Shelley during this brief exchange with Jake. Her eyes met no one's. Did she seem nervous? Meddlers? Peddlers? After she left, I had a few questions, too.

"Bud, how much does Shelley know about all of this?"

"Most of it. The letters, the threats, I mean. I haven't talked to her about your Sherlock Holmes stuff," he said with a wink. He certainly got a kick out of saying that. "She's a smart cookie, though, and probably figured out some of that on her own."

"It seems to me that the culprit's anger is directed at Mr. Bildar and not you, Bud, or even the school. Though the school would be affected should this next threatened act of vandalism come to pass. What do you think, Jake?"

"I think we should assume that the note is true and our suspect is merely waiting for us to leave before assaulting your lab. So . . ." A quick, knowing look passed between us. "We'd better stay a few extra days, but remain out of sight, so folks think we departed as scheduled."

We had a plan. Jake, Wendell and I would secretly camp out in the school's computer lab Saturday night and see what happened. Was that safe? Maybe not, but he dog would let us know if any one got close. The bird might blow our cover, though. We had less control over his actions. He would likely start squawking at the wrong moment, but we couldn't leave our little bird alone. That was our current dilemma.

My To Do list began to take shape. It was essential to vacate both vehicles from the campsite to create the illusion that we'd left town. Alternative parking spots needed to be found. Since we'd be using the car to transport ourselves and our meager sleeping and eating gear to and from the school, we wanted that spot to be close by, but still hidden. Jake would find a more distant location for the RV.

"Bud? You will be the only one that knows of this plan. Are you good with that? Can you keep it all under wraps?"

"Sure, Jake. Sure. You can count on me."

"No custodians working this weekend, right?" We both took note of his affirmative nod. "No school safety officers coming by either?"

"Hell. They are never around when you need them. So probably not."

That was not the answer Jake and I had hoped for. Oh, well. We'd cross that bridge when . . .

"So, if someone does show up, that's probably our man."

"Or woman," I added, not wanting to ever be accused of discrimination or sexism . . . and then there was that gravely, witchy sounding voice on the phone.

An uncharacteristic, sheepish expression appeared on Bud's face. "Oh, you guys might want to leave for a while. We're conducting one of the required fire drills today—district orders and all. It's not pleasant. The lights flash; the noise is almost unbearable."

"Thanks for the warning. Let's go get some lunch, Linds."

The next order of business was to call the Director of Elementary Education in Albuquerque, New Mexico, our next stop, and make certain that delaying our start time by a few days would not create any great difficulties for them. I made the call while Jake drove. The woman who answered the phone in the director's office didn't think it was a problem. She said she'd call back within the hour if the postponement resulted in a cancellation of our visit.

We found a cute little restaurant not far from the train station where we had a light lunch. All during our meal, dozens of memories about fire drills rose to the surface of my thinking. I felt fortunate that we'd escaped participating in this one. *Thank you, Bud.*

"No one likes them, Jake. It puts the kids on edge, breaks up the continuity of the day, and there are always a few kids in the bathroom at the time. They really panic, so do the adults that must try to find them. They are downright stressful. And . . . in most districts, the drills are timed. Timekeepers don't press the stop button until everyone, except for the principal or office manager, is out of the building."

"Of course. Why didn't I think of that?"

"Huh? What? Are you going to clue me in, Jake?"

"The first of May, an unscheduled fire alarm, the May Day basket. That all happened within the school building, during the school day. And the principal did not pull the alarm. So, who did?"

"Jake, when you dusted for prints a few days ago, did you dust the fire alarm pull-downs?"

"Sure didn't. But I'm on that tonight."

Finally, we may have stumbled upon a breakthrough. I called Bud to let him know of our plan so he could be there to let us in. Then we drove back to the campground for a semi-relaxing afternoon before our evening detective work commenced.

THIRTEEN

Jake

As we sat outside enjoying the crisp fall weather, Lindsey explained to me that though custodians rarely cleaned the pull-downs for fear of setting them off accidently, districts usually made annual checks of the fire alarms within the schools. So, dusting for prints could reveal our perpetrator or, if the pull-downs had been cleaned or examined by district personnel, nothing at all. We'd soon find out.

We waited at one of the side doors while Bud entered through the front entrance and deactivated the security system's alarm. *Amazing! He'd learned how to do that ... or had he known all along?* From this point on, we hoped our presence would go unnoticed.

"Bud, how many fire alarm pull-downs are in this building?"

"Five, maybe six."

"Okay. We'll look around. This won't take very long."

"I'll just wait in my office and pretend to be working."

I knew Lindsey was rolling her eyes just then, and I wasn't even looking at her.

We got to work, no pretending on our part. I wasn't surprised that there were no visible prints on the red-colored alarms. No problem. The black fingerprint powder I had with me should do the trick. Within ten minutes we'd found and dusted the pull-downs for prints, then snapped photos with my phone of the black arches, loops, and whorls that clung to the red, shiny surface of each alarm.

"I've got some good ones! Clear, adult-sized prints. That's one step in the right direction."

"What now?" Lindsey asked.

"We send them out by FedEx to Wally, my unofficial partner-in-crime-solving, down in Tucson. He's good. This will be easy. And, if any matches exist, we might have this little mystery wrapped up in forty-eight hours. If they don't . . . then Albuquerque, ready or not, here we come."

Waiting for the results was really all we could do. Well, other than prepare for our computer lab campout; make that camp *in*. No cooking by the fire tonight. Dinner would likely be a deli sandwich, and we wouldn't be singing any *cozy* songs, either. We would be huddling, whispering in the dark on the hard, tile floor in a corner of the computer lab. Somehow, I hadn't pictured any part of our road trip looking like this.

Besides hoping for some luck with the prints, this was our last chance to solve the Flagstaff mystery. I could think of no other leaves to unturn, no other clues to investigate. And now a few second thoughts nagged at me. Second thoughts about including Lindsey and Malcolm on this stakeout. Yeah, that's what it was—a stakeout. Wendell and I could handle this.

Lindsey knew me well. Apparently, I was giving off some signals of apprehension, so she asked, "Jake, what's the matter?"

Not wanting to answer her question, I asked one of my own. "Tell me again why we are doing this?"

"Because I love to help teachers; and you, Sherlock, love to play detective. And, don't forget that we didn't want to be tied down to real jobs."

"Right."

"And we wanted to spend most of our time together. We are a team!"

"We are an excellent team, but I think we should split up for the computer lab stakeout. I've got a funny feeling about this and I would never forgive myself if you were harmed in any way due to my desire to play detective."

"All right. I'm convinced."

"Good!"

"I am convinced, more than ever, that we *should* be together on this stakeout. If you don't take me with you, I will sneak in on my own."

There I stood. Scratching my head, scanning my brain for a more persuasive line of reasoning. Nope . . . nothing there. It was time to go.

Bud met us and we all entered the building the same as we'd done the night before except tonight the interim principal went home as soon as we were settled in among the computers. We even brought Malcolm, but we covered his cage and set it in the hallway just outside of the lab.

The night was uneventful, almost boring, until about 11 p.m. when Wendell stood up, moved closer to one of the exterior windows, and sat cocking his head back and forth, listening. Our human ears heard nothing . . . until it began. Then we all heard it, heard everything. A giant's electric razor? A dental drill on steroids? It was definitely a piercing, eardrum damaging sound. And then it got worse.

It was enough to make me howl. I didn't, but Wendell did. Then he barked and growled more ferociously than ever before. He even bared his teeth like a wolf—albeit a wolf with a big, round face.

Shining my heavy-duty flashlight toward the direction of the noise, all I could make out was someone wearing dark, bulky clothing and a baseball cap running from the scene. Not much to go on. The dog had kept us from harm, but he'd also scared away the intruder before we could identify him.

"Jake, look at that. Our visitor was cutting a small hole in the bars covering the lab's windows. I wonder why? What good—or bad—would that do?"

"It does explain the horrible noise. Sawing through metal is never a pleasant sound. I wonder if he'll return tonight?"

Needless to say, we did not sleep well and arose with stiff, aching bodies. We'd take a quick look around outside and then go pick up the RV and head back to the campground. Our perp knew we were still here, so there was no point in hiding. We might as well enjoy the woodsy setting the rest of the day.

"Jake? What is that?" she asked, pointing to a dark, oval object about ten feet from the recently vandalized window bars.

"Stay back, Linds. I'm not sure but . . ." Just then my cell phone rang.

"Hey, Jake. We got something."

"Wally? That was fast." I grabbed Lindsey's hand and we walked over to sit on the steps just around the corner of the building. I wanted her and Wendell away from the mysterious object that resembled . . . a grenade.

"Can I put you on my cell phone's speaker?"

"Sure, Jake. This is your show."

"What have you got?"

"One of your prints was an obvious match for a person previously convicted of several petty crimes: mostly shop lifting, disorderly conduct, and, get this, peeping Tom offenses, or should I say Tomasina?"

"I don't get it."

"Your likely suspect is a woman. A woman who has lived most recently in Yuma, Arizona, but also in Boise, Idaho and Blythe, California.

Feeling proud and sure our mystery was about to be solved I said, "I'll bet her name is Judy Jillstrom."

"Oh, uh . . . No. Sorry. It's not. It's Jacqueline J. Sullivan."

I could almost feel that rug being pulled right out from under me. Had to regroup my thinking. "Wally, do you have any information about the woman's teaching career?"

"Nope. No mention of teaching. Looks like she might have worked at a daycare in Boise doing housekeeping tasks."

If the prints were not Jill's, then to whom did they belong? There was no one named Sullivan on the school's roster, but a woman with that name had her hand on one of the fire alarm pull-downs.

"Thanks, Wally. Is there any way to find out what the J stands for?"

"Can I call you back? That might take a few minutes."

"Of course. Just one more thing." I proceeded to describe the object Lindsey had spotted right before Wally's phone call came in. My suspicions were correct, but we were not equipped with the knowledge necessary to deal with a grenade safely or even determine if it was 'live' or not.

After tossing a few ideas around, we came up with a suitable arrangement. I'd make an anonymous call from a pay phone—we'd seen one not too far from the train station and noted how rare they were nowadays—to the local police just saying that we saw a suspicious object near the lab on the back side of the school. Surely it would be gone before the kids arrived Monday morning.

"I guess our gal really had planned on taking down Mr. Bildar's lab after all. It wasn't just an idle threat. At least she didn't attempt that when children were in the building." With Lindsey, the kids always came first.

"Yes. And she would have accomplished that without setting even one foot inside the school. All she had to do was push that grenade into the hole she'd cut and BOOM! The job would be done. Good thing we were there."

"And it was a great thing she ran away before she'd finished cutting the hole or pulling the pin."

"Linds, we don't know that our late night lab culprit is the fire alarm puller."

"Well, if they are not one and the same, that would mean we have two culprits, right?"

My cell phone rang again. It had to be Wally. "Any luck with the J?"

"As a matter of fact, yes. The J, the initial for her middle name, stood for . . . Jill. So the print belongs to someone named Jacqueline Jill Sullivan."

Lindsey's eyes grew wide and my jaw was in need of some propping up. Even in our state of surprise, almost disbelief, some puzzle pieces were coming together.

"Pretty sure Jacqueline Jill Sullivan is a teacher at the school. A woman with a few loose screws, no pun intended."

"None taken, Jake—'cause I don't know what the heck you are talking about."

FOURTEEN

Jake

Tiny beads of sweat—his telltale sign of stress—
formed on Bud's brow as we waited for Jill to
arrive. The poor guy was so uncomfortable. The
only concrete proof we possessed at this point was her
fingerprint on the fire alarm pull-down, but the mound of
circumstantial evidence was sky high.

"Good morning, Ms. Jillstrom. Please have a seat,"
said Mr. Farley as he closed his office door.

"This better not take long. My students will be coming
in soon," said Jill, her eyes darting from Bud to Lindsey to
me, and back to Bud.

"No problem, Ms. Jillstrom. I've hired a sub for you
today."

Her look of annoyance changed to one of fear, but not
for long. She sat, though not still; her leg swung back and
forth like a swift pendulum.

"We know what you've done, but we wanted to give
you a chance to tell your side of the story." My vagueness
had purpose.

Jill's eyes squinted and stared, her lips tightened, and I braced myself for an explosion of anger. What we got instead . . . was sobbing. She held her head in her hands and cried. Bud now mopped his profusely sweating face with a handkerchief; with compassionate eyes, Lindsey watched the disturbed woman; I merely pressed play on my tiny recorder . . . and we waited.

"I loved him. He was the first and only love of my life. In the beginning we just talked about school, but eventually, things got personal. *Sob. Sob. Sniff.* We even fucked right there on the couch you're sittin' on, Bud."

Jill smirked. Lindsey and I gasped. Poor Bud would have had a cow, if that were possible. The multiple moods of Ms. Jillstrom were emerging. She continued on and on.

"But soon after he came in to do my March observation, I felt he was slipping away and we were drifting apart. I could not let that happen." She raised her eyebrows and turned her head toward Lindsey, then me, then Bud, giving each of us her hideous, with a hint of mischievous, glare. The glare became a smirk just before she spoke again. "I just wanted him to spank me for taking the bricks and the plants. The spanking was one of my favorite things."

Her fiendish grin said it all. We were far beyond the boundaries of normal here.

"He acted like he didn't know it was me. I gave him plenty of hints. Then he had the nerve to fill out the paperwork for my Plan for Improvement. I knew what that meant. Oh, yes. That was a short path to losing my job." Ms. Jillstrom stood up, crossed her arms and asked, "Are we done yet?"

I ignored her question and asked my own. "So, you became angry and wanted to hurt him?"

"Yes, of course. And I did that very well. I'm no idiot, you know. No improvements needed there. The only harm done was that my Jack—Homer to you—looked like a stupid fool that couldn't run his own school. But even my creative efforts, and you must admit that I am extremely creative, did not win him back. So, I went straight to his bitchy wife—I was doing him a huge favor, really, but he didn't see it that way—and told her all about our little escapades. Boy, did she flip out."

Jill grinned devilishly from ear to ear and found this part of her story hilarious—like a comedienne laughing at her own jokes. The woman did not have a moral or sane bone in her body. And to think children spent week after week, month upon month with her. That had to stop. Lindsey would see to that.

"The next thing I knew, I couldn't find my Jack, and you're here, Bud." She smiled coyly at the interim principal, looking him up and down, and batting the lashes that framed her dark eyes, then said, "You're no Bud Light, are you?"

Good grief. Do I detect flirting? Is she flirting with him after all she's done? Bud was not smiling. In fact, he was wearing a deer-in-the-headlights look on his face. Couldn't blame him for that.

"So, Ms. Jillstrom, or is it Sullivan?" I asked. Her coyness morphed into a sudden look of shock. "We'll come back to that. Why did you continue? Why threaten and attempt to vandalize the computer lab? Your 'Jack' was completely out of your life, gone from the school. Right?"

Jill tapped her pouted lips with her index finger. "I thought Bud could fill my Jack's shoes."

She turned toward him, stared him down like a wolf just before attacking its prey, though no wolf was capable of forming the seductive, sickening smirk that followed. "Besides, he looked to me like the spanking type. I thought you, Mr. Farley, would figure out my threat and want to make me be a good girl. But no . . ."

None of us wanted to go down this unexpected, twisted path, especially not Bud. We men were grateful when Lindsey interrupted sweetly.

"Jill, I know this must be hard for you. We are almost done talking. Would it be all right if I asked just one more question?" Jill nodded, probably thinking that Lindsey was the only friend she had at the moment. "Have you siphoned any gasoline from an RV lately or come out to where we've been camped?"

Jill uncrossed her arms and repositioned them on her hips. Her mood was about to swing. We all saw that coming.

"That was two questions," she replied, her tone riddled with annoyance. "I would never stoop so low. Besides, I am a career woman; I can pay for my own gas. And, I couldn't care less where you park your showy, I-am-better-then-you-are vehicle."

Finally the woman said something that made sense and I could tell by the look on Lindsey's face and the shrug of her shoulders that she felt there was no need to proceed with that line of questioning. So I took the last few questions in a different direction.

"So, Ms.—what is your name? Your real, legal name?"

The woman slumped back down onto the chair and stared blankly at nothing. She had no reply.

"All right then . . . where did you get the grenade and how many more do you possess?"

The blank look turned to panic, even horror, for a few seconds before spiraling down to resignation and defeat. Sobbing soon followed.

"I want a lawyer."

We had it all on tape. Everything but the body language. Three witnesses could attest to that, though, if it ever became necessary. Man, she was one wacky, dangerous woman. I made the call to the police; Lindsey called the superintendent's office. Bud was too distraught to think straight about anything right then. And, really, I couldn't blame him.

Because of Sunday's grenade issue, the police were more than happy to take her in for questioning and file a restraining order to keep her away from the school and Mr. Farley until they, themselves, could dig deeper into the case. Between the superintendent and the head of the Department of Human Resources, it was determined before the end of the day that Jacqueline J. Sullivan AKA Ms. Judy Jillstrom did not have any of the necessary qualifications to teach. Her job would be terminated immediately.

Lindsey approached with a bottle of Wild Horse Merlot and two glasses made of real glass. This was no paper cup kind of night. We were going to celebrate. I popped the cork and poured. Lindsey toasted first.

"To you, Jake, for out-Sherlocking, Sherlock."

That was not really possible, of course, but I did make it my business to know what others did not know. And . . . I liked that.

"And to you, Lindsey, for your patience, your brilliance, and for being the prettiest Dr. Watson that ever was."

She flashed her beautiful smile right at me, up close and oh so personal.

"I have not lived these few years with Sherlock for nothing, you know."

"One down . . ."

"And two to go."

We clinked, we sipped, we kissed.

"Do you feel like a real detective now, Jake?"

"Oh, yeah. I'm feeling it. I'm on a roll. We're on a roll. Homer Jay Bildar, The House that Jack Built, Jack and Jill, Jacqueline Jill Sullivan, and the related follow-up notes certainly took us far beyond the theft of a few bricks. I'll bet my sister, Julie, would love to get inside of Jill's head. We'll have to tell her all about this someday."

"Jake, could we get in trouble carrying on unofficial investigations like this?"

"Well, I don't know. Maybe. But we'll cross that bridge if and when we need to. Don't worry, baby."

"I just had another thought."

"And . . . ?"

"I was thinking that perhaps we've been bad. Very, very bad."

She was up to something—I could tell by the mischievous look on her sweet, beautiful face—and she waited for my reply. What should it be? Sometimes, I was clueless. I knew that. Then came the light.

"Oh . . . Ooooh! So, I guess we're going to do something different tonight?"

"Yes! Yes we are."

"But what about Wendell? He won't like that and he might misinterpret our playful actions."

"I suppose you're right. Oh, well."

Sometimes I just need to shut up. It's the thought that counts, or so they say. There's always tomorrow.

We would head for Albuquerque in the morning and meet with the Elementary Director in the afternoon. Our projection of running two days behind turned out to be just about perfect. *Stop thinking and get some rest!* I held Lindsey in my arms and we both drifted off to sleep.

\\

He had a knack—or a curse—for remembering scraps from the past: conversations, visions, sounds, even written words. Some were important and affected his life in ways he didn't always understand, others were insignificant. The most pertinent ones, however, haunted him by appearing over and over, day or night, without any prompting or conscious remembering on his part.

"What kind of 'food' will you work for?"

"Greens. I like my greens."

"I thought that might be the case. Hop in."

NEW MEXICO:

THE BIG BANG

FIFTEEN

Lindsey

We were on the road again, ready and willing to leave Flagstaff behind. Fortunately, we'd had closure at least as far as our obligations were concerned, but I knew the events that had transpired there were far from over for the school district, the local authorities, Bud and Jill. Though we never knew Homer J. Bildar, AKA Jack, we hoped he would find a way to rebuild his own house.

"I know we wrapped up Bud's little mystery, Jake, but I can't get Jill out of my mind. Is there any way she could have intruded on our privacy at the campground and tinkered with our RV?"

"I suppose it's possible, even likely. Who else could it be? I don't think we will ever know for sure."

"You're right. She wouldn't admit to it when we asked, but we know she has no problem designing malicious plans and carrying them out."

"Hey, Linds. Want to drive? It's hardly fair that I'm having all the fun."

"No, thank you. This thing is as big as a ship and I have no desire to take the helm. If you need a break we could pull over at the next rest stop. I'm sure Wendell would love to take a little walk around."

He wasn't tired. He was teasing me, but we did exit the interstate to top off our gas tank. That's when I spotted the hand-made sign pointing the way to a farmer's market. Pulling off the paved two-lane highway onto the dirt road, we saw stands set up off in the distance. As we drove closer, it became obvious that a variety of growers had fruits, vegetables, nuts and even flowers for sale. What a nice addition to our day.

My cell phone rang just as we'd stepped out of the RV. Jake and Wendell went on ahead to check things out.

"Well, that was odd," I said finding my guys at a picnic table, one of them crunching an apple. "Our next stop has been delayed."

"I bet someone is just confused since we had to push back our start day. You know how often communication errors occur. What exactly did the caller say?"

"Not much, only that the group of teachers who were to attend the workshop is—and I quote—'not available.'"

"We need more information than that."

Jake was right, we did. So I returned the call. No luck. No answer. Looking through the Albuquerque folder, I found the direct line for Mrs. Janelle Rubio, the Director of Elementary Education, and tried again.

As soon as I identified myself, a breathless voice rattled off that there had been a bomb threat and they were in the process of evacuating dozens of schools. She assured me it was probably nothing, but at this point they had to assume the threat was real.

"Can we meet two days from now?" There was a sense of urgency in her voice.

"So Thursday?"

"Yes."

"Is there anything we can do to . . ." Cut off. Nothing but the sound of silence hung in my ear.

I recapped the conversation for Jake whose eyes lit up at the mention of a bomb threat. Shaking my head I added, "We don't do bomb threats," just in case he had any ideas.

"We dealt with a grenade," was Jake's comeback.

"Not on purpose!"

Looking at me through laughing blue eyes and with the innocence of a child, he wiggled his eyebrows before saying, "Excuuuuuse me for enjoying my work."

He could be so funny at times.

We purchased a mixed bag of organic apples that included galas, honey crisps, and heirloom winesaps. The vender threw in a recipe for apple pie. Then, thanks to Jake's quick thinking, we were off to Santa Fe, New Mexico. It wasn't far from Albuquerque and since we'd never been there before and had been handed a couple of extra days to play, this spontaneous side trip would be icing on the cake, or rather, the ice cream on the pie.

Finding a place to park the RV with the car attached to the back was a challenge. Just driving on the narrow streets of Santa Fe kept Jake on edge. We should have looked for an RV park first. Oh, well. Too late.

"Jake. Over there. A parking lot with a sign saying: RVs welcome. No overnight parking."

That would work for now. We'd move it later. We learned that a parking attendant would be on the premises until 10 p.m. so we cracked open some of the windows, allowing Malcolm a hint of fresh air, and we took Wendell with us. The town square was almost a mile away; all three of us would benefit from the exercise.

Venders lined the sidewalk's edge sitting on colorful, hand-woven blankets with their jewelry, handcrafted toys, books, or artwork. And musicians? They were everywhere. Best of all, was the delicious aroma of a multitude of edible items that permeated the crisp fall air. Wendell's nose never stopped sniffing.

He wasn't crazy about the mariachi band playing across the street in the square or even the small ensemble playing pan flutes. He wanted nothing to do with them. But when we walked by a young girl singing and playing a guitar, he stopped, he sat, he listened. His reaction to her reminded me of the time he went to school to be an unofficial Sit-Stay-Read dog where he listened to children read. One little girl in particular read Wendell a poem she had written about the death of her military dad. She was so strong, but also very sad. Wendell adored her. I was witnessing a similar connection now.

Jake snapped a few photos of our dog with his new, musical friend; it was a precious sight. The girl's light brown, gently waved hair draped halfway down her back as she sat bare-footed on the sidewalk playing her guitar with amazing skill and singing like a pro. I placed a five-dollar bill in her tip jar and turned to go. I told Jake that I really wanted to find a cozy little bar and sip a Santa Fe margarita.

"Come on, Wendell. Come!"

He didn't budge, even when Jake gave his leash a gentle tug. Finally, he stood up. Good! No . . . not so good. He merely rearranged himself so that, instead of sitting, facing the singer, he was lying down right at her side. Hmm. That was a little out of the ordinary. Yes, we could have forced him to get up and come with us, though we've never had to use force before, and didn't like the idea now.

"Let's go, big buddy," said Jake using his *we're gonna have some fun now* voice. Nothing. He gazed up at her with his heartwarming, loving dog eyes. This sweet, young thing, resembling a flower child from the 1960s returned the look of love and appeared to be singing to him, only him—our dog.

When the song came to an end, I assumed we could move along, all three of us. But the girl said, "The next door down, if you go upstairs, has *the* best margaritas . . . but dogs aren't allowed." I wondered how she would know about margaritas; she looked to be about sixteen years old. "He can stay with me while you get a quick drink."

Jake shrugged, waiting for me to say something. It was my call. I knew that. "Well . . ."

"We will just be upstairs, Linds." Jake pointed to the neon sign in the window above us blinking *Coyote Wells*. "And we already know he's great with dog sitters." His wiggling eyebrows complemented the boyish grin that now filled the face of Wendell's original dog sitter. If only he could see himself.

It was Wendell that really made this decision. He placed his paw on her leg and gave us a look I couldn't even describe; we nodded at each other and dashed up the narrow staircase to get our best-ever margaritas.

"Thank you. We'll be back in less than ten minutes," Jake called out. She waved and began to sing another song. Wendell wagged his tail. All was right with the world.

The drinks were not only delicious, they were large, and even sipping as quickly as we could, fifteen minutes had passed before we'd returned to our dog. Our dog, our dog Wendell was GONE! The girl was gone, too. A horrible, sick feeling soared through me. This was far worse than the time Anthony, my first husband, took Wendell from me. At least then I knew where the dog was. Now, I had no idea.

I waited restlessly at the spot where Wendell and the girl had been, and Jake scoped out the surrounding area.

What was I thinking? How could I have left Wendell with a complete stranger in an unfamiliar town? With my vision now blurred by copious tears and my mind swirling with fear, I barely noticed the small Indian woman sitting on a blanket with her jewelry. She flapped a piece of paper in my direction, but I failed to see the significance of her actions. She was persistent, not taking no or my lack of response for an answer. Standing, she placed the paper in my hand and closed my fingers around it. Thinking she had given me a flyer or some kind of advertisement, I didn't read it right away.

Through my tears, I was able to see Jake making his way toward me—Wendell was not with him. My heart sank to an all-time low.

"Lindsey, we will find him. It isn't like a one hundred and sixty pound mastiff can be kept hidden for long."

He took my hands in his . . . and found the piece of paper. Whatever it said prompted a new course of action. Jake pulled me to my feet and, hand in hand, we went running across the square.

Still worried, my heart and my feet raced along. This sudden action did not ease my feelings of distress. "What are we doing?"

"We are going to get our dog!" His voice was so confident, his stride so decisive as he led me through a dark, narrow doorway.

I was not yet in sync with Jake in the area of confidence. It seemed we twisted and turned down one dark hallway after another. I felt like a mouse in a maze. Finally, we stood in a clearing that resembled an old hotel lobby where Jake momentarily glanced around before leading us into a bar far darker than the hallways. I blinked, trying to focus.

And there they were, up on the small stage—the singer and her groupie. We lingered in the back of the bar for a while calming down, catching our breath and watching this amazing sight.

"What did that note say?" I eventually asked. Jake read it to me. It said: Sorry. I didn't realize the time. Had to go to work. The dog is with me at the Adobe Moon Hotel in the bar. See you soon.

The plan had been to retrieve our dog immediately and make our way back to the RV, but the song she was singing was about a huge, friendly, tan dog that she'd just met. A dog that had transformed her solo act into a duo. Interesting. At the end of this tune she put down her guitar. She and Wendell came straight over to us, both looking quite pleased.

With my arms wrapped around my big, lovable companion, I asked the girl, "So they allow dogs in this place?"

"No. I said he was my drummer," she giggled and patted him on the head. She had no idea that we thought he'd been stolen. And why should she? She had left us a note explaining where he was. "Did you like his song? I just wrote it for him."

"Yes, I liked it very much. How did you do that so fast?"

"I make up songs all the time, and I had extra inspiration today," she stated, looking at Wendell.

"You're amazing," Jake said, adding another bill to her tip jar. "What is your name?"

"Bethany. Bethany Michaels. You've got a great dog there!"

We thanked her and said our good-byes. She gave Wendell one last scratch behind his ears and bounced back onto the stage to continue her performance.

The whole experience left Jake and I exhausted. We needed to begin the walk back to the RV. We walked and talked and wished that Wendell could talk, too, and tell us what was going through his big head during his time with his new friend, Bethany. She was so sweet and nice. Almost too nice—no one is *that* nice—and we wondered if she might be a little stoned. After all, the Colorado state line was just to the north.

"She is so incredibly talented." My creative wheels were spinning. I'd love to team up with her—seemed she could use the money—or someone like her to put some of my original poems, chants, and stories to music. Perhaps creating CDs could be next year's project. Hmm.

After having spent less than eighteen hours in Santa Fe, sleeping half of that time, Jake announced that he felt compelled to head south to Albuquerque a full day before our re-rescheduled meeting with the Elementary Director would take place.

"You know, Jake, if we hadn't spent those few extra days in Flagstaff, we would have been there to experience the bomb threat."

"Like they say, timing is everything. For once we got lucky and the timing ticked in our favor."

I hoped he was right. I also hoped that the bomb threat had nothing to do with us.

\\

He was tired. The work had become more tedious recently. Boredom had set in, too, but he wasn't sure what his next move should be. He'd gotten used to taking directions, orders really. He wanted to do his own bidding now, not someone else's, but this desire complicated life and filled him with paralyzing anxiety.

He recognized the vague fuzziness, the twinge of discomfort in his head that had recently come calling far more frequently than before. He knew what was to follow: words, conversations or pictures from his past. Since their inception he'd considered them to be significant signs, important messages, but were they?

"Any luck?"

"Yep."

"Well . . .?"

"I'm lookin' right at him. Yep. It's him."

SIXTEEN

Jake

No one expected us to arrive today. We were twenty-four hours early for our meeting with Janelle Rubio, the Director of Elementary Education. I knew she might not be available, but at least we could look around, get our bearings. And, I liked the idea that the element of surprise was on our side.

Lindsey and I strolled into the district's main office building and up to a counter located just below a sign that read 'Information.'

The man behind the counter peered at us over the top of his half-glasses and without a trace of emotion said, "No dogs allowed in here."

I turned on my charm. "Oh, it's okay. He's a service dog. He'll be fine, but thanks for your concern."

"Where is his service dog jacket? He needs to wear a jacket."

That's when Lindsey jumped onto my make-believe bandwagon and began to participate in the nonsense I'd started.

"You are absolutely right." Her tone sweeter, more innocent than usual. I hadn't realized until now what a talented actor she was. "We should go back and get it. It's in our RV that's parked just a few blocks away and . . ." She handed the man Wendell's leash—the dog was attached—and we turned to go.

Before we'd taken two steps from the counter, Mr. Information recanted his original statement and allowed our service dog, even without his jacket, to remain with us in the building; said he'd make an exception, but only for today. With that issue out of the way, he finally got around to asking how he could help us. So Lindsey filled him in briefly about her training sessions with the teachers. I asked if we could see Mrs. Rubio for just a few minutes.

"The director didn't come in today, but I can page her assistant for you."

We heard her before we saw her. The sound of high heels meeting the tiled floor, approaching with firm conviction from the long hallway to our right, could not be ignored. She wouldn't be sneaking up on anyone today.

We assumed the sound was familiar to Mr. Information because without looking up from his computer he added, "Ready or not, here she comes." *Was that humor or a warning?*

If I had to describe this woman, I'd say she looked like Marilyn Monroe at the height of her career but younger, slimmer, and with darker hair. She reached out to shake my hand and said, "Hi, my name is Marlow Mahoney."

"I'm Jake and this is Lindsey Lark, the consultant that will be working with your third grade teachers beginning this Friday."

"Yes, I know who you are." She glanced briefly at Lindsey and Wendell, then looked right into my eyes.

"Please, if the three of you will follow me, I'll show you your meeting room. It isn't far."

Lindsey whispered in my ear, "How can she walk so fast in those heels?"

I just shrugged hoping she wasn't able to read my mind right now because my own thoughts had more to do with her very short, tight-fitting apparel and I wondered how she could even sit down. Mrs. Rubio's assistant had a lot going on and, needless to say, my eyes were not on her shoes. *It's OK to look, right?*

"Here we are. This is it."

Lindsey's eyes scanned the room. "This will do nicely. It's perfect. Not in use today?"

"No, there wasn't enough lead time to rebook it after all the delays. Do you have any special requests regarding the physical set up of the space?"

Lindsey and Ms. Mahoney spent a few minutes discussing tables and chairs, but Mrs. Rubio's input was necessary when it came to some of the materials that would be used.

"I'm not sure where she is today, but I'll send her a text message of your arrival and your questions. Today's been a calm day around the admin building. A welcome change from the previous two days, almost relaxing, quiet . . ."

BANG! POP! POP! ZIP! BANG! CRASH! ZING!

Pretty sure we added to the unexpected, explosive noises with our own sounds of shock and surprise. Wendell bolted and was the first to take cover behind a table near the far wall. We were right behind him. Ms. Mahoney distanced herself from the explosive sounds, but remained standing and used her walkie-talkie to call for assistance.

"Explosion in the Annex, room 114. Bomb in the Annex, room 114. Does anyone copy?" Then, turning toward us almost apologetically she said just loud enough to be heard over the continuing sounds of detonation, "The bomb threat was for some of the elementary schools, not a district meeting room. This should not be happening."

She was one cool cookie, her tone so business-like, so matter-of-fact. Not a hint of panic could be heard in her voice.

I had questions. "So, this location where the workshop would take place was never searched?"

"Probably not. They focused on specific school sites. That's what I heard. Not my department. No 'need to know.' You know how that works."

"Sure. So ... this building, this room is not kept locked?"

"That's correct. It's not locked during regular business hours. Only our Legal Department gets that kind of security. They are all safe and sound, snug as bugs in their double locked wing of offices."

The noise had been sudden, loud, and over before help arrived. I could not stand by and do nothing any longer. Cautiously, I moved closer to the opposite end of the room where the explosion took place. There I found a kitchen-like cove containing an industrial sized metal trash barrel. In and around it were remnants of used fireworks—lots of them. The burning, smoky smell from this pyrotechnic display still lingered.

Ms. Mahoney was on the walkie-talkie again. "Explosion over. No injuries or major damage, but send a school safety officer and a custodian. We've got a mess here."

We left her with the mess and headed back to the RV. Was there some reality to the bomb threat after all, or was this a completely separate incident? Either way, it seemed to me this episode was meant to frighten or disrupt rather than harm anyone or anything. But frighten and disrupt who or what and . . . WHY?

"Jake, if we'd kept to our original schedule, I would have been conducting a workshop, standing just a few feet from the explosion, with eighty third grade teachers."

Our eyes met and locked. We'd developed a talent for riding the same wave, being on the same page, whether for business or pleasure. I knew one thing for sure: our time in Albuquerque had started with a bang!

SEVENTEEN

Lindsey

Why didn't I smell the coffee? Jake usually jump-started our day by preparing the morning drink as soon as his eyes opened. And, why was it so quiet? No whistling came from Jake, no tail thumping from Wendell and not even a peep or a squawk from Malcolm. Curiosity got the better of me; I threw on my sweats so I could take a look around.

Upon opening the door of the RV, all the missing sights, sounds, and smells were found. My loving trio turned and gave me a what-took-you-so-long look. Jake handed me a blue tin cup of coffee he'd percolated over the fire and a piece of something he called cinnamon bread, though it looked more like a snake.

"Try it, Linds. It's good. I just made some dough, sprinkled it with sugar and cinnamon, wound it around a stick, held it over the fire and . . . *voilà!*"

I had to admit it wasn't bad. A little crunchy, slightly charred, but that made it perfect for dipping into my coffee. "Thanks, Jake. How long have you been up?"

"Not sure, really. It was dark when I started the fire. And this is the second pot of coffee. And . . ."

"You drank a whole pot of coffee? Jake, that is not like you."

"I had some help." He took his time with the details, first sipping from his tin cup then taking a bite of his twisty bread. He could be such a tease. "We have neighbors down at the end of the loop." And he pointed in the direction of a small airstream camper. "A retired couple, I'm assuming. They didn't say much, wouldn't stay long, but seemed nice."

We discussed our plans for the day. Other than the sixty minutes we'd spend with Mrs. Rubio going over the details of my workshops and Jake's investigation, the day was ours. As much as I'd love to lounge around in the delicate fall sunlight reading one of the six novels and four magazines I'd brought along with me, I could tell Jake was feeling antsy and needed to move around. And, I knew why nothing sedentary would do today.

When Mrs. Rubio had returned her electronic application several months ago, she stated that she wasn't comfortable sending the "subtle investigation" portion of her request in writing or talking about it on the phone. So Jake hadn't a clue what he was in for and that fact was finally getting to him. I'd do what I could to lessen his tension.

"Jake, I'm having second thoughts about our work here. The combination of the explosion and the fact that we don't know what Mrs. Rubio is hoping you will do, makes me a little uneasy."

The last chewy bite of cinnamon bread in Jake's mouth delayed his response, but by the thoughtful look on his face, I knew he had one.

"The unknown is often unsettling. Let's meet with her and see what she has to say. We can always back out. We have no legal obligation to do any investigating; that's the beauty of the subtle, covert aspect of what we do."

"All right. I like the sound of that. On the other hand, though, I'm not so sure I could get out of my teacher training workshops. The district must have hired subs for those teachers and are locked into paying them. I'm not sure how that works here, especially with all the delays that have occurred. Every district is different."

By 10:00 a.m. we'd packed a lunch, filled our canteens, and agreed to embrace the mindset that everything was going to work out just fine. We took off walking toward the western end of the loop and the trail marker we'd noticed just before dusk last night. Our late arrival time yesterday was due to the fact we'd had trouble finding a decent place to park the RV. Most of the locations we looked at were set up more like RV sales lots than campsites. We could not spend a week in such a setting. Then we found this one. Yes, it was a twenty-minute drive from where I would be working, but being here among the trees, with mountain views, hiking trails, nature in every direction, trivialized the length of the drive.

"Come on, Wendell. You can come, too."

Nature was our drug of choice. We loved to surround ourselves with trees, flowers, streams—just about any natural outdoor venue would do as long as we were away, the farther the better, from buildings, traffic, or hordes of humans. In a matter of minutes, we'd regain that euphoric, spiritual connection we valued so dearly.

Even Wendell acquired a springier bounce in his four-legged walk out in this cool, wooded area. He did slow down as we passed by that airstream trailer, though. Something there held his interest for a few seconds. Perhaps a scent our human noses could not detect or the sound of . . . what was that? A cartoon? A TV show? As

Jake would say, *Ah, ha!* We heard some dog whimpering, whining. Either they had a dog or they might have been watching reruns or a DVD of the old *Lassie* show.

EIGHTEEN

Lindsey

Refreshed and rejuvenated from our hike, we were not only ready, but also anxious to begin our work in Albuquerque. Jake had suggested that we drive our Jeep Liberty into town this afternoon. We wouldn't be gone very long today and it was easier to maneuver the car through city traffic, plus, the pets could remain in the cool, forested area until we got back.

Unlike the need for off-campus meetings at the small Flagstaff school, we both felt comfortable talking with our new client in her office at the district's main administration building. After a quick pause to get directions at Mr. Information's counter, we headed toward the elevator.

A petite, dark-haired woman greeted us and introduced herself as Mrs. Rubio. I guessed she was in her early fifties and likely Hispanic. And though she looked incredibly tired, she was friendly, and before long insisted that we call her Jan.

"I would have brought you in, Lindsey, even if I hadn't needed Jake's services. My teachers' weakest area is writing. They know that and they requested the help. So you'll have a willing and eager audience."

I smiled. That was good news. An unreceptive crowd would have made success far more challenging.

"Every quarter for the past two years I've received the Innovative Teacher Awards Newsletter so I've kept up with your expertise, Lindsey. And because my goal for our students is to increase their competency in writing as well as their interest and enthusiasm for writing, your Art Journal lessons and concepts seemed like the perfect way to begin."

The more we spoke with Jan, the more we liked her and respected her knowledge of elementary instruction. I had the feeling that she'd worked her way up the rungs of the educational ladder, beginning with real classroom experience.

The next five days, preparing eighty third grade teachers to effectively conduct Art Journal Writing Lessons in their own classrooms, as well as to teach this process to the other educators at their schools, would be fun. I couldn't wait to get started. And I could see out of the corner of my eye that Jake couldn't wait to get started either. If we hadn't switched this discussion to his investigative project soon, I think he might have ascended the curtains like a cat, a curious, anxious cat. As it was, he could barely sit still.

"Jake, I'm not sure where to begin. My problem—my suspicions—are complex, yet I have very little factual information to share with you."

Up to that point, she'd told us nothing. Jake, though patient with me and our pets, had no patience when it came to his own work. He reminded me of a wild mustang at post time . . . objecting to the unfamiliar gate that prohibited any forward movement. Finally, Jan's words had some substance that Jake could relate to. The mustang mellowed.

"I have a hunch that funds are being skimmed from the teacher salaries budget line. Maybe skimming is not the correct term, but money is disappearing and no one in the finance office seems to care or is willing to reevaluate the math with me. I used to work in finance and I know something fishy is going on."

Jake scratched his head. "Embezzlement? Is that what you think is happening? That might be a little out of our 'unofficial' league and, possibly, beyond our capabilities."

"You don't have to solve this mystery or prosecute anyone or . . . oh, I don't even know. I just don't know." Her subtle anxious feelings were now obvious. Her stress level soared to heights an eagle would envy. "I just need you to snoop around and find some facts. Facts! I need facts. I can't go to the authorities, the superintendent or the legal department with just a hunch. And I especially cannot go to the school board."

I understood that issue, but Jake didn't and asked, "Why not?"

"Let's just say that some of the members are a little difficult to work with this year."

"Do you have anything in writing for me, Mrs. Rubio, that might add some detail to your hunches? That would really help me. Otherwise, I'm not sure I can find what you are looking for."

She took out a folder from her briefcase and handed it to Jake. "I made you a copy of everything I have including some of the budget pages as well as my thoughts, ideas, and additional hunches."

We walked back to the Jeep and as Jake opened the door for me, he paused in thought before saying, "There is something she's not telling us. Something important."

NINETEEN

Lindsey

Light, cheery, classical music gently filled the room as the teachers began to arrive. I had seen to that. I'd learned a lot about creating a welcoming atmosphere for presentations or workshops during my time as a presenter with the Innovative Teacher Awards Company and its owner, Elisabeth Meriwether. I added my own knowledge of healthy eating and provided a variety of fruit, nuts and mineral water. Admittedly, I felt pangs of guilt as we set out the carafes of coffee and boxes of donuts, but coffee and donuts were expected. They just were. *Oh, dear. One of the glazed donuts is calling my name.*

Jake made sure I had everything I'd need for the day and Wendell took on the role of greeter. He sat at the open door's threshold smiling as teachers entered. The teachers smiled back. He'd surely steal the show if I let him stay. Our dog loved attention.

I introduced myself, then Jake, then Wendell—and mentioned that our bird was back in the RV probably sleeping. Hands went up.

"Questions already?" I laughed. Having learned several years ago how important names were to the majority of people, I'd supplied nametags not only for my benefit but for the participants, too. This group of eighty teachers represented over a dozen schools, so many of them did not know each other by name. I called on one of the women whose hand was raised. "Okay. Melody, let's begin with you."

"Do you think I could get a photo with you, your husband, and your dog? My students will want to know where I've been and what I've been doing. That would help me explain my absence and I know they would love to see that photo."

All eighty heads nodded in agreement and the room buzzed with conversation. I needed to find a way to make that happen, but definitely not today. I waved at Jake as he and the dog left the room. Things calmed down a little after that and I said I'd check with Jake and his schedule and maybe we could fit in a photo shoot next week. That seemed to make everyone happy for the moment. That and the donuts.

Then we had a frank discussion about our fears, our failures, and our successes when it came to the teaching of writing. During this time I took questions from the audience . . . and lots of notes. If a question could be answered quickly and easily, I answered it right away. That was seldom the case, though. The remainder of their inquiries would be answered during the course of the workshop. We were off to a mighty fine start.

No problems—educational or otherwise—reared up today, but I did catch myself looking over my shoulder and keeping an eye on the entrances to the Annex, room 114.

TWENTY

Jake

My heavy lifting was done for the day. The last box of materials that Lindsey would use this sunny Monday morning now rested on a chair in her meeting room. The teachers straggled in and headed directly to the coffee and donuts before selecting a seat at one of the round tables.

I was helping Lindsey hang up a poster-sized Post-it containing the day's agenda when Ms. M&M (that was my private nickname for Marlow Mahoney) hurried in waving an envelope. And yes, today I noticed her spiky-heeled shoes.

"Oh, good. You're here, Jake. I just wanted to swing by and give this to you or to Lindsey, if I didn't see you. But there you are, so here you go."

She handed me the envelope before departing and said, "Tootles. So much to do. Monday's are crazy around here."

She talked so fast, not taking a breath, and moved so quickly, I didn't have the opportunity to thank her. But I did watch her walk away, though the word 'walk' didn't do justice to describing her departure. It was more of a stomping, swaying, marching movement.

"What did she want?" Lindsey's eyes sparkled with curiosity.

"Nothing. Just delivering a note . . . from Jan, I think."

"Oh, okay," said Lindsey shrugging her shoulders. "Thanks for driving me into town today. Got to get started now. I'm going to take the teachers through the Art Journal lesson I'd named 'Arthur's Thanksgiving' and then we will create adaptations for all the grade levels. Fun stuff, but it will take every minute we've got today to accomplish that."

"My pleasure. You know I promised the guys I'd work from home today, so I'd better get going, too. Can't wait to get back to the RV, nature, the pets . . . but I will be back at 3:30 sharp to pick you up. Miss you already," I said backing toward the door, feeling incredibly charming, and knowing that a room full of women were watching me go.

On my return drive to the campground, I thought about my day of research surrounded by fresh air, fragrant pines, and my loyal pets, and couldn't wait to begin. Most of the weekend campers had already pulled out. Only a few small pop-up trailers and the airstream camper remained. Ah, all was quiet, except for the chirping birds and chattering squirrels—just the way I liked it.

The Elementary Director, Mrs. Janelle Rubio, was right. The budget line for teacher salaries was shrinking every pay period more than it should. That appeared obvious to me. How could others in the finance department not see that? I realized that this phenomenon, however, did not fall within my realm of expertise, but I could do basic math and the addition and subtraction right here in front of me, did not add up . . . or subtract down.

Jan's hand-written comments were on separate pieces of paper attached to the budget sheets with paperclips. They alluded only to the possibility of a form of sabotage against her, which led her to the conclusion that someone was out to get her fired. Maybe she was right, but I still had nothing to validate her hunches or her conclusions about that aspect of the issue. Upon closing the folder, I remembered the envelope I'd received this morning. Perhaps it contained some useful information. *Now where did I put that?*

Of course, I found it in the car, the very last place I'd looked. Before sitting back down, I poured myself a glass of sun tea—a mixture of oolong tea, rooibos and orange peels—developed especially for Leos like me. I'd drink it slightly warmed by the sun for now, and add some ice later as the day heated up.

"Ouch! Dang! That hurt!" Wendell was soon at my side checking to see what had happened. "I'm okay, just a paper cut on my finger that wants to keep bleeding. It sure does sting, though." I told myself to slow down as I got up to retrieve a small bandage.

I opened the envelope from end to end, and, in the process, figured out why I'd been such a klutz the first time around; the envelope appeared to have a thick, extra layer of glue keeping it closed. Good! I relinquished all thoughts of my own klutziness to the universe and now removed what I'd assumed to be more information from Jan.

What I found was another envelope displaying my name above the address for the district's administration building. My curiosity grew. And my thoughts traveled back to the threatening letters Lindsey and I had received last year. We had our own educated hunches about the author of those letters, but no actual proof. So, I hesitated a moment before opening that inner envelope, then took great care with the process, not wanting another bloody finger. Inside was a letter; not just any letter, but a very . . . flirty letter. That was a first. In my entire life, I'd never seen, let alone received, a letter like this one.

Dear Jake: I hope this letter finds you well and happy. You deserve to be happy. My letter may come as a surprise to you, but it really shouldn't. After all, you are a very desirable, handsome man, a man that any woman who was even half alive would want. I am no exception. Just thought you should know.
Your Secret Admirer

I shook my head and could feel my own face frowning. After reading the words several times, trying to come up with the *who, what, where, when, and why* of it all, the only thought that surfaced was WTH? I needed to talk to Lindsey, so I sent a text message to her phone and hoped she'd see it.

LINDS—GOT SOMETHING U MUST C. WILL B THERE IN 30. JAKE

They were just breaking for lunch when I walked in.

"Jake, what a nice surprise. Did you come back to join me for lunch?" The warmth of her smile echoed in her voice. She was really glad to see me. Don't think she saw my text message, though.

"Uh, sure. What sounds good to you?"

"Well, there is not much time. How about we just snack on some of those healthy, unpopular treats that I keep bringing in? Got plenty of those."

We sat there alone in the meeting room. I took a few bites of cheese and apple slices. When I could not wait another second I said, "Linds, remember when Marlow Mahoney dropped off an envelope this morning? I think you should see what it contained." I handed over the letter and braced myself, not knowing what her reaction might be.

At first she giggled and said, "Is this a love letter? Maybe one of the teachers has a crush on you." But then she reread it and as its content sank in, her eyes grew troubled. "You received a love letter . . . with drops of blood on it." Her tone was oddly devoid of expression. Perhaps she was experiencing a little emotional shock or disbelief. Or had suspicions or thoughts I had yet to think.

Holding up my bandaged finger hoping that would suffice for the presence of blood, and speaking the words *paper cut*, I explained what I could about the letter, which wasn't very much. I posed the question: "Who knows we are here? It was sent here to the admin office's address!"

"Obviously, Jan Rubio and Marlow know we are here," contributed Lindsey.

"And that Mr. Information guy," I added weakly, doubting that he would have a crush on me. Then again, you never know, till you know.

"Jake, every single teacher at this conference knows we are here." She stated the obvious again, and then her eyes became glassy—almost dazed—with a far, far away look. "Laura. Laura knows where we are. We always update her regarding our location."

I'm quite sure I'd let out a long, heavy sigh just then, and suddenly I could relate to the common phrase about the wind being taken from one's sails. Not wanting to believe that Lindsey still thought about the drawings her best friend had created last year, I tried to change the subject, but unwanted, flashback memories of that unfortunate event floated to the surface of my thinking.

Lindsey had told me about finding several sheets of paper that contained pink, purple, and red drawings of a

romantic nature. She saw the words *Jake &
Laura* and *Mr. and Mrs. Lee* written over and over—some
within the shape of a heart, others heartless. Laura had
been in our home watching the pets. Lindsey knew that.
She also knew Laura's handwriting. Things got ugly. The
two women came to blows. Literally!

If this was the trip my own brain took me on, I could
only imagine what Lindsey was going through right now.
With the arrival of this letter, was she frightened or
jealous or both? I watched as she stood up slowly—no
wind in her sails either.

The teachers were returning from lunch now.

"It's show time. Got to put on a happy face and get
things going again."

She turned and walked away from me, not looking
back.

I knew this letter might upset her, it upset me, but she
was taking this awfully hard, and I deemed her response
as overreacting. *Why? Does she not trust me?* I wondered.
I could not leave things like this, so I went to her, took her
hands in mine, brought them to my lips, giving them a
gentle kiss while looking intensely into her worried eyes.

"The pets are comfortable, their needs met. I will be
parked right outside in the car. Text me if you need
anything. Otherwise, I will see you at 3:30."

She acknowledged my statement with a solemn nod,
and I walked away feeling uncertain about . . . us.

TWENTY-ONE

Lindsey

My normal enthusiasm was nowhere to be found. An unusual midday slump had taken over and I knew I could not blame this down-in-the-dumps feeling on the weather. I could blame it on the letter. *Focus! Focus!* Why was I suddenly dwelling on that stupid letter again?

Eighty teachers were waiting for me to begin. That was my sturdy, sensible, intellectual side talking. My emotional side whispered into my ear that someone was trying to steal my husband. And that someone, if not Laura, could be right in this room.

Listless and off-balanced, I pulled out my outline to remind myself what came next. The eager energy radiating from the teachers forced me out of my funk. I asked everyone to make one huge circle around the tables, handed out some percussion instruments—shakers, rhythm sticks, clickers, and even a couple of cowbells—and led the group in a rousing, reverberating version of the chant we learned the first day of the workshop. It was loud. *Cowbells? What was I thinking?* The activity proved to be energizing and fun!

"You will notice a stack of papers in the middle of every table. The top sheet on each˙stack will have a letter or a number. K, 1, 2, 3, or 4/5. I am asking that each of you select a table and there you will begin to write an Art Journal Lesson Plan for the grade level depicted on that top sheet of paper."

I recognized that panicked look. With the exception of the teachers that managed to find a seat at one of the '3' or third grade tables, all the others would be planning for a grade they did not currently teach.

The room was suddenly silent (and I hadn't yet collected the percussion instruments) when one of the seasoned teachers spoke up.

"Third grade is the only grade I've ever taught in my entire career. I can't imagine thinking like a kinder teacher or a fifth grade teacher, not to mention understanding the needs of the students. I don't know what they are supposed to learn in the other grades."

A few other women nodded in supportive agreement. And I understood that embarking on something new, unfamiliar, produced fear or at least a feeling of insecurity.

"I completely understand. That is why there are stacks of paper on each table. In those stacks you will find several copies of the writing standards New Mexico's public schools follow. Also, there are examples of lesson plans for the corresponding grade level and pages from several, easy, *How to Draw* books."

The tension in the room lessened, but was not yet gone. What could I say to empower each and every teacher?

"How many of you rely on official teacher guides when deciding what to teach each day?" Almost every hand went up. That explained a lot.

"How many of you follow the lessons in those guides exactly as they are written? Come on. It's not a trick question."

No hands, not even one, went up.

"No, of course you don't. And thank goodness you don't. You modify and adapt the lessons to your students' needs and abilities. Right? There is no need to worry about creating a perfect lesson today. Besides, there is no such thing because your students have diverse learning styles and abilities."

Finally, smiles and nods pervaded the room. With the hurdles eliminated or at least lowered a bit, the teachers jumped forward and happily created make-and-take lessons for their table's assigned grade level. They would share those lessons later this afternoon during the weekly professional development meeting back at their own schools.

I felt the corners of my lips turn upward. I'd become a victim of their contagious enthusiasm.

TWENTY-TWO

Jake

S itting in the small car yesterday afternoon while waiting for Lindsey and attempting to solve the declining budget line mystery was less than satisfactory. So today, the back of Lindsey's meeting room served as my office, at least until it was time for my appointment with Jan at 11:30. I didn't accomplish much, but then I did not know what else I could do until Jan and I met. There was little to go on and nothing related to the budget was jumping out, waving flags, or appearing suspicious, other than the budget itself. Questions. That's all I had.

Pretending to work, I listened to Lindsey teaching teachers. She was an expert in her field, but without a hint of superiority or inflated ego. Again, she was amazing, and so genuine. No wonder adults and kids alike loved her. She was the one deserving of a love letter, not me. *Don't go there. Don't even think about that.*

Time to go. As I tiptoed out the door, dozens of teachers shouted, "Bye, Jake." I gave a little wave, a silly grin and headed next door for my meeting.

"Have a seat, Jake. Would you like some coffee or soda or . . ."

"Water, if you have it, would be great, Mrs. Rubio."

"It's Jan. The only time I'd prefer to hear 'Mrs. Rubio' is in the presence of teachers or students."

"Okay, I'll work on that. But before we get into the disappearing money mystery, I have some questions about that letter you had Ms. Mahoney bring by yesterday. Do you know where it came from? When you got it? Anything—"

"I wouldn't know about that. My assistant handles all the mail and messages that come to this office. She only gives me the ones that I need to attend to. Sorry that I can't help you there."

"Uh, no problem." Something about her answer bothered me, but I couldn't put my finger on it.

I asked Jan why the teacher budget was so important to her. She was quick with her answer and passionately informed me that the teacher to student ratio and the quality of the teachers was paramount to the students' success.

I blurted out, "I don't get it!" What I really didn't get was the emotional side of Janelle Rubio that was inching toward the surface again.

I could see this topic was a raw one for her, cutting right to the bone. But why?

"When the budget shrinks, so does the teaching force, and then the district's academic scores go down. I am held responsible for those scores, my *raison d'être*, if you will. Cuts were made and that should not have happened."

I searched her face for a hint, a clue. I needed that fictitious light bulb to shine above my head because I still didn't get the emotion I saw. "Jan, talk to me."

Silence. Nothing. Then a tear—not mine; I'm not the crying type. Oh, dear. The floodgates opened and tears streamed down the cheeks of the high-ranking, school official sitting before me.

"So, I take it, it's personal . . . this whole thing."

She let out a heavy sigh before speaking. "I care about the students; they always come first. I also care about the teachers—the ones that lose their jobs and the ones left with far too many students in their classrooms. And, yes, I care about me. This job is my life."

Jan mentioned her family and how they'd always been her moral support. Then, after a few awkward moments of silence, she tossed in the fact that she no longer had any family—none at all. *Was that significant?* She rapidly moved back to the topic at hand. She'd had a relatively successful run in the field of education, but that had begun to change with the arrival of the new superintendent. He'd been critical of her right from the start, accusing her of using old-fashioned, outdated methods.

She admitted to me that keeping up with the constant changes, especially in the use of technology in the classroom, had been difficult, even stressful. That was the main reason she campaigned for the hiring of an assistant.

"I can see that this particular budget is shrinking more than the debits reflect, but aren't most budgets shrinking nowadays? Isn't that the current norm?" I'd hoped to draw more information from her. The more she'd talk, the more I'd learn.

"Generally speaking, your thinking is correct, Jake, but our enrollment numbers have increased over the past two years. The budget is directly related and affected by the number of students enrolled."

I was beginning to get that part. More students should equal more money. Money seemed to be disappearing and not showing up anywhere else. Or maybe neither Jan nor I knew how to decipher all the financial paperwork. It was overwhelming, baffling.

"If only the Director of Finance would talk to me, but he won't. I am the proverbial *thorn in his side* and he is too busy brown-nosing all the important people in the district, even in the city. Everybody loves him. He is ambitious. I think he wants to be the next superintendent and, apparently, he has the credentials."

I enjoyed my public claim to fame as Lindsey's helpful husband, but I wasn't comfortable blowing my cover. That was never part of the plan. Now, I couldn't think of a way to move forward without doing so.

"Well, Jan. Maybe the Director of Finance will speak with me."

TWENTY-THREE

Lindsey

On the drive home—we did consider the RV our home on this road trip—and after sharing a few of the highlights of my afternoon—kept the lowlights to myself—I asked Jake about his meeting with Jan. None of this budget mystery interested me much until he asked, "Why do women want to tell me all about their families and their personal problems? Answer me that, Dr. Watson."

Jake could always make me laugh, even after a long day. "Okay, Sherlock. Here goes. Women tell you personal things because you are a very nice person and you're good looking. Even hot! Nice and hot is a combination that is hard to ignore. That is normal. And, yes, I'm speaking from personal experience. But . . . and this is a BIG but, (Stop laughing, Jake. Stop laughing right now!) Nothing about that love letter was normal."

"That was some segue, Linds, from nice and hot to the stupid, friction-causing letter. You're right, though. The arrival of that short letter was strange and inappropriate. I doubt there is anything more to it. But we're a team and we'll handle that issue together, if we need to handle it at all."

Jake unlocked the door for me before unloading the car. I hurried up the RV's steps prepared for dog kisses and bird chirps. We hadn't been away from our pets for this many hours in months. Wendell always greeted us with exuberance; Malcolm's reactions to things could be a little harder to read.

"Jake! Jake! Something is wrong," I shouted, and I'm not a shouter.

Wendell sat in the driver's seat trembling, panting—do dogs hyperventilate?—and the side window near his face displayed vertical streaks, scratches as if he'd tried to scratch his way out of the RV.

"What the hell happened here?"

"I don't know, Jake, but it couldn't have been good. Look at poor Wendell. I've never seen him this upset. And even Malcolm is not doing well. Some frantic flapping must have occurred to leave that many feathers on the bottom of his cage."

Our first order of business was to comfort these guys. That took a while. Jake refilled the water dishes—the huge one and the tiny one—we put on some soft and mellow classical music, and patted and rubbed Wendell. It was harder to comfort a bird, but we let him out of his cage and he sat on my head for a minute before moving to Wendell's.

"I sure wish these guys could talk. They know what scared them."

"Malcolm does know a few words and phrases and, thanks to your leisure time addiction of watching sports on TV, he can even sing a little bit of the 'Star-Spangled Banner'." I knew that wouldn't help in this situation, but now that our boys were acting more normal, I felt my own tension lessening and my typical, grounded self returning.

Wendell sat by the door and gave it a paw tap. Of course! The poor dog needed to pee; he'd been cooped up inside for almost eight hours. Jake got up to let him out.

"Wow! Did you see that, Lindsey?" Jake called. "He leaped out of here, missing the steps completely, and now he's dashing all around the RV. Put Malcolm in his cage and come out with us."

By the time I'd coaxed Malcolm into the safety of his cage, I found Wendell and Jake in close proximity to the left front tire. The tire was obviously lacking air, Wendell felt the need to dig, sniff, and lick, while Jake stood by scratching his head, which meant he was attempting once again to make sense out of the senseless. Wendell came closer to me—the dog treat in my pocket might have had something to do with that—allowing Jake a better look.

Instead of coming up empty handed, he came up with a bloody hand. As much as the situation we now faced was bad, it wasn't as bad as I'd just made it sound. The hand was his own and though it did have blood on it, I quickly learned it was not Jake's.

In this age of blood borne infectious diseases, I insisted he go and disinfect his hand immediately. He was more than happy to do that. In fact, we all went back inside. Wendell did not need something or someone's blood in his stomach any more than Jake needed it on his hand.

"What do you think happened, Jake? We couldn't have run over an animal, right? We haven't driven the RV in several days. And Wendell would have noticed the blood before now."

"The blood is not from an animal, Lindsey. It is from the person that slashed our tire who, in the process, slashed a part of his or her own body as well."

I watched as he carefully transferred blood from his hand to the special strips he'd retrieved from his crime scene investigations kit; the kit he'd been issued during his Forensic Psychology Internship last year. It was like watching an episode of CSI without any dead bodies. I suddenly felt the urge to knock on some wood—real wood.

"Do we have enemies, Jake? Does someone want to hurt us? Are all these RV issues connected? Are we being followed? Should we call the—"

"Whoa. Slow down girl. As soon as I get these samples stored and packed properly, we will tackle your great questions . . . one at a time.

We generated a list of possible enemies. It was neither long nor strong. My former husband, Anthony, got top billing because he had already tried to harm, even kill Jake, Jake's sister Julie, and me over 18 months ago, but he was still locked up, doing time in the state of Washington for arson. So his involvement seemed unlikely, probably impossible.

Second runner up was Sean. (He used to be Shawna, the woman Anthony left me for until he discovered her cleverly disguised transgender issues. All of which triggered some major mental problems and sent those problems hurdling to the forefront.) Sean gave up living his life as Shawna almost a year ago. The authorities have yet to tie him to any of Anthony's past threats or criminal deeds, but they haven't completely exonerated him either. His involvement seemed unlikely, too, though not impossible.

"We don't have any enemies, Jake. Not really."

"Well. Apparently, we do. At least one. We just don't know who he—"

"Or *she*, is."

"I stand corrected. I will dust for prints next to cover all of our bases though I think our best option lies with the blood. But I'll need to request a favor, a huge one."

Jake hoped to bypass the normal order and timeframe for obtaining a typical DNA analysis. His plan was to call Lad in Oregon. He lived with Jake's psychiatrist sister, Julie, and I knew him to be trustworthy and well connected when it came to doing the impossible. If anyone could pull off the blood analysis quickly, it was Lad.

TWENTY-FOUR

Jake

"Hi, Julie. How've you been?"

"Good. What's up?"

She'd never been one for small talk. So I got right to the point and began to explain our situation, but she interrupted me.

"I suppose you've heard about Anthony?"

"Uh, no. I don't think so. Tell me, and tell me quickly because bad things are happening around here." I said a quiet prayer in my head that the man was still behind bars.

"He comes up for parole in thirty days. Lad thinks they might actually let him out because they were never able to pin an attempted murder charge on him."

"Good. I won't have to worry about his sorry ass for at least a month. But someone is harassing Lindsey and me by messing around the RV. It's a long story; aren't they all? Today was the last straw. The culprit slashed one of the tires and himself in the process. I want to run a DNA analysis on the blood and I need Lad's help."

"He just walked in. Hold on."

Then I could hear her say, "It's Jake . . . with a problem." Lad and I were speaking within seconds.

I told our story, at least the parts I felt were pertinent to our personal harassment. Then Lad filled me in on the status quo regarding Sean and Anthony. Sean's phone was still tapped, and there was above-the-norm surveillance on Anthony's activity in prison. It was noted that Anthony gave Sean some papers on a few occasions and that he did spend a lot of time writing, but no one seemed overly alarmed about the way he passed the time. He was a model prisoner. That was about it.

"Jake, take your package of blood samples and prints directly to the FedEx office at the airport to ensure it goes out tonight. We'll talk again soon." Like in the past, Lad was all business, a man of few words. Tonight I had a greater appreciation for that character trait than ever before.

We all piled, squeezed really, into the small car. No one would be left alone until we figured out what the heck was going on here. The sound of an old cartoon—I think it was *Scooby Doo* this time—came from the airstream trailer as we drove slowly past it.

"They must have a kid with them."

"Could be a grandchild, but I haven't seen anyone but the two older folks." Lindsey's eyes remained focused on the trailer until it was out of view. "Maybe that child has a disability and can't come out."

"I think we should pay them a visit when we get back, if it's not too late. And we can ask them if they saw or heard anything today. They must have heard Wendell barking."

Our pets were not themselves. Sitting there in the crowded backseat, Wendell whimpered softly and Malcolm was completely silent. Neither behavior was typical.

We arrived at the FedEx office at the Albuquerque International Sunport in time to ship my package of evidence to Lad. Once again, we were put in a position of waiting—not one of my strong points. Even Lad needed several days, maybe a week, to work his magic through governmental departments calling in favors from old friends. In the meantime, I'd need to be ready to fend off our unseen, unknown enemy.

TWENTY-FIVE

Lindsey

Back home, sitting around our campfire, we noticed that our neighbor's airstream at the end of the loop was dark, not a hint of light could be seen. All was quiet, too. Early-to-bed people, I assumed. We decided our visit could take place another time and agreed that, more than likely, they were not part of our problem. Jake, however, couldn't keep from stating that 'no stone should go unturned' and 'everyone is a suspect until proven otherwise.'

"I was just thinking, Lindsey . . . what's with us and letters?" It dawned on me that I might have lifted the lid to Pandora's box. Regrets? Probably, but it was too late. "First, there were Anthony's threatening letters last year, then Jill's follow-up letters in Flagstaff, and now a love letter in Albuquerque. That's a lot of letters in our lives."

"True, but I am more concerned that someone might have followed us all the way from Flagstaff, Arizona, to this campground in New Mexico. That is serious, costly,

115

and time-consuming harassment. Who would do something like that?"

We considered everything . . . and came up with nothing. Though we did reconfirm our plan to stick together whenever possible—all four of us.

Jake turned toward Wendell and Malcolm. "Well, guys, I guess we are all going to school with the teacher tomorrow." Then, lifting one eyebrow, he looked me straight in the eye and added, "Hope you have something planned that will keep us entertained."

"I'll have to think about that."

And so I did. I thought while Jake put another log on the fire. Hmm. A familiar rhythm began to keep time in my head—no, not from the Merle Haggard song, but from my own version of a nursery rhyme—and extended down to my tapping foot: This was the fire that Jake built. This was the log ... those are the sparks ... these are the holes, burned into the shirt ... Jake! Your shirt is on fire!"

He'd felt the heat just as I'd spotted the tiny flames, and pulled the shirt off over his head. I noticed just a few pink marks, no blistering, and he said it didn't hurt. I said he was a sight for sore eyes standing there, shirtless, by the flickering flames. Even though 'it didn't hurt,' I retrieved and applied a cold, damp cloth to his bare chest wondering all the while how a guy who doesn't work out at a gym maintained such ripped abs.

Looking down at my own midsection, I knew I would not be accused of having well-defined abdominal muscles. In fact, for the first time in my adult life, I thought I might be gaining a few pounds. No, I hadn't been standing on a scale, but my clothing felt a tiny bit snugger lately. We had been eating out more, I rationalized.

"Jake, am I starting to look fat?"

Who said that? Surely it wasn't me. Oh, God. It was me. I'd said it—out loud. And I could tell by the expression on Jake's face that he was giving much thought to his reply. What a smart man.

"You look beautiful, Linds. I don't see those extra . . . ounces, but if it would make you feel better, we could hike them off when we get to Estes Park."

He must have noticed my slight weight gain or he wouldn't have said that. Yes, indeed, he'd noticed and then tried so hard to be sensitive and kind about it. I vowed then and there to get back into shape—wedding day shape—beginning tomorrow.

Images of taking high altitude hikes with Jake had been nestled in my brain ever since we'd accepted the small Rocky Mountain town's application. I'd even cut out a picture of Bear Lake and taped it to the fridge at home.

"I just hope snow won't be a deterring factor. We didn't bring any snow gear."

"Lindsey, if we need snow gear, we will get snow gear."

I still couldn't wrap my thinking or my spending habits around the concept of wealth, at least not at the level of affluence enjoyed by the Lees, which trickled down to Jake, to us. In attempting to come to terms with the ability to buy whatever I wanted or needed, I vowed to give every purchase some serious thought. I would not let myself become frivolous nor wasteful. Still, it was like living in a fairy tale. And I suppose, in a way, I'd asked for that. Never thought I'd get it.

"Can you believe it, Lindsey? Most of my life I resented my family's wealth."

That was something difficult for me to imagine. I had no frame of reference. What I did know was that Jake needed to talk about this, and he continued . . .

"I understand now that my perception of the real world was limited and I lacked traditional family togetherness including love and affection. My father was so busy being a wealthy man, hovering over his land, cattle, and oil investments as if they were his real children, I rarely saw him.

"And Mother claimed (often) that hiring people to do the cooking, the cleaning, the running of errands, the gardening, the travel arrangements, the flower arrangements, the chauffeuring of us kids—well, you get the idea—was such time-consuming, difficult work, she barely had the chance to get her nails done or attend a school function. Her nails always looked perfect, though.

"They were both into creating the appearance of perfection but neither seemed to realize that *perfection* involved things far grander than mere monetary wealth."

"Your parents were wonderful at our wedding."

"Yes, they were. Both Julie and I were shocked; she'd even whispered in my ear, 'Who are those people?' because their behavior was not typical. You, Lindsey, brought out the *family* gene in them, at least for our wedding day, that had been lying dormant for as long as I can remember."

I was part of that family now, though it hadn't really sunk in yet. At a loss for words, I sat quietly by the fire with my own immediate family: Jake, Wendell, and Malcolm. We were a family in every sense of the word. *And, please, let no man (or woman) put that asunder.*

TWENTY-SIX

Jake

We doused what was left of the glowing embers, removed anything that might attract wild animals to our campsite, and headed inside. It had been quite a day for both of us, and I needed to replace the slashed tire in the morning before we could go anywhere. Fortunately, Lindsey's workday didn't begin until noon tomorrow when the teachers returned after having had the experience of teaching their first art journal lesson. We could sleep in!

With that pleasant thought, new energy surged through my veins. I got my second wind and began to make a plan for the next phase of our evening.

"Hey, sweetie? Why don't you hop in the shower while I finish cleaning up the kitchen area?"

As soon as I heard the water splashing down, my man-of-the-house-on-wheels mode kicked into high gear, but I wasn't cleaning. I could do that tomorrow. Next to our bed, I set out candles, some wine—from a bottle, not a box—some body lotion, and, last but not least, some extra fancy lubricating oil I'd been saving for a special occasion. Every inch of my baby's body would feel good tonight.

"You think you'll fit in here?" was Lindsey's comment when I joined her in the RV's small shower. It was tight, but we managed. We even washed each other's hair and backs. However, dropping the soap right now could be problematic . . . or delightful. Hmm.

Eventually, we stood face to face.

"Oh, Jake. I think it would be best if I didn't touch your chest." Genuine concern came from her voice as her eyes reconnected with the pink spots, the minor burns from the popping sparks, that were more visible now that we were illuminated.

I appreciated her concern and explained that it looked worse than it felt. Then I complimented her rhyme.

"What rhyme?"

"Best and chest. In addition to alliteration, you use rhyme a lot, too. You don't know you do that?"

"I guess I do rhyme, sometimes, but not always on purpose. It's more like a coincidence. You will know, without a doubt, when a purposeful rhyme comes from these lips."

My second *hmm* of the evening just came from my own lips.

"Come on, Jake. You're in luck. Come with me. I want to—"

"Lindsey!" I had to interrupt.

"What?" Her tone was one of pure innocence, but I knew better.

"You know what!"

"Oh. You thought I was making a rhyme?"

I'm not a guy that's into giggles, but when Lindsey's the giggler, I love it!

"Well . . . maybe I was."

Her laugh was contagious. She got me. And then she repeated and completed her purposeful rhyme.

"Come on, Jake. You're in luck. I want to gaze out the window 'cause I'm moonstruck."

She got me again.

Next stop, our bed.

"Oh, my. You've been busy. Does this mean the dishes are still in the sink?"

"Yes, ma'am. Priorities. I've got my priorities."

"I like the way you think, Mr. Lee. And, yes, tonight you are Mr. Lee. Sherlock is *persona non grata* for a while.

It was late, we were tired, so my plan was simple. We'd sip a glass of wine by candlelight and I'd take great pleasure in arousing Lindsey in a sweet and gentle way using my new oil. Then we'd drift off to sleep in each other's arms feeling loved and contented. A perfect way to end the day. It was the best of times …

Even with only the flickering light of two candles I could see her beautiful smile just before my lips reached hers. She seemed as eager to touch me as I was to caress her. She lay panting, her chest heaving. My plan was working. She writhed beneath me, gasping in sweet agony. Then she cried out.

"Stop! Stop! It hurts so much."

I was right about the agony, but wrong about the sweet.

"Baby, what's the matter? What's wrong?"

"My insides are burning, really burning. I don't know why, but it is so painful."

This was a mystery to me, too. So I began my questioning. It's what I do.

"Do you think it was something you ate?"

"No, Jake. It is not my stomach that is on fire."

Oh. I wondered if she might have an infection down there, or maybe an allergy to my new oil.

"Lindsey, except for the lubricating oil, nothing is different. And that stuff is supposed to make you feel good, really good."

From her expression, there was no doubt in my mind that she was in pain, terrible pain that seemed to worsen with each passing second. Neither of us was the type to 'freak out' but that was exactly what we were doing.

She demanded that I turn on the light so we could read the fine print on the bottle of oil. Damn! I'd made a mistake. Oh, my gosh. A GIANT one. It was oil, all right. High intensity massage oil called Hot Stuff! Its main purpose was to heat up the skin to help relieve severe muscle pain. NOT FOR INTERNAL USE. I quickly brought Lindsey some ice wrapped in a wet towel.

"Maybe another shower would help, Lindsey." I felt so bad. Causing her pain was the last thing I ever wanted to do.

"Tonight I wish the RV had a tub, but I'll try a shower."

I didn't think either of us would be falling asleep anytime soon, so after putting Lindsey back on ice, I stared into the freezer hoping to find a quick and easy snack that we'd both like. That cartoon light bulb hovered above me, and the idea sprang from my tongue.

"Lindsey, we've got Popsicles in here." I wondered if they could be used therapeutically in this . . . situation.

She appeared to be contemplating my offer of a Popsicle. So, I continued.

"Would you rather have cherry or grape?"

I wasn't sure, but I think she glared at me. So I prepared some chamomile tea and a healthy midnight snack of veggies and cheese, instead. I still thought the Popsicle might have helped.

"I'm very particular about what goes into my body," she said before taking a bite of a carrot.

Hmm. Was she regaining her sense of humor, being sexual, getting me back, or none of the above? Hard to tell. One thing I knew for sure . . . we'd both suffered burns tonight.

TWENTY-SEVEN

Lindsey

Today's session began with lunch. The teachers clamored in with boxes and materials of their own just as Jake and the dog walked out toward the parking lot, back to the RV. The RV was Jake's office today. Wendell and Malcolm were his assistants.

The sight of my guys reminded the women of the impending photo shoot. There was more talk of that than of their lessons. Now that I was looking around, it became clear that none of these teachers had needed reminding. Did I detect a profound increase in the level of mascara, blush and lip-gloss today? Definitely! Hmm. I jotted a note to myself on a mid-sized Post-it: "Allow time to re-apply gloss & blush prior to photo shoot".

"We don't have much time and we have lots to do. So grab a box lunch from the back table; we need to get started—and yes, we will make time for photos with the dog."

I explained how we would proceed. No one was required to share here today, but I'd hoped several would.

To encourage that, I'd given a simple handout yesterday containing suggestions for the sharing of their lesson.

"Who would like to start us off?"

There were no volunteers. I waited. Nothing. So . . . I had an idea.

"Everyone, quickly share at your table what you drew during the guided art portion of your lesson and what the writing focus was. You have five minutes." Ah, the buzz was back.

"Okay, time's up! Now that you've heard a little bit about your colleagues' lessons, I would like one person from each table to restate or summarize your group's discussion. Let's begin with a kinder lesson."

The hesitation that had existed a few minutes earlier had reversed itself. Now everyone wanted to share.

In the kinder classrooms the teachers read a very short version of *Cinderella* and then guided the students through the drawing of a pumpkin.

"How did that work for those of you that implemented the kinder lesson?"

A dozen hands went up.

"The drawing part went fine, but when students were asked to add their own details to the picture, they all went Halloween on me. Cinderella was left in the dust."

The nodding heads let me know that many of the teachers had the same experience.

"Were the students engaged? Did they write something to go with their pictures?" Again, lots of nodding. "Then it was successful. One of our goals is to help students see themselves as writers, and that is more likely to happen when they are able to have enjoyable writing experiences. It seems you gave them that.

All of the teachers kept with the Fairy Tale theme for their lessons. Apples representing the poison apple in *Snow White* were drawn in the first grade classrooms and the students were asked to write a sentence describing their apples. A frog from *The Frog Prince* was drawn in second grade. The students wrote short rhyming poems to go with their pictures. A small house from *Hansel and Gretel* was drawn by the third graders. They wrote descriptions of their candy houses.

The fourth and fifth graders were guided through the drawing of a wolf from *Little Red Riding Hood*. They were asked to write a paragraph about their pictures. Many of those paragraphs were about werewolves. And gruesome details—snarling fangs, dripping blood—had been added to their original drawings of the wolf. Oh, well. Halloween was fast approaching.

TWENTY-EIGHT

Jake

Pacing back and forth inside of a motor home is neither gratifying nor helpful. I speak from experience. But I did not dare pace outside in this district parking lot either. That would not only call unwanted attention to myself, someone observing my obsessive circling of the RV—*can one pace in a circle?*— might think I was in need of a psych evaluation.

One last pass through of all the materials Jan had given me proved to be a total waste of time. There was nothing I could use. Nothing. And, I was not accustomed to seeing only brick walls between me and a solution, but there they were: brick walls covered with graffiti. How many different ways could the word failure be written? I needed to clear my head; my imagination was taking a dim, fruitless path.

I stood. I stretched. I stared into the fridge, reaching first for the wine, then the soda, and finally settling for a small bottle of sparkling water. I sat back down, but my eyes looked up just in time to see the mini-skirted, spike-heeled Ms. M&M strutting her stuff toward the far corner of the parking lot.

Of course, that action alone was not necessarily unusual, but I did think she had her own parking spot much closer to the main building. Then again, there were some trees down at that end of the lot; maybe she'd wanted some shade. I hated it when my logical assumptions consisted of plain old common sense, but then … Oh, yeah! She wanted shade all right. Always better to meet a man in the shade. She had my attention!

I must have begun verbalizing my thoughts because suddenly I could feel Wendell's hot breath as he now sat a little too close to me, cocking his head from side to side attempting to understand my rambling.

"Hey, buddy," I whispered. "Got to snap some photos. Go lie down."

I crouched just below the back of the padded bench in the dining area, zoomed in with my full-size camera, and clicked away, capturing images of the man handing Marlow an envelope. That by itself meant nothing and could be completely innocent except for the fact that the man kept looking over his shoulder and appeared to be troubled, nervous, maybe angry? I couldn't be sure from this distance.

However, I was far more certain when it came to getting a read on the pretty woman: the words sexy, smug, and arrogant came to mind like a flashing neon sign. As if I needed that. It didn't hurt that I had a head start when it came to her profile—her mighty fine profile. Uh, yes, I was chuckling. Sometimes I got a kick out of my cleverness because . . . it was so rare.

They turned and parted ways. *Oh! Do I follow the girl or the guy?* I was feeling the urge to follow somebody. Finally, some action! The girl, of course, since she is the one with the envelope. Mentally, I replaced my basic detective hat with one badass spy fedora. (They both looked a lot like my black baseball cap.)

After slipping my other, small camera into my shirt pocket, cracking open all the windows in the RV, and grabbing the leash, the dog and I headed out. Wait. Ms. M&M knew Wendell, and there was nothing inconspicuous about walking with a one hundred and sixty pound dog. She'd spot us right away.

Take two. Action *sans* the dog. Ol' Bud would be proud of me, while taking full credit of my use of *his* word.

I'd followed her for almost three blocks, still amazed at her ability to walk in those shoes, and remained on the opposite side of the street. She continued past several houses that had been converted into small businesses, a few restaurants, and a used furniture store. I thought I detected her pace slowing as she approached a bank. Yes, she slowed, stopped, and subtly looked in the window.

I ducked out of sight in the recessed entryway of a dingy-looking bridal shop. That would not have been my first choice, but you know what they say about beggars. I pretended to be talking on my cell phone when it vibrated into my ear. That was a new experience for me. One I never needed to have again. Scared to death by my own phone.

There I was trying to get my heart to work properly and read a text message from Lindsey, when I saw Ms. M&M, my reason for being out here in the first place, walk into a pawnshop. A pawnshop? I glanced back at my phone and read the text: TIME 4 FOTOS. BRING IN THE CREW. I was torn, but knew what I had to do.

"Jake, you're sweating!" was Lindsey's greeting.

"Yeah. Sorry. Took Wendell for a walk and we were several blocks away when I got your text. So we hurried back and here we are," I said feigning innocence.

She eyed me up and down, and Wendell, too. "Well, lucky for you, I won't require any Bible swearing with regard to the truth, the whole truth, and nothing but the truth . . . for now." I sure was relieved when she turned around, blew me a kiss, and gave me her best *I love you* smile. I reciprocated immediately with my very own *I love you more* look of endearment.

The first photo included all the teachers, plus Lindsey, Wendell, and Malcolm. That was when I discovered I could scratch *photographer* off of my list of part-time careers. Lining up, organizing, and keeping the eyes of eighty-one teachers, a dog, and a bird open at the same time, was a challenge I had no patience for.

On the first day of the workshop, the teachers had formed eight groups of ten that would occasionally work together on specific activities. Now, each group wanted their own photo, too. Lindsey must have seen the slight look of apprehension on my face because she scooted up close to me and said in a soft voice, "Don't worry. I will get each group set up quickly." Then she added for all to hear, "Frisky Squirrels, you're up first. Potent Peppers, you're on deck."

Each group saved a space in the center where Lindsey would stand; Wendell and Malcolm held their end positions. The dog loved to *sit* and the bird, well, what choice did he have? All went well until one of the teachers in the last small group insisted that I be in the photo, too. I shrugged and without giving it much thought handed the camera to Lindsey.

Walking closer to the group, the young woman who'd requested my presence waved me over to stand by her side and proceeded to snuggle up as if the photo were only of the two of us and we were a couple, an item. From my vantage point I could see an abundance of head shaking and eye rolling coming from the teachers standing near Lindsey.

One of the senior members and lead eye rollers muttered, "Good grief, Veronica." Then she raised her volume for all to hear. "Lindsey, I think I can handle clicking the shutter. Go on. Go get in the picture, hon."

I made room for Lindsey right between Ms. Flirty and me. A little shuffling took place as everyone adjusted to the additional person. Seconds later, more shuffling as Wendell nudged himself between Ms. Flirty and Lindsey.

"Smile everybody!"

Almost everyone did.

After uploading the photos from both of my cameras to the laptop, I took a look. Couldn't wait. Besides, Lindsey wouldn't be ready to head home with us for about thirty minutes, and I needed something to pass the time. Shots of the Flagstaff campground came up first. It was a beautiful site. I'd taken lots of pictures of Lindsey in front of the RV, by the fire ring, walking ahead of me on the trail—that was one of my favorites—but even more of the dog. Wendell sitting, standing, walking, sniffing, lying on his side, and . . . wait. Is that an airstream trailer in the background? I hadn't noticed it at the time, but then, why would I? It had no significance then. The one here at our campground north of Albuquerque probably didn't either, unless . . .

I clicked quickly through photos taken in Santa Fe and around our current camping location. Whoa! Back up. There in the background of a photo of Lindsey and the pets was a rather tall man standing about ten feet from the airstream trailer and, even from a distance, I knew it was not the older man that I expected to see. Who, then? A visit to the airstream would happen this afternoon. I had questions.

Photos flew by after resuming my quick clicking strategy until Ms. M&M appeared before me. I had to study those; she was part of my investigation. *Good shots; she's very photogenic.* I zoomed in. Pausing on a close up of her legs was purely accidental. Talk about flawless and well-shaped. She must work out. Wait just a minute. Was she wearing those magical pantyhose that the girls at Hooters wore to make their legs appear perfect?

"Jake!"

I quickly clicked to the next photo. *Damn!*

It was none other than Ms. Flirty and her group. Lindsey was looking over my shoulder now.

"Well, with that too-short, too-tight, too-revealing little dress, no one would accuse her of looking like a teacher today."

Had I noticed that?

"Jake, do you think she could be the author of your love letter?"

I should have been the one to ask that question.

TWENTY-NINE

Jake

Due to my Tuesday evening massage oil blunder, last night was a night of snuggling. I liked that, even read an Internet article that stated how valuable that activity was when it came to keeping depression and anxiety at bay. Not that I needed any help with those conditions, but I did have concerns about failing when it came to solving Jan's budget mystery—depression?—as well as worries about our own safety with regard to the RV vandalism—anxiety? Hmm.

With that said, I had to admit that I'd hoped for more than snuggling tonight. That hope now reappeared in a physical form, a prelude, when I gave Lindsey a slow kiss goodbye. Ah, timing is so important. Teachers walked in, we both were in need of taking a breath, so our passionate kiss came to an end. Our eyes held each other as I inched toward the door, and, if I was reading her expression, her signals, correctly, she'd recovered from Tuesday night's little mishap. Hopeful! I was very hopeful.

Today I'd parked the RV in that shady corner at the far end of the lot. It was farther from the entrance to where Lindsey's workshops were being conducted, but the pets would be more comfortable and far safer than if we'd left them at the campground. Lindsey had said that I could bring them in to be with her if I needed to be away from the vehicle for very long.

My mind bogged down and was stuck in the muck as I wondered about the evidence we'd sent off to Lad. For now, all I could do was wait, which was not one of my strong suits. Not expecting to receive any information about the tire-slasher's identity until sometime next week, if at all, I'd try to stay focused on the budget mystery. That was my challenge for today.

One thing was for sure. Jan expected me—because I'd offered—to pay a visit to the district's Director of Finance. Today was the day for that unannounced meeting. It was now or never. So, I began to formulate a plan of action.

Step 1: Find the director on the district's website to see what he looked like. Sometimes I gleaned helpful hints about a person's personality from viewing their physical appearance. Step 2: Find out the exact location of the office and how to get there. I wanted to avoid Mr. Information's counter, if possible. Step 3: Go! Go! Go! Step 4: TBD at the conclusion of steps 1-3.

Implementation of the plan would commence just as soon as the coffee was ready for consumption. Okay. Here goes . . . Laptop powered up, district website found, Department of Finance link just waiting for my click and . . . Eureka! Struck a vein! Pure gold. That was way too easy. There he was—the man. The Director of Finance. He was also none other than the man in the photo giving Ms. M&M an envelope. And now that man had a name. Robert Bentley.

Perhaps their brief meeting meant nothing, nothing at all. Would the Assistant to the Director of Elementary Education have official business with Mr. Bentley? I didn't know, but I would check on that. I had a hunch that what I saw at the far, shady end of the parking lot yesterday would not qualify as official business, though the envelope at the scene appeared to carry some importance.

The Finance Department took up the majority of the third floor of the main administration building. Skipping the elevator, I walked up the three flights of stairs hoping to rid myself of the twinges of nervousness that had invaded my body the second I left my current comfort zone—the RV.

What right did I have barging in, unannounced, to a high-ranking, district official's office? None. None at all. And yet, here I was—a total stranger—ready to call his bluff based on my own mere assumptions. My only ammunition? A few photos.

The pace of my heartbeats quickened; the pace of my walk did not. At the far end of the corridor I could see the nameplate above the door. It read: Robert Bentley, Director. My physical body headed toward it but my brain traveled the distance via a variety of distorted tangents. What if he wouldn't invite me into his office or take the time to talk with me? What if Ms. M&M and Mr. Bentley were an item, a couple? If so, their brief meeting was none of my business. He would think me a lunatic, call security, and have me escorted from the premises. That would not make my day.

The door was open. Mr. Bentley sat facing the window, talking on his cell phone—not his office landline. *Ah, ha!* That could mean he was having a personal conversation on company time. *Good grief, what is the matter with me?* I was grasping at those proverbial straws again.

Feeling desperate, I needed a break in this case, which wasn't likely to occur without the kind of luck only a friendly leprechaun could provide. Too bad it wasn't the season for those little green men. Nope. It was the season of things like witches, black cats, jack-o-lanterns, ghosts and goblins. In my entire life, I'd never heard of any of them offering up the slightest bit of good luck. Quite the contrary.

I wasn't hiding, but I did stand back a ways so it wouldn't appear that I was eavesdropping on his conversation. I also did not want to startle him though I didn't know how to avoid that issue. I was fairly certain that the likes of me rarely stood at his doorway. I doubted he'd mistake me for a teacher, a banker, a custodian, and especially not an accountant. So, who would he think I was? Before I could head off on another terrible tangent, Mr. Bentley swiveled around, slipped his cell phone into his pocket, and waved me in.

After introducing myself as a concerned citizen with questions about missing funds from the teacher salary budget line, Mr. Bentley let out a long sigh, stood up, and closed his office door. Apparently, we were going to talk—really talk.

Mr. Bentley rambled on and on about basic math and accounting strategies—if his purpose was to baffle me, he'd succeeded—then, he admitted to making some mistakes. Mistakes that he intended to correct. He even thanked me for coming and acted as if our conversation was over. He was good. Very personable. Most people would likely have gone along with his charming dismissal, but I was not like most people.

"I think we both know there is more to it than that," I said, opening my envelope, removing just a few of the photos, then observing the man across the desk sink back down into his chair, holding his shaking head in his hands. Mr. Bentley said nothing. Fortunately, Lindsey had taught me the value of 'wait time' so, I waited, and the strategy worked like a charm.

"It started out so innocent, so simple. I have a wife and four kids whom I love dearly, but we were going through a . . . a difficult time. She'd lost that lovin' feeling, and I had not. So when Marlow cast her spell over me—do you know her, Jake?"

"Not well, but enough to picture her seductive abilities. Please go on."

"As you've probably guessed, we had an affair. She was incredible! Of course, I felt guilty as hell, but she was so savvy about the ways of the world, our careers, and the need for complete secrecy that I thought it would work, at least for a little while. You know, till my wife's problems abated."

I could not believe how clueless this smart guy was when it came to relationships and loving his wife. I could believe, however, that Marlow was more than capable of seducing this man and getting what she wanted from him—money. I wondered if Mr. Bentley would get around to explaining how that went down. I hadn't yet shown him the photo in which he handed Marlow the envelope or the one where she entered the pawnshop.

"I assumed we'd eventually go our merry ways. I knew she wasn't looking for a husband. By the time I discovered all she wanted was a partner in crime, it was too late. I wanted no part of that, but I was in too deep." Suddenly, a horrified look swept across his face and with a shaky voice he asked, "Did my wife hire you to get photos of me . . . with . . . her? Oh, my God. I'm ruined. My life is ruined."

"No, Mr. Bentley, I don't know your wife; we've never met or even talked."

"Oh, that's a relief. But then, how are you involved with all this?"

"Come on, Mr. Bentley. When money disappears from one of the largest budget lines and you, the Director of Finance, refuse to talk about or explain that to another high-ranking district official, you've got a whole flagpole supporting dozens of red flags waving wildly."

"Mrs. Rubio, huh?"

I nodded.

"Marlow said not to worry about her, that she'd soon be gone."

"And you were good with that?"

"No, Jake. I wasn't good with any of that, but, like I said, I was in too deep—way too deep. Can you help me? I really need your help. She's got me by the short—"

"I get it."

We talked some more. The guy, who seemed like a nice guy, was in deep shit. I suggested that he call a meeting with the superintendent and the school board and tell the truth, come clean. He didn't want to hear that. He wanted to make it go away with no consequences. Life rarely worked like that. I did feel bad for him, though.

He filled me in on a few more details, many of which I did not need to know. After all, I was neither a district official nor a member of law enforcement.

"So, would I be correct to summarize this situation by saying that it all began with a sexual affair between you and Marlow; she then blackmailed you and demanded hush money; and then proceeded to help you skim money from the district, which you handed over to her? Is that about it?"

He nodded and I could see he'd begun grieving for all he was about to lose. And for what? Wanting to make use of the dormant testosterone moving sluggishly, impatiently around in his body?

THIRTY

Lindsey

Good-byes were hard for me. In less than an hour my time with the Albuquerque teachers would be over. That was the bittersweet aspect of conducting the workshops, the trainings, and the consulting. For now, teachers shared what they'd learned and what their next steps might be.

One forward-thinking teacher spoke up. "I would really like it if we, this group, could meet once a month to share ideas and more lessons, and help each other with any difficulties that might arise as we ask our colleagues to add something new to their already busy days."

Eyes widened, heads nodded. The woman's idea was well received by all and now other participants spoke up, too. Using those eyes in the back of my head that most moms and teachers have, I noticed that Mrs. Janelle Rubio had just entered the room. I gave everyone a few minutes to discuss and jot down some additional details so their great idea could become a reality.

"Hi Jan. I'm so glad you could stop by today."

I wasn't surprised to see her. After all, this was her baby, her plan to help teachers teach students to become better writers. We both hoped everyone here would learn to love and come to know *the joy of writing*, then pass it on to their students.

"You have some wonderful, effective, and positive teachers here. It has been a pleasure to work with them."

"And I've had outstanding feedback concerning you, Lindsey, and I hope to bring you back someday, which is why I've brought this box of books, your books. *Lindsey's Art Journaling Lessons: Teacher Guide*. One for each participant."

Jan helped me pass them out. It was exciting to watch the joyful reaction of the teachers as they each flipped through their own copy. The room filled with smiles and thank yous.

"Let's thank Mrs. Rubio. She is the one who brought me here and arranged for each of you to have your own book to keep."

A standing ovation was followed by hugs, tears and more good-byes. As the women filed out the door I was reminded once again how much I loved working with teachers—even the flirty ones in short skirts.

Jan lingered, even hovered, fairly close to me as I packed up my presentation materials. Jake and I would leave tomorrow and, so far, we had no news—good or bad—regarding the missing money. But it was far more than that. Other problems had trickled down from the shrinking budget: crowded classrooms, the diminishing academic progress of the students, and the very security of her job. She was desperate for some answers. Who could blame her?

"Lindsey, I haven't heard from Jake in almost forty-eight hours. Is everything okay?"

Though I had only lived with my mom and dad for the first eight years of my life, they instilled in me how important it was to be trustworthy and truthful. I'd try to live up to their teachings but still answer Jan's question with caution.

"We've been slightly distracted by a few little mysteries of our own, but rest assured Jake is on it! He's been working on your issue day and night, especially the last forty-eight hours. Sometimes, Jake's silence is a good sign. That could mean he's in hot pursuit of key information."

Just then I felt my phone vibrate from inside my pocket. Looking down I saw that a text from Jake was coming in. "It's Jake. Let's see what he says."

"Okay. I hope he has some news."

"He must be in a hurry. He's used a lot of texting short cuts, so I'll translate for you. It says that he'd like all three of us to meet tonight. He wants to know if you would join us for pizza in the RV at the campsite at seven o'clock. And he added that it was IMPORTANT!"

"That sounds good! Tell him, I mean *text* him that I will be there. Would it be okay . . . would you mind . . . could I watch you do that? I've never texted before. I need to learn how."

It appeared that Jan assumed the news was good. And it might be. But I had to admit that my assumptions would remain on shaky ground until the facts were in ... and the pizza eaten.

THIRTY-ONE

Jake

The evening with Mrs. Rubio held the promise of excitement, the possibility of celebration, and I was as giddy as a kid with straight A's on his report card waiting to share the newly discovered information with her. However, my idea of setting up a pizza picnic outside by the fire fizzled when I realized how darn cold it was. No problem. The thin crust, pepperoni with bell peppers and mushrooms pizza would taste just as good inside the RV.

"She's here!" Lindsey called out from the sleeping area where she'd gone to exchange her school clothes for jeans and a sweater.

I greeted her at the door and gave her a hand up the steps. She, too, had made a wardrobe change and now we looked like triplets standing there, dressed down, in our jeans and sweaters. I made a mental note: With the addition of jackets, which we had, sitting around the fire after dinner might still work.

Lindsey quickly tossed a simple salad while the two take-and-bake pizzas cooked in the oven, teasing us with a delicious aroma—we'd all worked up an appetite today. This was our first experience *entertaining* on the road, and visions of a perfect evening lessened my therapeutic need for naked snuggling, though I certainly wouldn't turn it down should Lindsey be in that sort of mood later.

"Mrs. Rubio, would you like some red or white wine?"

"First things first, Jake. Unless there are students or teachers lurking outside, I insist you call me Jan." She waited. I waited, then figured out what was expected of me.

"Yes, ma'am. Jan it is."

"And water will be fine for me, thank you."

"I could make us some hot tea, if you'd like."

"Oh, Lindsey, you read my mind. That would be perfect."

Pizza and hot tea? That combo would never have occurred to me, but what do I know? On second thought, I knew a lot about tea . . . and about what our next course would be.

"Lindsey, sweetie, mix a little oolong and chamomile together." That would help Jan relax, de-stress while remaining wide-awake. Was worth a try.

Lindsey insisted that we eat at the *kitchen* table by candlelight and said it was the next best thing to dining outdoors at the picnic table by firelight. Ten minutes now remained on the oven timer. There we sat—one wine drinker and two teetotalers—waiting for dinner in the cozy, semi-darkness.

Silently, we sipped our drinks of choice . . . so silently that this tiny slice of time could qualify as one of Lindsey's 'pin drop' moments from her classroom days. Feeling that we needed to move things along, I broke the ice, the silence, the sound barrier, something . . . and began to tell the story of today's discoveries. I would share the photos, my notes, and the transcription of the tell-all conversation I'd covertly and illegally recorded earlier, after we'd eaten and Lindsey was ready to give up the ambience provided by the candles.

"Jan, I want you to know, upfront, that what I learned over the past few days should prove very helpful to you. Your thinking was on the right track. You were wise to follow your hunches."

She nodded and produced a small smile. "Does your dog need to go out?"

"What?"

Jan's question caught me off guard. That was the last thing I expected her to say right then. But now that I took a good look at Wendell, I knew something was up. He was in his *guard dog at attention* mode with his nose to the door. Putting a finger to my lips, giving the ladies my 'quiet' signal, I moved closer and listened, wishing I had the ears and nose of a dog. A low, throaty rumble emerged from Wendell's still-as-a-statue body—my cue to grab the gun.

I knew the night sky offered little illumination this evening, and I needed to exit the RV if I was going to get a visual on … what? Hey, it might just be a raccoon or an owl that caught the dog's interest. This wasn't a movie, a TV show, or even the plot in a scary novel, so there didn't have to be a bad guy out there. That's what I kept telling myself. But it would be stupidity rather than courage to refuse to recognize the possibility of danger.

My intention was to sneak out, unseen and unheard, and take a look around. Just as I cracked the door open, the oven timer beeped loudly (the epitome of bad timing). Lindsey jumped up to silence its call and remove the pizza, and Wendell bounded out the door nearly knocking me over. So much for sneaking out.

A strange, whimpering cry coming from the direction of the picnic table became a shrieking, pulsating scream upon Wendell's close up and personal arrival. I wasn't far behind, but still could not make out the source of the noise. Wendell added barking to the odd cacophony, but it wasn't his fearful, protective bark. It was more of a *there's a squirrel* bark. His reaction surprised me, even confused me.

Within minutes Lindsey, Jan, and our airstream neighbors, all attracted by the commotion, surrounded the picnic table. The older woman turned to me and apologized for the trouble. Now I was completely confused. Then she began to talk to the mysterious thing under the table.

"Jimmy, come out. No one will hurt you. The doggy is nice. We are not mad."

Jimmy? Hmm. The Jimmy under the table didn't budge. His grandmother, mother, guardian?—we did not yet understand the relationship—quickly lost her patience.

"Jimmy! Come out of there!" Her voice was harsh with anger. "Right now! Don't make me get the stick."

Wendell whined, Jan gasped. Lindsey took immediate action.

"If you would all take several steps back, please, I'd like a moment with Jimmy."

Almost hypnotically, we all did as we were told, and watched from a distance. Though with the absence of a moon tonight, there wasn't much to see. At first Lindsey merely sat on the picnic table's bench seat positioning herself so she would not invade Jimmy's space under the table. When her presence did not cause any further unrest from the boy, she began to hum a gentle, familiar version of "The Bear Went Over the Mountain". Leave it to

Lindsey to calm and comfort an upset child. So far, so good.

Next, she reached under the table and offered him her hand. He took it and within seconds we could see the boy—the boy who wasn't a boy. Lindsey held the hand of this adult-sized man as if he were one of her kindergarten students and guided him to the far side of the table where they both sat facing the forested area. No words had been spoken, yet.

"I wanted to try one of pop's cig'rettes."

"Well, I've heard that smoking is very bad for your health," added Lindsey, remaining calm and sweet.

"Pop smokes."

"Maybe they care a lot about you and just want you to be healthy. Do you like pizza?"

"Uh, huh, if it has cheese."

Lindsey was able to get Jimmy to walk with her to the RV. He didn't look in the direction of the rest of us who were standing idly by waiting for . . . an outburst, or the other shoe to drop? We didn't really know what would transpire next, but the boy in a man's body kept his eyes on the dog.

"Want to pet him? His name is Wendell."

"I thought he was the monster mama sent to get me. I am not supposed to go outside."

"No, Jimmy. He is a good and friendly dog."

Jan and I heard every word of that part of their conversation. At least now we knew a little more about the relationship. The couple from the airstream might be Jimmy's mother and father though they looked older than the typical parents of a son Jimmy's age, but then, what was his age? He could have been thirty or forty or—. They stood about ten feet away, shifting their weight from one foot to the other like two adult black bears reared up on their hind legs for a better look.

Jan moved closer to me. "Do you mind if I speak with the mom and dad? Their adult son has obvious mental deficiencies and it seems they could use some help."

"Since Lindsey has the Jimmy portion of this strange evening under control, let's have a chat with our neighbors. I have a couple of questions I need to ask them anyway. But Jan, you talk first. They are likely to prefer what you have to say."

I could tell that she didn't want to appear pushy or to frighten them off, so she requested that they exchange contact information at this point. She let them know they weren't alone and there was help available should they ever want it. All they had to do was call her.

Well, *everyone's a suspect* was my mantra in the midst of any mystery. So, that included Jimmy. Could he have slashed the tire, cutting himself in the process? I could see that happening. He had opportunity. He was here all the time, though he was also closely watched. Momma Bear and Poppa Bear looked like the type that might nap much of the afternoon. Did he have a motive? Maybe. He was a mentally challenged man who was likely frustrated and possibly filled with anger.

"Do either of you or your son own a sharp knife capable of piercing a tire?"

Okay, I suppose that might have been a little too direct, abrupt, but why beat round the bush? And, that was a simple question requiring no more than a *yes* or a *no*. They both shrugged and bobbled their heads from left to right. Did that mean yes or no? I moved on.

"Has Jimmy come home with any blood on his clothing or cuts on his body recently?"

Even in the dark Jan's look of shock and disapproval was impossible to misread. And now Momma and Poppa Bear grabbed their great big Baby Bear and hurried back to their camper. At least Baby Bear was no longer hungry or thinking about cigarettes. He'd finished one slice of pizza before my questioning began and Lindsey had wrapped up a second slice that he now clutched tightly in his hand while being whisked away.

"Good night," I called to them. "We can talk again tomorrow." Yeah, like that would happen.

The three of us—well, five, if you count Wendell and Malcolm—reorganized ourselves back inside the RV with all the lights turned on, and a few windows cracked so any approaching sounds might be detected. We were still a little on edge.

Lindsey reheated a few slices of pizza in the oven in case we (humans) regained our appetites, and then she was the first to speak up.

"Jake, do you think Jimmy might be the one that slashed our tire?"

"I think that is a viable possibility."

Jan remained silent for now but listened intently as Lindsey and I bounced our thoughts and ideas back and forth like a singles game of tennis.

"I didn't notice any cuts on his hands, the most obvious place for a tire-slasher's cut to be." *Lob!*

"But what if he was wearing flip-flops or no shoes at all? He could have dropped the knife on his foot while in the process of slashing the tire." *Break point!*

"I think we'd have seen the prints of bare feet, Lindsey, had they been there . . . and that theory doesn't explain the blood on the tire and wheel well." *Fault!*

Visions of Jimmy and the tire-slashing incident played over and over in my head. With each replay a new detail or question appeared. The tennis match? Over. I was now having an internal debate with myself.

If Jimmy did sneak out, with a knife, maybe Poppa Bear went looking for him, found him, and a scuffle ensued. Maybe he hadn't meant to cut the tire . . . though

149

cutting through sturdy rubber would take some effort. Not sure that could be accomplished accidentally. There would be no winner in my debate, at least not tonight.

Lindsey, using her steadfast sensibility, stated, "He might not be involved at all."

"You're right. We don't need to speculate any further right now. Lindsey, did he touch anything besides the slice of pizza?"

"Just a glass of water. Why?"

"There might be some DNA or at least a good print there. Guard the glass until I can bag the evidence."

Poor Jan. She had no idea what was really going on here. Then again, neither did we.

"You both live exciting lives. A little too exciting for me, though."

Exciting lives? That is the understatement of the day!

I went through the packet I'd prepared for her. She agreed that there was more than enough evidence to take to the authorities now, but the situation was far more complicated than she originally assumed. So many indiscretions had occurred by at least two district employees—the use of company time for personal pleasure, blackmail, and embezzlement. Her new dilemma? How to proceed. What would her next move be?

"Jan, in my estimation, Marlow Mahoney created and implemented the lion's share of the inappropriate and criminal activity. Using her sexual attributes she lured Mr. Bentley into her wicked little web. She thought she could bring both of you down. But first, she'd take full advantage of her own money tree that was growing so nicely, slowly ruin your leadership reputation, and bide her time until she was awarded your job. Oh, she is one smart cookie.

"She knew the Superintendent and the Director of Finance were longtime friends. She also knew Mr. Bentley was well liked and respected. No one would suspect or even check on the work he did for the district unless evidence was dumped in their laps. He was the perfect pawn for her corrupt caper. If anything went awry, if they were discovered, she'd blame everything on Bentley."

Jan's eyes glazed over as she listened to my soliloquy. Lindsey made more tea for her, leaving out the chamomile and adding some strong, black tea this time. The woman needed to be wide-awake for her drive home.

"I humbly suggest that you have a conversation with Mr. Bentley, a confidential, off-campus conversation, because you will need him to back you up, be on your side. He will need the same from you. I really do believe that he wanted no part of this; he's a family man that made some mistakes and got in over his head. Marlow will find it more difficult to manipulate—she is an expert—and convince anyone with authority over these despicable acts, if you and Mr. Bentley are on the same page, the same team.

"You don't need to take any other action, Jan. Once you turn this packet of evidence over to the authority of your choice, they decide how to proceed. I do have a backup copy of everything, just in case."

We walked her to her car and said our good-byes. This really was good-bye; we'd be leaving Albuquerque in the morning. She started the engine, opened the window, and with tears in her eyes said, "Thank you, both. I don't know what I'd have done without you. And, about the undocumented, somewhat covert payment arrangements for your services, Jake—I believe you called it a *tip*—I have my own money tree, a family tree, and all of its leaves are completely legal. And . . . I'm a big tipper."

Two down; only one to go.

THIRTY-TWO

Lindsey

What a day this had been; a day and night of ups and downs, questions and answers . . . the rollercoaster aspect of the past twelve hours had taken its toll. I desperately needed some rest.

The interior temperature in the RV was warmer than usual, probably due to the heat generated by the oven during the pizza cooking and later, the reheating. I climbed into bed wearing only a little white tank top and watched Jake strip down to his boxers. He was wearing his boxer boxers. Confusing, huh? Boxer, not as a type of fighter, but as a breed of dog. He couldn't find any underwear designed with pictures of mastiffs and thought the boxers (the dogs) were the next best visual representation of the dog he so loved. Personally, I'd prefer to be looking at Snoopy right now, or the real thing … not photos on fabric of dogs.

Jake sat on the edge of the bed. "Lindsey, we've got to ship Jimmy's prints and DNA sample to Lad first thing tomorrow. I'll give him a call, explain about our bizarre evening, and let him know another delivery is on its way." He hadn't even noticed that I'd climbed onto his lap and was nibbling his neck. "I'd be surprised if Jimmy was in a database, so without our samples, Lad would find nothing. However, if that was Jimmy's blood on the RV, Lad's government friends should be able to connect that blood to the prints and DNA we gathered tonight. We need to know one way or another."

"You're right, as usual, Jake." Running my fingers through his hair, I held his head so we were looking eye to eye before I whispered, "No need to be looking in the wrong direction or worrying about someone that is not involved."

"Our list of odd circumstances, unexplained events, keeps growing and that nags at me." My husband had a one-track mind tonight. Well, so did I. Next I tickled his ear with the tip of my tongue . . . with no results. He continued down the same track. "The broken RV steps, the siphoned gasoline, the slashed and bloody tire, and let's not forget the letter. Linds, did you notice the airstream trailer in Flagstaff?"

"Jake, stop it! That's enough detective talk. Please take a break or we'll never be able to sleep tonight."

"Okay. If not detective talk, what do you suggest?" Finally, I had his attention.

"Hmm. How about . . . pillow talk."

Jake thought for a moment—he's such a thinker—then grabbed two of the small, decorative pillows from the head of the bed, held them together forming a mouth, a pillow mouth—I know, who does that??—and proceeded to make the pillows talk as if they were a puppet and he, the ventriloquist. I didn't want to laugh, this was too goofy even for me, but I couldn't help myself. I laughed out loud uncontrollably right before converting that pillow puppet show into a pillow fight!

Jake could be so funny at times. He also had a talent for being sweet and gentle when such conduct was called for. Pillows went flying, to be sure, but no clobbering took place. My fight could be more accurately named a pillow toss. No clobbering, but . . . eeeww. Slobbering. A few pillows were already dog-dampened. Wendell had joined the fun on the bed and now more than pillows flew. *Are those feathers?* Upon closer examination of the floating objects, I was relieved to discover the feathers were from the punctured pillows and not our bird, Malcolm.

Laughing, Jake rolled and wrestled with Wendell. "Hey buddy, you need a bath."

"I agree. He's not feeling fluffy," I added after giving the dog a good tummy rub.

"Linds, Wendell is not a fluffy dog. Never has been; never will be." A few seconds of silence passed. He was thinking again . . . then came the intense eye contact followed by a mischievous grin. "Are you feeling fluffy?"

My turn to think . . . "I was, but I'm over it."

We laughed, we hugged, but then all of a sudden, a sick sensation took me by surprise. I did not feel well. Saliva built up in my mouth and I didn't know whether to run to the bathroom or lie very still. Something was happening to my body; I could not control the horrible, sick feeling. Attributing this untimely onset of illness to the pizza or the many school germs attached to the teachers I'd just spend a week with, I told Jake I'd be fine—but I wasn't so sure about that. I needed to lie down and get some rest. Tomorrow was a traveling day.

Just before closing my eyes, I'd noticed a different kind of look on Jake's face, a look I hadn't seen before.

"Jake? Is everything okay? Are you all right?"

"Yes . . . No. My mind won't relax. Your workshops, our school investigations have all been successful so far. But there are still so many unanswered questions about the events in our own lives. I'm worried and feeling my own onset of nausea."

Tonight called for a celebration, but here we lay sick and tired and a little scared about the future. A spoonful of sugar would have been nice, instead of the invisible tureen full of troubles that had replaced my collection of fall leaves as our table's centerpiece.

"I'm so sorry, Jake. We'll both feel better in the light of day and with the arrival of some answers. We only need a few. "

This was the first night since we'd lived together that hadn't ended with a kiss.

ROCKY MOUNTAIN HIGH

THIRTY-THREE

Lindsey

On the road again and, thank goodness, we were feeling fine! With the sky a brilliant blue and dotted with small, puffy white clouds resembling a herd of sheep, I could cheerfully say, 'Life is good' and mean it. Leaving Albuquerque behind, at least in the physical sense, provided a new beginning, a fresh start.

Jake and I had come to the conclusion that perhaps the RV issues were not personal attacks on us. *Was that a conclusion or just a hope?* We were merely in the wrong place at the wrong time. Maybe we'd been reading far too much into these mishaps because of our inclinations and interests in mysteries. That made sense. This early morning discussion, just saying these things out loud, gave us a brighter outlook on our future and a much needed feeling of lightness.

An hour into our drive, heading north on I-25, an eerie silence passed between us as signs proclaiming the nearness of Trinidad, Colorado popped up along the side of the highway. Flashback memories of a miserable time in my life surfaced and now hovered above me like Pig-Pen's persistent dark and dusty cloud.

Trinidad reminded me of the beginning of the end for Anthony, my ex-husband. The day he and Shawna—the woman he'd had left me for—were packing to fly to Trinidad together for her final 'cosmetic' surgery. That was also the day he'd discovered her gender deception. The shock, the lies, were more than he could cope with.

Speaking softly I broke the silence. "Are you thinking what I'm thinking, Jake?"

"Pretty sure that I am." Looking straight ahead, he whispered, "It's like we are traveling through an ancient burial ground each holding our breath to keep from being discovered."

I think Jake had just added a scene from *Jeremiah Johnson*—he knew that movie inside and out—to the bigger memory at hand. We had the same event in mind, just different points of reference and ways of expressing our thoughts. My Pig-Pen to his ancient burial ground. Oh well, to each his own. It wasn't until we were several miles beyond the small city's exit ramps that we were able to laugh and release the temporary tension we'd felt.

"I know, Lindsey, that everything about Anthony and Shawna's relationship was hard on you, and, yes, that's putting it mildly, but we never would have met and fallen in love if she hadn't lured him away. So that cloud, albeit a messy, stormy one, did contain a silver lining."

I knew Jake was right. Things did happen for a reason, though sometimes, that rationalization, that blind faith, was difficult to come to grips with.

Though his eyes remained on the road, he reached across the console and took my hand in his. This small gesture, this skin-to-skin contact with the man I loved, infused me with hope and renewed my strength.

Even though our 'planned' mini-vacation was cut short by several days due to our extended time in Flagstaff, and the additional delays in Albuquerque, we still had several days to play before our initial meeting with the Curriculum Specialist in Estes Park would take place.

We pulled off I-25 and headed toward Red Rocks Park. Our first stop? The visitor center where we'd hoped to get information about hiking trails, dining opportunities, the local flora and fauna, and, of course, RV camping facilities.

Jake and Wendell waited for me outside while I made sure Malcolm would be comfortable and safe. From the window above the sink I noticed a very sturdy looking, uniformed woman marching toward Jake. Then, with an equally sturdy tone, she spoke.

"That dog must be on a leash at all times."

"Uh, okay. But he's just sitting here at my side right now. In fact he's kind of leaning on me like we're attached . . . like Velcro. That'd be even better than a leash."

I could tell right off that she didn't appreciate his humor or his effort to be charming. This woman would not be charmed. Not by Jake or anybody else.

"Rules are rules. Follow them or move along."

Jake looked up and saw me at the slightly opened window. I saw his grin and his wiggling eyebrows and knew he was not done with her.

"Have a nice day!" I heard him say, knowing the odds were not in her favor when it came to *nice*.

The three of us headed over to the visitor center's main entrance where we were greeted by a sign stating that only service dogs were allowed inside. Jake grinned again (oh, dear) forcing me to do *it*. Yes, now I had to do *it*. There was no alternative. I gave him my most

HIT THE ROAD, JAKE!

convincing *teacher look*. It worked! I still had it. Jake sat down on a bench with our leashed dog while I went in search of information.

That didn't take long. No lines to wait in. Not many visitors today because the concert season, the park's largest draw, had recently ended and some of the other services were in various stages of being shut down for the winter.

"The good news is that we won't have to fight the crowds. The bad news? There's not a lot left to fight for."

"What should we do? We need to be out and about doing something. Right, Wendell?"

Wendell woofed. He's so smart; I'd give anything to know what he was thinking sometimes.

"I suggest that we hike up the Trading Post Trail, which I was told is only one-point-four miles. And, we can take the dog, if he's on his leash. It is definitely a single file trail, though. It said on the trail map that most of it is only thirty inches wide. Do we want to do that?"

Jake and Wendell looked at each other . . . then they looked at me. One of them gave a positive nod. The other one smiled and drooled.

"That should put us back here right about time for *linner*." Jake was really on a roll today.

"Linner?"

"Yes, of course. Come on, Linds. If the meal between breakfast and lunch is brunch, then the meal between lunch and dinner is linner. After that we can move the RV, drink some wine and continue our unfinished pillow talk. What do you say?"

"Yeah . . . well, your suggestions, though wonderful, are directly affected by the bad news portion of the information I'd been given back at the visitor center. Bottom line . . . At this time of year there is not a single spot where we can camp with our RV. Let's take our short

hike and I'll fill you in. Then after *linner* at the Ship Rock
Grille, we'll head north."

Every now and then an activity or event or just about
anything takes longer than originally anticipated. That
was the situation with today's short hike. The distance
we'd walked was not the problem. The steepness and
narrowness of the trail slowed us down. Then, of course,
there was the dog on a leash. Poor Wendell. He was so
accustomed to walking at our side that he didn't take well
to walking either behind us or in front of us. We loved the
trail, the landscape, but by the time we got back,
our *linner* could legitimately be referred to as dinner or, I
conceded . . . *late linner.*

It wasn't until we'd taken Wendell back to the RV,
headed over to the Ship Rock Grille, and sat down to
order that I got around to explaining our camping options,
none of which were located in Red Rocks Park. Oh, we
had plenty of options, but I'd call most of them city
parking lots rather than campgrounds. Only one was
agreeable to both of us and that one was the farthest away.
Jake waved to the waiter. We ordered elk sliders, sweet
potato fries, and apple pie à la mode.

"And we need that—TO GO!" Jake seemed a little
anxious about driving the RV in the dark on a narrow,
winding road. I couldn't blame him for that.

The waiter looked at Jake as if he'd asked for the
moon instead of a To Go order. "You want to take your
apple pie à la mode in a doggie bag?"

"No. Of course not. Can't you put it in a Styrofoam
container?"

"Oh, sure. That's what we use, but still it will melt
and—"

I entered the back and forth banter and thanked the
waiter for his concern. "We'll eat our dessert first, but
we've really got to leave ASAP."

With our destination established in the memory of our GPS, we proclaimed, "Gold Canyon State Park, here we come." It wasn't very far—less than fifty miles, but it also wasn't long before a new dose of reality became an unwanted, bitter pill for us to swallow. Our cell phones, GPS features included, did not work consistently in this hilly, mountainous area. Being tech-savvy wannabes, we'd made sure that we knew how to operate the GPS feature on our Smartphones before we'd embarked on this journey, and we'd counted on using it—instead of paper maps—for any driving directions we might need along the way.

Now, with sketchy, intermittent cell and GPS service, we were limited to relying on our recall talents to make correct turns. That did not always work and we found ourselves backtracking more than once. To make matters worse, our adorable flock of fluffy cloud sheep from earlier in the day had since transformed into an ominous herd of dark cloud goats. The dim light of the premature dusk made deciphering the road signs an added challenge.

Poor Jake looked exhausted by the time we found a campsite suitable for our RV. Though we were the only campers there, few sites had enough space for our vehicle. We shoved one night's fee into the slot of the steel, self-service pay station. All we wanted and desperately needed was a good night's sleep.

THIRTY-FOUR

Jake

If it hadn't been for the cold nose and the hot breath against my ear, I'd still be sleeping. Who needed an alarm clock when you had a dog? Definitely, not us. I turned over, kissed Lindsey on her neck and stroked her cheek with the tops of my fingers.

"Good morning, sunshine. Wendell and I are going out for just a few minutes."

"Okay. I'll uncover Malcolm and put on the coffee."

The minute we returned and stepped back into the RV that *loving feeling* almost knocked me over, the feeling of true love, forever love, love that extended far beyond the hot moments of physical passion. Don't get me wrong; I loved those hot moments. I loved them a lot. But here stood Lindsey, her smile so captivating. That alone would've been enough for me. She was in the midst of creating an atmosphere of pure joy and happiness. That's what I'm talking about.

The voice of John Denver filled our traveling home with upbeat, toe-tapping energy. *When did she get that*

CD? Malcolm, who'd been fairly quiet on this road trip, was singing along. So far his favorite lyrics were: feather bed, feather bed, and more feather bed. Sometimes that bird scared me. He picked up words so quickly. He's one smart bird, that's for sure. I think in another life he might have been something other than a bird. Not sure how that worked. And I could swear he and Wendell communicated with each other. Not sure how that worked either.

Fresh cool air slipping in through the window, happy music, dark roasted coffee and—"What is that smell?" By the sudden and uncharacteristic frown on Lindsey's face, I knew that I must have made a mistake.

"A smell? There is a smell? You know, Jake, smells are not good. Garbage smells, tarring a roof smells, a doggie bag (and I don't mean from a restaurant) smells . . ."

"Okay. I get it and I'd be happy to rephrase my question. So, what is that wonderful aroma?"

"Probably the cinnamon."

"You are baking something for our breakfast?"

"Yes, I am. But not from scratch."

I sniffed the air once again. "Are there buns in that oven?"

We sipped our coffee, ate our aromatic cinnamon rolls, and tapped our toes to "Thank God I'm a Country Boy." Malcolm's word of choice from that song was 'fiddle.' He said that often. So often, in fact, we were tempted to cover his cage, and Wendell went to the opposite end of the RV for a dog nap.

Usually, Lindsey and I would check our cell phones and the Internet for messages and information while we drank our coffee. Not today. No cell service or Internet, not even Wi-Fi to hook up with at our camping location in the Gold Canyon State Park. But that was fine with us.

Just different, that's all. Jarred our routine a little, and added a sensation of being really far from home.

Estes Park would be today's destination, with a stop somewhere along the way for a nice picnic and maybe a walk on a wide path. We'd take the scenic route, which was longer, but we'd gladly trade a few more hours of driving on a beautiful, wooded, and winding road with a quicker trip on a traffic-filled highway.

"Linds, I'm going to just give the exterior a once over and make sure nothing went awry while we slept." With every passing day, the desire to be the protector of my little family, the hero to my lovely wife, intensified.

"I am willing to bet that everything is just fine. Wouldn't our dog have told us if there was a problem?"

"We'll see. Come on, Wendell, or maybe I should call him Dr. Watson. He does seem to know when trouble is around."

"Nope. I'm not giving up my title just yet. He could be Wendell, dog detective, though. Or how about Wendell, the sniffer dog. There are dogs trained especially for that purpose."

I scratched my head, waiting for a brilliant comeback to pop up. "I'm pretty sure all dogs sniff stuff." That wasn't the brilliance I'd hoped for.

"Well, not all dogs have jackets that identify them as sniffer dogs. I could make one."

"But most of his work is *undercover*. He can't go around announcing that he's doing detective, sniffer work."

I took great joy in our playful bantering this morning. With all the strange situations that erupted on this trip so far, we'd not had our usual amount of fun. We always attempted to find the sunny side of any situation because we were both positive people, but lately, the stress and tension affiliated with our work was taking its toll.

However, it seemed none of the problems or threats from our recent past had followed us. I'd count my blessings today. No Post-it note needed.

"All is well on the outside and the dog agrees with my assessment. Right, Wendell?"

"Then, it's Estes Park or bust!"

I wish she hadn't said that.

THIRTY-FIVE

Jake

The day could not have been better. I knew that. I also knew—at least I had a very strong feeling— that our work in Estes would be fun and our time there, like a vacation. Even the drive toward the Rocky Mountain town was more fascinating that I could ever have imagined.

To the west, a few scattered clouds hovered around the not-too-distant mountain peaks and were encased in a bright, intensely blue sky; I didn't realize the sky could be *that* color. Apparently, the postcards I'd seen and assumed were artificially doctored up using an editing program … were real. Awesome! The air's crispness combined with the scent of fallen aspen leaves uniting with the soil, delivered the unquestionable message that winter was just around the corner.

"Look, Jake. There's a sign pointing to a ranch. Let's go take a look."

We turned off Highway 7 and onto the dirt road. It was a ranch. A horse ranch. Lindsey's eyes grew big as if she were a kid walking into the It's a Small World ride at Disneyland. Several people waited near the corral decked out in their crispy, new ranch attire, which I thought looked more like costumes. So, I concluded this was a *dude* ranch. Or a horse ranch that allowed dudes. *That is the Texan in me talking.*

We got out and stepped closer to the stables and corral. Wendell would get his walk in a while. We were greeted right away by a . . . cowboy. A real one, I think, who tried to convince us to saddle up with his next trail ride that was about to head out.

Lindsey pulled me aside and I braced myself for her response.

"Jake, if it's all right with you, I'd prefer to just look at and pet the horses today. They are so magnificent and I love being here near them. I just don't want to be *on* one of them. Maybe, when our work in Estes comes to an end, we could come back. What do you say?"

"You, my lady, are a wise woman." And I was a relieved man. Just because I was from Texas, didn't make me a cowboy, or even a good horse rider, much to my cattle baron father's dismay.

We drove a little farther north just past Allenspark and found a perfect place to have a picnic. It was far enough off the paved, two-lane road that we felt comfortable letting Wendell out—no leash needed here—and Malcolm, too, though he'd stay in his cage.

"Jake, I think I hear your phone's ringtone."

Running back to the RV, glad to know that we were once again in business and connected with the world, I quickly learned that I'd not run fast enough. I'd missed the call. It seems I'd missed several calls. Then my phone vibrated, telling me that this caller had left a message. Good!

The voice message was plain, direct, and urgent. It said: It's Lad. Where the hell have you been? Call me.

Stepping back outside, I did just that. He answered right away. The first words out of his mouth were not "Hi, Jake." They were, "Do not put me on speaker phone."

"Okay." I silently mouthed the word *Lad* so Lindsey would at least know who the caller was. His urgent tone still baffled me. Lad was usually a cool, calm, collected guy even when the likelihood of danger was present. He couldn't possibly have DNA results this soon. Could he? Or maybe something else had happened. If that was the case, that *something* had trouble written all over it.

"I've been trying to reach you for almost twenty-four hours."

"We are on our expected path and almost the expected schedule, but we've been in remote areas, locations blocked from cell satellites. What's up? Is Julie okay? You sound stressed." I'm sure I sounded stressed, too. The information I'd hoped Lad would find, shouldn't be this upsetting to him. I was uncomfortably curious.

"I was only stressed when I could not reach you or Lindsey. Now, I'm just being serious, though you may be stressed before this conversation is over."

Lindsey looked on, her palms toward the sky, and gave me her own version of a *what's up?* look.

Lad continued. "Seems we've both got brother issues."

"What the hell is that supposed to mean?"

"We got the analysis back and this was no ordinary analysis. My FBI friends went all out for me on this one."

"We all know that you've got a fraternal twin brother and he's none other than Lindsey's ex-husband, Anthony. That alone is weird enough." I could feel Lindsey's eyes glaring at me. "But *I* do not have a brother."

"You are half right about that. But it is highly probable that you do have a half-brother."

"No! I just have a sister, a whole-sister named Julie, with whom you are well acquainted, I might add. Is this a new twist on the Brothers Grimm? A play on words? Some kind of a joke? Because if it is, it's NOT funny. No laughing going on here."

"Jake, have you ever known me to joke?"

"Good point."

Lad shared with me that Julie, my psychiatrist sister, his live-in girlfriend, was in a bit of a funk herself, now soaking in their hot tub trying to come to grips with the meaning of this discovery. Selfishly, I hadn't thought about Julie yet. If this person was my half-brother, he was hers, too.

"Lad, is this finding, the blood analysis, one hundred percent accurate?" I'd wanted to know who had slashed our tire, if possible, but not if it meant finding a skeleton in my family's closet.

"No, but it is close. Identifying siblings is easier and far more accurate than identifying other relatives. With that, plus the fact that he was already in several systems because he'd begun his own search looking for his biological mother, I'd say our odds are ninety-nine to one that this is our tire-slasher and that he just happens to be your half-brother, too."

I know I'm a pacer; I pace. That's what I do . . . but not usually at such a break-neck speed. Anxiety and negative energy must have been exuding from my pores because Wendell, wanting no part of me, had placed himself on Lindsey's lap—well, his front half; that's all that fit—and Malcolm had become silent, which isn't typical especially when he has wild birds to chirp with.

"Holy crap! This cannot be. We would have known. At some point, Julie or I would have found out we had a half-brother."

"And this is that point—you just found out."

Lindsey's eyes popped out of her head and her jaw dropped to the ground. Having heard only one side of this conversation must have been confusing for her. Though the other side held no comfort, only more trouble. She clutched the big, lovable head in her lap. He didn't seem to mind. I quit my egocentric pacing and sat down by Lindsey. She leaned into me and I gave her head a gentle kiss though my ear was still glued to the phone.

"So, he is the one who cut himself while slashing the RV tire? Oh my God. That's not very brotherly. What the hell? Does my mother even know this guy exists?"

"Jake. Come on. Think about it. Try to keep up with me here."

"Yeah. Okay. But do you think she knows that he's looking for her? That he's surfaced?"

"I doubt it. We couldn't find Evelyn in the DNA system, not that he'd have access to that anyway. He probably hasn't located her yet but he's definitely trying to. With information about the approximate birth date and birth location there are search engines can sift through the past with uncanny results."

"Lad, I really am trying to keep up, but it just doesn't make sense yet. How does the tire-slasher's blood get tied to me?"

"You were in the system, Jake. My associates said that you entered yourself last year by submitting several DNA samples."

"You're right! I'd completely forgotten about that. It was part of a class assignment during my forensic psychology internship. That ties us together biologically, but that doesn't explain how he found me."

"And that is the nastiest fly in this messy ointment. I don't think he was looking for you, but somehow he found you. And . . . it doesn't seem possible that he'd know the two of you are blood relations. Those facts alone defy my reasoning at this moment."

Lindsey had written something in the dirt with a small branch. It was the word JIMMY. I nodded. I got it. Lad needed to know about Jimmy. Could he be the man that was my half-brother? If he was, we'd at least know who to look for, or who to stay away from. But he didn't seem capable of putting two and two together let alone this complicated caper. I wondered ...

"Lad, my phone is breaking up; maybe it's my battery. I'm not hearing you very well. Can you hear me? Do you know the guy's name?"

"Barely. Working on it . . . Call me . . . settled. We need . . . And be careful. Don't know . . . up to . . . harassment or . . ."

My phone went dead probably from all those hours it had spent roaming for service. I should have turned it off or kept it charging while we were driving. I didn't get to tell him about Jimmy and the odd evening we'd had with him and his keepers. I'd meant to call Lad yesterday, but forgot. I'd intended to make that call this morning to let him know another package would be arriving on Monday. Forgot to do that, too.

"Jake. I'm really tired all of a sudden. Could we just go in and lie down for a little while?"

"Sure, babe. I like that idea. Lad's phone call zapped me of my strength. A short nap sounds perfect. I'll get Malcolm."

I did my best to recreate Lad's half of the conversation for her. We'd begun this day with a feeling of lightness, but repeating the details dissolved that lightness for both of us faster than a tablet of Alka-Seltzer plopped into a cup of boiling water.

With Lindsey's head resting on my shoulder and the dog snoring lightly at my side, just a few more thoughts pounded at my over-worked brain.

Yes, it is true that I love to play detective, but not with my own life or with Lindsey's. That hits too close to my heart. And now ... I wish we were home.

THIRTY-SIX

Lindsey

It was dark. I didn't know where I was at first, but I knew who was whispering 'rise and shine lovely lady' into my ear. Mmmm. I rolled over to wrap myself around him. A little skin on skin was a good way to start the day.

"Ouch! Jake! Rough jeans and a wooly shirt?"

"Yes, ma'am. Got work to do. If you recall, it was dark when we arrived last night and we decided to simply park the RV and get set up and hooked up in the morning. Well, it's almost morning, the sun will show up any second now, and that's what I'm about to do."

When planning our trip, I'd discovered that many of the RV camping locations in and around Estes closed at the end of September. There had been few options and I knew then that a reservation would be necessary. Considering our requirements: dogs allowed, less than a fifteen-minute drive to the school, and plenty of room— we didn't want to be parked on pavement or be able to see into a neighboring camper's windows—I was prepared for disappointment, but hoped for the best.

Back in Tucson, when I'd received confirmation of our reservation, I learned that our location was a ten-minute drive west of town and a mere five-minute drive to the entrance of the Rocky Mountain National Park. And, dogs were allowed. I pulled on my jeans and slipped into a sweater, then added a jacket after noticing the frost on the front window of the RV. Now . . . to check the nearness of our neighbors.

"Jake, what are you doing?" I called to my guys who were at the far end of the campground.

"Wendell and I thought we should take advantage of the fact that there are only two other RVs and one truck in this entire campground. We're scouting for the best spot. Come and check out this one."

Oh, my gosh! Any spot here would do, but Jake was right. He'd found *the* perfect one. Nestled by a scattering of pine trees, with views of snow-capped peaks, this space felt like it was ours. And the best part? It was right on a clear, bubbling river. Wendell's feet were already wet and, I suspected, his thirst quenched. Wow! What a water dish. It was only a matter of time before more than his feet were wet.

Jake moved the RV to our little slice of heaven. Heaven for a week. The chilly, fresh, pine-scented air plus the babbling sound of the river as it danced over the rocks helped us focus on the important things in life. We would rejoice in the moment. The *now* was really all there ever was, and our *now*, that very moment, was so magnificent, it defied definition.

Not needing to report for *work* until Tuesday, we decided to take a short, local hike today and maybe head into the national park the next day. While I packed up a few snacks, our small first aid kit, bottles of water, and dog biscuits, Jake let Malcolm out of his cage so he could have some bird fun before we left. He'd created his own RV routine for his play time, which included flying the interior's length and back about four times, perching on the steering wheel for a few minutes, and then sitting on Wendell's head (the dog didn't seem to mind this). At some point during the head-sitting, Malcolm determined he'd had enough and would go back into his cage. Everyone was happy.

"Jake? You're bringing your handgun on the hike? That's a first." Having so little experience with guns, I preferred pepper spray or a baseball bat.

"Yes. I know everything feels pretty good right now, but we still need to be cautious, vigilant. The tenuous tone in Lad's voice yesterday sent a chill up my spine. Besides, we might meet a rabid bear on the trail. You never know." He smiled, attempting to make me think this was no big deal. I knew better. And his thoughts were not on bears.

"Well, if we were to meet that bear, that little gun won't do us much good, but if that's what you want to do, it's all right with me." I'd made an online purchase of bear spray—there really is such a thing—before we'd begun our road trip . . . just in case. Though, at the time, I was only thinking about bears. Now my thoughts were not on bears either.

Sure, I joked about the bear and the gun, putting on my worry-free, brave face; I didn't want Jake to be more concerned about my welfare than he already was. Deep down, I, too, knew we weren't out of the woods yet. Should we meet up with a feral human, our feral human, that little gun might come in handy. And, I'd be Jake's backup, packing my own weapon. *If it slowed down a bear, what would it do to a human?* I was going to tell Jake about the bear spray, but he'd already headed out the door.

Walking past the two RVs and the one truck at the opposite end of the loop, I wondered if anyone was home. All three vehicles were closed up tight without any signs or sounds of human inhabitants. Perhaps they were not the outdoorsy type—a bit too much irony there—or they were off on side trips. That was fine with us. We liked having the place to ourselves.

Since we had no idea how long the trail was or if it would loop back, we agreed to take a four-hour hike. Two hours in and two hours out. Wendell went with us. He stayed on the trail, though there were times the trail was hard to see. Jake said that was likely from lack of use.

This was not a forest service maintained trail. In fact, it might've been a game trail used only by deer or coyotes. It was beautiful, though. The only sounds other than our own boots and paws on the ground were birds singing, an occasional squirrel screeching our arrival to all its friends, and a gentle breeze tickling the tops of the pine trees.

A branch snapped, broke. That was no squirrel. Jake and I froze at the sound. We didn't breathe, though our hearts raced briefly until . . . Jake pointed at the deer up ahead.

He kneeled down, face to face with Wendell and whispered, "Shh. Deer."

It took one look at the three of us and bounded away as if it had springs for legs. We were very proud of our leash-less dog for freezing right along with us. Most dogs would have run toward the deer. But then Wendell was not like most dogs.

We'd reached the halfway point of our hike and were ready for a break. Jake glanced around, then led me over to a shady area covered with a bed of soft pine needles about twenty paces from the trail. It was a perfect spot to rest and eat our snacks.

Using a downed tree trunk for a bench, we dined on homemade trail mix comprised of almonds, peanuts, dried cranberries, and a few chocolate chips. I'd brought along a Ziploc bag of cut up celery, carrots, and radishes, too. Wendell ate several dog biscuits, drank some water, and then begged for a carrot — a carrot that he chewed up and spit out. I guess he had second thoughts about the vegetable.

Getting ready for our hike back down the hill, I placed any uneaten items into my pack. Then I noticed that while I was packing, Jake was unpacking.

I didn't know if Jake was ever a boy scout, I'd have to ask him about that, but he definitely came prepared today. I watched as my prince charming, my mountain man, proceeded to spread out a blanket on top of the fragrant pine needles and blew up two small pillows.

"Looks like we are going to take a serious rest, a real nap. Are you that tired, Jake?"

"No, but I'm still a little hungry . . . and I want you."

Oh. Ooohhh! I got it. "Right here? In the forest?" Gleefully shocked, I awaited his reply.

"Uh, huh. Right here, right now, with my beautiful forest nymph."

Jake began to undress me, slowly. I was about to be naked in the forest. Mixed feelings darted around my brain; an internal debate ensued.

This is so romantic. *No, this is crazy.* I am so much in love and now I'm a little hungry, too. *Again, no. And keep your mouth closed or you'll be satiating your hunger with pine needles, squirrel fur, or worse.* But the faint soapy, sweaty scent of Jake had my undivided attention. *No, no, no. Bugs will bite you.* Be still, my conscience.

"Jake, someone might come hiking up this trail and see us."

"Hmm. Good point. I've got the perfect solution. I'll be on top, so if a stranger walks by, he'll only see my good-lookin' . . . you know."

Being forewarned of this precarious position with regard to things falling from the sky and into my mouth, I will definitely keep my lips together, unless Jake is kissing me.

"Lindsey, don't worry. I will protect you with my life, and my gun, and my incredible intelligence and—"

Enough talking. I pulled his shirt over his head, which stifled his words not to mention the laughing, and then proceeded to unbuckle his belt. He liked that. Oooo! He liked that a lot. Heavy breathing and all, he managed to articulate one last, reassuring comment.

"And, besides, we've got our very own sentinel. He'll stand guard and let us know if anyone or anything approaches."

I gave Wendell a wink and a smile and hoped that he'd really do that because we were now at the point of no return.

Jake wasn't on top, at least not yet. He'd guided me to his lap and wrapped me in his arms. My legs encircled his waist. This experience was a first in several ways. Let me count them.

1) Naked (not even socks!) in a forest far from home.

2) No place to hide anything. The midday sun revealed everything.

3) To be continued . . .

Playful and sweet was the way I'd describe our typical, everyday lovemaking. I liked that; I loved that. But Jake set a new tone for today and it was one of powerful affection and deep love. A Romeo and Juliet kind of passion . . . without the tragic aspect.

Any lingering thoughts of falling squirrel fur quickly evaporated as we began to explore the details, the intricacies of each other's faces, lips, even fingertips. I'd never known Jake to be so intense and yet so gentle. In this moment, he was my world, my everything.

Jake, with the skill and confidence of a choreographer, guided me to our next position—a version of spooning, though we were not on our sides. I was now on the bottom, but *not* looking upward. My view? The blanket. Jake hovered just inches above me before snuggling close, skin to skin. He knew me well, so this arrangement came as a surprise and I wondered, with a hint of apprehension, what his next move would be.

With one arm around my waist he kissed the back of my neck, my ears, my shoulders as we knelt on hands and knees together. The call of the wild took over and my apprehension vanished into thin, high altitude, air. My animal instincts kicked in—didn't know I had them— trying to catch up with Jake's, and we rocked rhythmically as one.

No pillow talk or sweet words were uttered. Lost in our own tiny space on the planet, we were too breathless to speak. Then, another surprise . . . in one swift and masterful movement I found myself gazing up at Jake's loving face, which was framed by pine tree branches and glimmers of sunshine. He'd made it to the top without skipping a beat or the rocking rhythm, and so we continued. Oh, the sounds of love. The heavy breathing, the not breathing, the moaning, the groaning . . . the groaning? The groaning wasn't us.

I tapped Jake on his back and whispered, "Jake, I hear something."

"Me, too, my forest nymph babe, and I'm loving what I'm hearing."

"Then you are not hearing what I'm hearing."

"It's probably just another deer or . . . wait, I heard it. That was neither a deer nor a *squirrel*."

181

That was no longer a funny word, still interesting to Wendell, but not funny to us. The groaning, the creaking, was like something from a monster movie and it was getting louder and closer. We noticed that the dog was sitting, staring specifically in one direction. He didn't look terribly anxious, but he was, without a doubt, alert and listening to the noise, too.

Our magical moment was gone. We'd find it again some other day, but for now, we needed to get back to the safety of the RV. A low-pitched squeaking noise that reminded me of *fingernails on a chalkboard* (really big fingernails) joined forces with the groaning for a few seconds. The combination sent chills up my spine. Wendell's bravery waned and he whimpered. He had no frame of reference to make sense of all this. Well, neither did we. If Jake or I had been sitting on the ground, Wendell would have suddenly transformed into a lap dog. No laps were available so he merely leaned up against me. I gave his ears a rub and a tickle, just the way he liked it. We were all feeling tense.

"Jake!" I didn't need to yell, he was only a couple of feet away hurrying into his clothing, but I couldn't help it. I wanted to run. With his pants now on, he was ready to comfort me and the dog before taking on the woodland monster. We knew the general direction the sounds were coming from, but still we saw nothing.

Then came the snapping, the splintering, the crashing. We stood paralyzed . . . it took a few seconds for us to comprehend the source of those sounds. The ground beneath us trembled with each impact. *Boom! Thud! Thump!* Then, it was over. What followed was an eerie, profound silence.

A dead, medium-sized pine tree had fallen in the forest and taken two smaller trees along with it. We all ran over to get a closer look at the phenomenon.

"You heard all that, right?" Jake had regained his sense of humor.

"Yes," I answered, now able to smile, too. "Three trees fell in the forest and I heard them all."

"But you know, we're lucky that I selected that spot over there for our *nap*." He pointed in the direction of our bed of pine needles. "Or this could have ended badly. We could have been killed."

"But it didn't. We're still here, alive and well. And I am very thankful for that."

"Let's go home. I need another nap."

THIRTY-SEVEN

Jake

Nothing like a good night's sleep to wipe away yesterday's frightful moments, and give me the strength to keep up with the lingering issues that would haunt me until they were resolved. I was able to inform Lad about Jimmy and the package containing his DNA and fingerprints that he would likely receive today. At least we'd be able to rule him out (or rule him in) after tests were done.

How would I feel about the results? Not really sure. I did want to know who was responsible for the RV vandalism — knowledge is power — but did I want Jimmy to be my half-brother? No. That was a definite no. I could not imagine Jimmy with all of his problems being part of the 'family.' *Darn! Unkind, selfish thoughts ... be gone!*

I unhitched our Jeep Liberty while Lindsey packed up a light lunch. Today we'd venture into the Rocky Mountain National Park and check out Bear Lake. My cell phone, the Internet, and our GPS were all working fine here, so I was able to learn which roads and points of interest were open this time of year, then get the driving directions. As much as I loved and craved being out in the wilderness, I liked it even more when I knew that the technology in my pocket was working.

We thought we'd leave the pets in the RV since we'd seen no signs of personal trouble in a few days, well, except for Mother Nature putting a few trees to rest. That *was* the plan . . . until the campaigning began. Wendell blocked the doorway and looked up at us with his best sad dog look ever. And Malcolm, who had fewer campaign options and abilities, put on quite a concert to gain our attention. It worked.

We drove to the Beaver Meadows Entrance where the ranger eyed us with concern. That was understandable. We had a giant dog and a small bird in our car.

"Sir, you must keep control of your animals at all times for the sake of other park visitors and"—he now cast his skepticism in Malcolm's direction— "there are predators."

What? Did he really think we'd let the bird out?

I said, "Yes, sir. Will do." But I thought, *I'd take a park predator over a psycho half-brother any day.*

After paying our entrance fee, he handed me several pamphlets, which I, in turn, handed over to Lindsey. She informed me that the one containing the 'pet' rules was on top.

"I suppose we'd better read those first. It's probably not a good idea to break the rules on federal lands."

Lindsey read out loud—she was good at that—as I drove onward, watching for Bear Lake Road. I knew we'd take a left there.

"Oh, dear. Wendell won't have much fun today. He is not allowed on any trails at all. Not even on a leash. But he can be on roadsides, in parking lots, picnic areas and campgrounds—on a leash."

Finding Bear Lake was easy enough. We parked, cracked the windows for Malcolm, and proceeded to walk all around the edges of the large parking lot with our big dog. Unaware of the limitations that had been placed on him, he seemed to enjoy himself. Lindsey and I had a glorious view of several mountain peaks and every now and then a glimpse of the famous, pristine lake. All in all, it was worth the effort even without the privilege of hiking.

We managed to make our minimal Bear Lake experience last almost forty-five minutes. Arriving back at the car, Lindsey announced that she wanted to use the restroom before we drove on to our next stop.

"Okay. I'll roll the windows all the way down for Malcolm till you get back."

"Sounds good. He will enjoy the additional fresh air. He might even hear a few birds chirping in the nearby trees."

She smiled and hurried off. A quick pit stop was a good idea. I should do the same.

"Hop in, Wendell. I'll be right back."

He wouldn't budge. He would not get into the car, and he was too large of dog to be picked up. He obviously had a plan and the plan was to stay with me.

"Okay. Come on, big buddy. I haven't read any rules against dogs in the men's room."

We'd only been gone a few minutes—I was almost finished—when Wendell's ears pricked up and he dashed out. Damn! I was less than half of a minute behind. From my second place position I could see Lindsey was already at the car and that the dog was fast approaching. Something was wrong.

"Malcolm? Malcolm? He's gone! Jake, hurry!"

Her voice quivered and by the time I reached the car, her body was halfway into the backseat frantically and futilely searching for the missing bird.

"Malcolm is gone, cage and all. Just vanished."

It was obvious to me that the bird was not in the car so our search needed to be expanded. I was about to ask a question or two when she turned toward me with glaring eyes.

"How could you leave him alone with the windows wide open? Why, Jake? What were you thinking?"

She was angry and blamed me for the bird's disappearance, but right now was not the time for blame or anger. If someone had stolen our bird, the theft had taken place no more than a minute or two ago. There was still a chance to find him. A caged bird does not just up and fly away.

"Lindsey, you and Wendell stay here. Jot down the license plate numbers of any cars or trucks that leave the parking lot."

Then I began running around like a small dog on an agility course looking into every parked vehicle, keeping my eyes alert for anything unusual. I came up with nothing. So I headed back to the car. Lindsey had jotted down some words about a few departing vehicles, but her mood was still one of sadness, frustration, and anger. Yes, the anger at me was still evident. Who could blame her? I had walked away, leaving the windows wide open and the doors unlocked. Guilty as charged, but who would steal a bird?

"Lindsey, I don't know what to do now."

She thought for a moment, sighing deeply and wringing her hands all the while.

"I don't either, Jake, but once we leave, all hope of ever seeing him again is gone."

She was right. I knew that. So I suggested that we circle around the parking lot multiple times, asking everyone if they had seen a birdcage containing a white bird. She nodded and we began this phase of our search.

We must have talked with several dozen park visitors. No one had seen such a thing and everyone agreed if they had, that sighting would have been so unusual, too memorable to forget. We were out of ideas and I could see tears welling up in Lindsey's eyes.

"Don't cry, lady."

A small boy, probably about five years old, left his parents' side and stepped closer to Lindsey. He motioned for her to bend down and proceeded to whisper into her ear. Lindsey looked up and cast her eyes toward the far end of the parking lot. Then, she smiled.

"Thank you very much," she said giving the boy a hug before grabbing my hand, pulling me back to the car.

"What did the kid say, Linds?"

"He said that I shouldn't be sad because the bird's just waiting for a bus."

How the kid's words made Lindsey happy was a mystery to me.

"The little boy's 'bus' is the shuttle. Look, Jake. There is something at the shuttle stop way down by the road; it might be Malcolm's cage."

"Let's go! I just hope there is something in that cage."

THIRTY-EIGHT

Lindsey

Malcolm! There he was: a bird in a cage waiting for a bus. The little boy was right. Copious feathers littered the cage—obviously, he'd been upset by whatever had taken place over the past ten minutes. Otherwise, my little white bird seemed okay.

We drove in silence to the Upper Beaver Meadows where the elk, supposedly, hung out. I'd already expressed my anger and anything else I might add right now would not be helpful. I knew that, but deep down, I wasn't ready to let it go. How could Jake have been so careless letting his guard down like that? Just because we'd had a few days free from any odd events, harassments, or intimidations—I really did not know what to call them— we still had to be cautious. Jake had taught me that, and then he didn't follow his own advice. Ugh!

"We're here, Lindsey. Do you want to get out of the car? "

I answered his question by opening my door, still feeling far too much emotion for any kind of response, no matter how brief.

"So, that's where we're at? We're not speaking? You are giving me the silent treatment? Why?"

"Because of you, Malcolm was stolen from our car. Only by the grace of God and a little boy did we find him alive. There. Are you happy that I'm talking now?"

I did blame Jake for the near loss of our bird, not to mention the trauma it must have endured. It was his fault, but now pangs of regret filled my heart. Why had I been so mean to him? He was obviously also shaken and frustrated by the near disaster.

"You know, Lindsey, I care about the pets as much as you do. Besides, what are the odds that there would be a bird thief at Bear Lake? And . . . that there would be a bird in a cage in a car waiting to be taken?"

"Rhetorical questions?" There was nothing humorous in the words we spoke. We weren't bantering today; we were hurting.

When we finally made eye contact, I had to look away. Jake's eyes were as cold as steel in an ice storm. I'd never received a look like that before. There we stood, uncomfortably speechless . . . when one of the male elks grazing in the meadow began to bugle.

Amazing! Shocking! We had read all about the habits of the elk that resided in the Rocky Mountain National Park and thought the mating call, the bugling, only occurred at dawn or dusk. So, this was a surprise. The eerie, unexpected sound forced both of us to our senses.

Jake took my hand; that's how we began. Then leaning against the car, he positioned me in front of him and encircled my waist with his arms holding me close. The ice that had clung to our souls for the past several hours began to thaw just as the sun dropped behind the treetops and the elk became shadows. Only then were we able to share our thoughts without the angry and emotional distortions that had previously prevented any kind of meaningful dialogue.

"Lindsey, did you write down the plate numbers of any departing vehicles?"

"Only three drove out: One red sedan and one blue van with Colorado plates and one grayish pick-up truck from California. I was too far away to read the plate numbers. Does it matter? We got Malcolm back."

Something nagged at Jake. I knew this from observing his head scratching, toe tapping, and stationary pacing. I know that sounded like an oxymoron—because it was. Jake could pace in place when he had to. Right now, he had to. He'd explain his thinking or begin thinking out loud any minute now.

"I don't think anyone wanted to steal the bird. Or, if they did, they changed their mind. After all, they had him. The hard part, the theft, had been accomplished. All they had to do was keep on driving away."

That got me thinking about motive. I could not put myself in the shoes of someone that would remove a caged, pet bird from a vehicle, so motives were slow in coming.

"If they didn't want the bird, Jake, why did they bother to take him?"

"I have a few hypotheses. Maybe the thief saw you watching them leave, writing something down and then worried about getting caught. That would be enough to change almost anyone's mind. Or perhaps Malcolm drove them crazy with his chattering and flapping so he-she-they dropped him off . . . at the bus stop."

We were back in business; our bantering almost up to speed. "Okay, now tell me what you really think." I was glad we could be serious and still maintain our sense of humor once again.

"I think someone wanted to upset us."

I quickly added, "So their motive was one of harassment? Like siphoning gasoline or slashing a tire?"

"Exactly! Or, it could still be one super wacky coincidence."

I couldn't resist asking, "Jake, can you picture yourself ever writing another detective story?"

"I don't know. Maybe. Why?"

"Because *The Bird Thief at Bear Lake* would make a terrific title for a novella."

THIRTY-NINE

Lindsey

J ake drove the small car into town today. We'd only
be there for a short time while I reconfirmed the plan
for the teachers and Jake obtained clarification
regarding what Marsha Brady expected of him; her
questionnaire had been strangely vague.

"Marsha Brady. Can you believe that?" *Good! Jake
had discovered something to chuckle about.*

I found her name worth a giggle, too. We'd each seen
reruns of *The Brady Bunch*. Not knowing the age of our
Ms. Brady, we wondered if the TV show had influenced
her naming or if that was merely a coincidence.

Awestruck! That's what we were. The inviting
ambience in the district administration building implied
vacation rather than work with plenty of indoor greenery
thriving in an abundance of natural light, and not a gray
wall in sight. I was concerned that I might see animal
heads mounted on some of the cedar walls in keeping with
the outdoorsy, woodsy theme of the town, but the walls
within my visual range were headless.

A pretty young woman sat at the reception desk listening politely to a young, athletic-looking man's story. Looking up, she stood and greeted us warmly.

"Good morning. I'm Lindsey and this is Jake. We have a ten o'clock meeting with Marsha Brady."

The receptionist muffled a chuckle of her own and the young man said, "Gosh darn. Those scoundrels did it to me again."

The young woman looked back at her computer. Jake and I turned to the man who'd spoken those words, hoping for an explanation.

"Sorry. Where are my manners? The women in the office love to mess with me. Come on back."

Jake and I shrugged our shoulders and followed, still utterly confused. We were escorted into an office with a view of the lake where the young man offered us a seat on the leather sofa and then sat down in a matching chair directly across from us.

"We are here to meet with Marsha Brady," Jake stated again in case the man hadn't heard me. He stood up and shook each of our hands.

"Uh, that would be me. My name is Marshall Brady. My application was missing the LLs, huh? The ladies do that to me every chance they get."

"Oh," Jake and I chimed together, beginning to understand.

"Yeah, I get that look a lot. Call me Brady, if you don't mind. I prefer to use first names, but since mine is Marshall, which reminds me of law enforcement, I just go with Brady."

"Well, it's nice to meet you, Brady. I'm Lindsey Lark, and this is my partner, Jake Lee. I don't think I've ever known or met a male elementary curriculum coordinator in my educational career. Sorry, if that sounded a little . . . sexist. It's just unusual, that's all."

"No problem. But the unusual is the usual around here. I've got friends with PhDs that are shopkeepers selling taffy or truck drivers making deliveries. Folks just want to be here; it doesn't matter what job they do because they live for their days off and the opportunity to hike, fish, or ski. This place is heaven on earth."

We agreed with Brady about that. He told us that he was hired two years ago and though elementary education hadn't been 'his thing' he'd agreed to take the job, knowing he had a lot to learn. He had the necessary credentials but his experience had been in secondary education.

"The elementary teachers here are enthusiastic go-getters. They have taught me more in two years than I learned in college, maybe, even in my life. And they let me know what they want to work on and who to bring in and I do it—they told me about you, Lindsey."

"Sounds like a good arrangement. Let's get to it, then. You mentioned that the school doesn't follow or have a specific writing program, correct?"

"Yep. We've got the writing standards as a guideline, but that's it. And as great as these teachers are, they came right out and said, 'We don't feel like we know how to teach writing or even where to begin.'"

"That's not an uncommon feeling. I hear it a lot."

Then I added that rather than a 5-day workshop I could put together a twelve-month workshop that would give all the teachers the knowledge they needed to not only teach writing, but to be writers themselves. I could see his wheels turning.

"I'm just kidding, Brady."

But . . . it wasn't a bad idea. That's really what it would take. *Maybe Brady can continue on with this professional development topic long after Jake and I leave. I can be his long-distance learning advisor.* Now my wheels were spinning.

Brady agreed with my plan to work with grade-level groups—kinder and 1st on Wednesday, 2nd and 3rd on Thursday, and 4th and 5th on Friday. The teachers, with my help, would create Writing Calendars that would map out each grade level's writing instruction for an entire school year. We would determine and fine-tune the content of the remaining two workshop days, next Monday and Tuesday, as we went along.

"Oh, I have some super, duper news," claimed Brady, looking and acting like one of the Brady Bunch kids. That made us smile. "The meeting room is not just a room. It's the Rustic Roof Guest Ranch. You're gonna love it! And it's only about a mile from here."

"How did we get so lucky?" I really did want to know.

"A miracle, I guess. The ranch is owned by one of the school board members and he strolled in here looking like the cat that ate the canary just a couple of days ago suggesting we conduct your workshops there. And *Voilà!* That's French . . . I think."

FORTY

Jake

Now it was my turn. The mystery, the fun, my part of this equation would finally begin. To say I was chomping at the bit, didn't begin to describe how I felt. Bring it on! I took a deep breath to calm my enthusiasm, not wanting to seem over anxious, then, "How can I help you, Brady? Your application didn't contain much information."

"Yeah, sorry about that. The office ladies do all the paperwork for me and I didn't want them to know about my little mystery. I don't need your services, but I think my friend, Gigi, does."

"And this friend is a teacher or school employee?"

"No. She works for the park service in the gift shop."

"Oh." I wondered if my expression appeared as puzzled as my mind felt. Lindsey and I shared an oh-my-gosh-what-have-we-just-stumbled-into look. That was not the way we usually worked. In fact, it had never occurred to us to help with problems outside of the school, the district or its employees.

"You or someone had hand-written the word *blackmail* on the form."

"Yeah, that was me. Added that right before I mailed the form to you. I didn't know what else to call it."

"Is your friend being blackmailed?"

"She's talked about blackmail since late last spring. I think I'm more upset about this than she is. She won't say much to me about it, but I know it bothers her."

"And now she wants to talk to me about her *blackmail* situation?"

I didn't understand his uncomfortable hesitation until he finally spoke.

"Let's say she is *willing* to talk with you."

Now I was the hesitator; this did not feel right, but I agreed to check it out.

"Okay. When and where?"

Brady scribbled something on a yellow pad and handed it to me. He'd written her name, a phone number, and her work schedule for the next five days.

"Will Ms. Gigi Guzman be expecting my call?"

"Not sure about that."

"Then make sure. We don't want any trouble." *That was the understatement of the day.*

Lindsey and I drove out to the Rustic Roof Guest Ranch before heading back to the campground. Horses! There were horses. Lindsey's eyes lit up. Maybe we could go riding next week after the workshops were complete and all the mysteries solved. For now, we walked around the corral; Lindsey petted a few horses, commenting on how their noses felt like velvet, and then we entered the office and met the manager. After showing us the room Lindsey would be using, he invited us to stay and have lunch. No hesitation there. Offer accepted.

Wendell and Malcolm were glad to see us; they always were. After letting the bird do his thing, out of his cage, but inside the RV, we decided to take the dog for a short walk. Even though it was only midafternoon, the sun had dropped just enough so that its warming rays were blocked by the tall mountains. Wendell gladly romped around, acting like a puppy. His joy was contagious. Lindsey began her own version of romping, which looked more like dancing, and I crouched down in a linebacker stance ready to tackle the dancer. And I would have if the dog's expression of sheer joy hadn't come to a sudden halt.

We both noticed his odd stance. We called his name but he ignored us. Instead he gazed, unmoving, off into the distance in the direction of our Sunday hiking trail. We called his name again. He didn't budge.

"I don't see anything. Do you see anything, Lindsey?"

"I don't think so, but he definitely does."

"Could be a deer." I said that hoping it was.

"Or a coyote."

"Or a raccoon."

"Or a tree getting ready to fall. He knows about those now."

"Or . . . it could be my gas-siphoning, tire-slashing, bird-stealing, crazy half-brother."

That just flew out of my mouth. I shouldn't have said that even though I was thinking it. We'd almost had a day without worry. Part of me knew this was probably nothing, but then we were learning to trust the dog and what he knew or sensed, and just now he'd sensed something worthy of his unflappable gaze. The pets would not be left alone at the campsite tomorrow. Of that, I was sure.

\\

Not yet in the mood to do today's dirty work, he made one stop, his usual stop, before carrying out the thankless assignment. He had to wait for a seat; he hated waiting. Some days he hated almost everything. Today was one of those days. He began to hum a familiar tune, causing others nearby to give him the finger-to-the-lips shut-up sign. *Go ahead. Make my day!* He wanted to slug someone, anyone. His humming continued in spite of the annoyed glances from others. Finally, a seat.

Stress and anxiety gnawed at his gut like a beaver frantic to build its den as the winter storm clouds rolled in. He tapped the floor with his heel, first one, then the other, then both. The further he got into his tune, the faster it went until it became unrecognizable. Then, the humming, the tapping, stopped abruptly, and his own brilliant words appeared in his mind.

Son of a bitch! It's about time.

A name. A number. Yes, no, yes, no.

Should I? Will I? Won't I? YES!

Hit return . . . Wait. Wait. Wait . . . Fuck me!

This is great! Greater than great! It won't be long now.

This could be it. I've hit the mother lode.

FORTY-ONE

Lindsey

My final workshop of the year was about to begin. I'd looked forward to being here for so many reasons: 1) It was Estes Park, Colorado. Who wouldn't want to be here? 2) The school's chosen topic was Writing Calendars. I loved helping teachers make a plan, a map, a calendar for the entire year's writing instruction. 3) There would be fewer than ten participants each day. With such a small cluster of motivated adults, we could make miracles.

As a former kindergarten teacher, I could spot those energetic, early childhood teachers a mile away. They were, without a doubt, a special breed. Teaching kinder or first grade was not for everyone. But today, as I watched the group grab some coffee, juice, or water before sitting at the table, something didn't look right.

"Welcome, everyone, and thanks for coming. I have to admit that when we set the dates for your workshop we forgot that your day would fall on Halloween. So please accept my apology if this has caused any inconvenience."

The teacher, Colleen—thank God for nametags—spoke first. "We are the ones that should be apologizing."

That was a peculiar thing for her to say and it piqued my curiosity. "Really? Tell me more." I said with a smile.

"We are not the kinder or first grade teachers you were expecting. We are the fourth and fifth grade teachers."

Ah, ha! Looking from face to face, their vibes, their tones began to make complete sense, and everyone at this large, rectangular table nodded resembling a shelf of guilty bobble heads.

"We apologize for making the switch at the last minute, but the K-1 teachers did not want to miss out on the holiday fun with their kids, and we welcomed the chance to avoid it."

I thanked Colleen for the explanation. It made sense, and I could adjust. No problem, but I'd need to remove my *cute* hat and replace it with my *cool* hat. Hmm. Did I have one of those? Additional comments from the teachers flowed freely.

"The older students aren't into pumpkins or cute little ghosts anymore."

"You can say that again. They want to dress up and act like Freddy Kruger or a zombie."

"Or some scantily clad pop star. And their parents let them do that."

"Remember last year when James came dressed up like an executioner and Frankie was his headless victim? Well, he actually had a head, it just wasn't attached to his body, and it dripped of fake blood."

OK. Time to move on.

FORTY-TWO

Jake

Gigi, Brady's friend, agreed to meet with me and suggested that we conduct our business in the town's dog park around noon. She would bring her dog, too. Having several hours to kill, and really no 'work' to do yet, I googled *blackmail* on the Internet. There I found far more information than I knew what to do with, especially since I didn't know the details of Gigi's problem.

It seemed the online sites could not agree on the origin of the word or the concept of blackmail, though numerous contributors mentioned the plight of Scottish farmers in the seventeenth century. Apparently, there were plenty of bad guys back then, too, demanding payment from the farmers to keep from being harassed or harmed by those asking for the money. The word *mail* was used back then to mean payment or rent and the farmers paid their extortionists with cattle (black cows = blackmail) or coins (silver coins = whitemail). The term blackmail seems to have survived a lengthy passage of time while whitemail faded away. Interesting, but not helpful.

Wendell, Malcolm, and I sat in the RV in the dog park's parking lot watching for the arrival of a woman about twenty-five years old, 5'6" tall, with long, dark, wavy hair. That was Brady's description of his friend. I knew that she'd have her female Rottweiler with her. No sign of Gigi yet, but Wendell had a blast, sitting in the passenger seat, watching three Labs romp around in the fenced area.

That's when it hit me. Wendell had not been in the company of his own kind during the few years I'd known him, and I wasn't sure what canine experiences he might have had before my time. I'd have to ask Lindsey. Today, however, his body language conveyed delighted excitement. I'd just have to wait and see what kind of dog behavior arose in him when he saw the Rottie, which would happen soon. *Here they come.*

"Hi, you must be Gigi." We stood about ten feet apart holding our dogs by their leashes.

"Well, that's what Brady calls me. I'll bet you're Jake."

"You'd win that bet. So if your name is not Gigi where'd he come up with that? From the old movie? The Maurice Chevalier song?"

"No, just a G for Gabby together with a G for Guzman. GG. I don't actually know what Brady was thinking, but that's my assumption for his invention of the nickname. Either way, he's the only one that calls me that. Gabby is fine. Preferred, really."

"Well then, Gabby, shall we see how the dogs do together before we get down to work?"

"Good idea. I never know with Willy . . ."

"She's a he?"

"Oh, no. Willy is short for Wilhelmina. She's great with people — nice people, that is — and with most dogs.

We entered the small double-gated area that prefaced the large, main portion of the dog park, unclipped their leashes and I held my breath. Gabby appeared to be breathing just fine. So far, so good. We proceeded into the large grassy area. Wendell and Willy had just begun the typical sniffing ritual when the three Labs already occupying the space galloped toward them. Willy stood firm. Her confident stance, not to mention her significant size, would have slowed me down, but the lovable Labs kept coming. So far, Wendell just watched. But then he stepped closer to Willy and stood by her side. What a formidable sight that was.

Now I was not only watching the body language of five dogs, I was watching Gabby, too. She was not looking at the dogs at all. She didn't strike me as the type that would let her dog be aggressive or engage in a dogfight.

"So, everything's okay here?" A little clarification would ease my mind.

"Probably. We'll know in about a minute." Gabby stood unruffled as if the three romping Labs were not headed straight for the two powerful sentinels.

"But you're not even watching Willy."

"I don't want the dogs to think I'm watching them, but I am. I definitely am. We don't want them to feel our concern or anxiety. That would only make matters worse. Besides, they're Labs. They might annoy our serious-minded dogs with all their pointless, playful romping, but they won't start any aggression."

Gabby was very calm; our two giant dogs stood their ground, their expressions intense, but they made no moves toward the other dogs. I was a little tense, though. The Labs stopped their forward movement about ten feet from our dogs as if they'd experienced a sudden epiphany. They turned around and bounded away. Wendell and

Willy got past the sniffing portion of their greeting and on to a little bit of play bowing with each other. I recorded some of the action on my phone so Lindsey could see her happy dog with his new, and maybe first, canine friend.

We sat on a bench with a view of the entire dog park. I had to admit, I was distracted. Not by Gabby, though she seemed like a nice, fit-looking young woman, but by the joy exhibited by our two dogs as they jumped over logs, ran up ramps, and drank from the huge water trough. But enough about the dogs. Time to get down to business.

"Brady really wants to get my little mystery solved. He's a bit protective by nature and he wants me to be his girlfriend and . . . "

"You're not his girlfriend? He seems mighty concerned about your safety."

"I guess I'm sort of his girlfriend. We go hiking and skiing together. Stuff like that. I'm just not ready for a real commitment right now. I take care of myself. I am strong, I have Willy, and I carry my pepper spray at all times. I don't actually need a man."

"So, how can I help you?"

Gabby explained that she'd been receiving blackmail since late last spring. And though she was not afraid, she would feel better if she knew what was going on. She wondered if the author of the blackmail was stalking her in some abnormal way. *Is there a normal way to stalk someone?* I needed clarification and cut in with my own questions.

"What does this blackmailer want you to do?"

"I don't know. That's part of the mystery."

"Okay. I'm a little confused because blackmail is a crime of threat. Someone threatens to reveal an embarrassing or disgraceful or harmful fact about another unless they receive the requested payment or action. Let me back up."

After a frustrating game of Twenty Questions (make that thirty) I learned that Gabby was not being blackmailed. She was receiving mysterious, unidentified mail that was black—notes written with metallic pens on black paper, put into black envelopes. The content of the notes was not what I'd call threatening, but what concerned her, and Brady, was the fact that the writer seemed familiar with some of Gabby's activities, thus, her use of the word *stalker* earlier in our conversation made sense. The notes were getting longer and longer and lately she'd started calling them letters. They arrived at her P.O. Box in town almost weekly. I gave her my number and asked her to call immediately when the next letter arrived or if she felt something was not right.

"I'll do that, for sure. And, maybe there will be some black mail waiting for me at the post office right now. Black mail with big orange handwriting on it."

She paused, waiting for my reaction. When all I had to offer was a puzzled look in my eyes and a frown on my brow, she explained.

"It's Halloween! A night of ghosts, goblins, and . . . black mail with orange lettering." She shook her head in disbelief as she and Willy made their way to the gate.

Halloween! I'd completely spaced that out and was surprised that Lindsey hadn't mentioned it.

"We've got to go, too, big buddy." Wendell's expression said a lot as he gave me a *What? We are all leaving now, just when things are getting good?* look. This was followed with persuasive, pitiful dog whining.

I was focused on the dog, so I completely missed the fact that Gabby had come back until she flung her arms around me in a full body hug and said, "Thank you. I feel better already." Then she was gone . . . again.

Thankful? Grateful? I'm sure that was nothing more than an expression of gratitude. Or had I just been on a double date?

\\

Sitting alone in his late model truck, looking over his next three assignments, his hands began to shake. Was he sick? Sick from germs, high altitude, or was it merely his miserable life? His head began to twinge, which meant a killer headache would arrive soon, followed by the words, conversations from his past. He didn't want to hear them, but they came anyway. He had to be patient, though, because the words he didn't want to hear were sometimes followed by his own brilliant, rhythmical sayings. That part, he liked very much. That almost made his suffering worthwhile.

"Here's the address. Deliver the box."

"That's all I have to do? You're gonna pay me for that?"

"Oh, yes. And we've only just begun. I have lots of work for you."

Need a doctor, got a doctor . . . one too many doctors. Yeah!

There was an old woman who lived in a shoe . . .

Gotta find that shoe and tell her what to do.

Along came a spider that sat down beside her. No, sit down by me!

FORTY-THREE

Lindsey

What an amazing, jam-packed, energizing day! The teachers had been extraordinarily enthusiastic and cheerful; I almost felt pangs of guilt being paid to have so much fun. Almost, but not quite. Tonight, this Halloween night, Jake and I would share the stories of our day.

Jake was upbeat and said his blackmail investigation had the potential to be interesting, even amusing. He needed that. We needed that. The icing on this cake? (Or, perhaps, the gravy on the kibble.) Wendell and his new friend, Willy. I wished I could have been there to see them playing together.

"Jake, I know it's dark already, but let's roast some turkey dogs and marshmallows tonight. The moon should be rising by the time you get the fire started and I've gathered the goodies. What do you say?"

"I say we get this Halloween party started! Do you have a costume?"

CRICKET ROHMAN

"I don't have an outdoorsy, cookout costume, but I might be able to improvise something later in the evening." *Oooooh.* From the quizzical smile on Jake's face, I wondered what picture had flashed through his mind.

The four of us—yes, Malcolm, too, but with his cage partially covered due to the chilly temperature—gathered around the fire ring. Wendell went to work; at least that's what it looked like to us. He circled the fire ring with his nose to the ground like a sniffer dog. He didn't have the face shape or the nose for that kind of work, but unaware of his limitations he continued to sniff, to circle, to lift his head and look around. To all this, he added a little whining and then a sneeze or two. We were clueless as to the cause of this sudden frenzy of activity.

Jake retrieved the lantern from the RV to shed some light on the area until the fire was lit and the flames could take over. The strike of a match, the hiss of pressure within the lantern, and then the glow of . . . Right away we spotted the object of Wendell's curiosity—a box lying in the center of the fire ring. At first we assumed that a departing camper had left some burnable trash, but there was a trash container at the far end of the campground, even a container for recyclables, and, this was our campsite. So, our initial ideas didn't make much sense. Curiosity got the better of Jake and he wanted to get the fire lit so he lifted up the box.

I screamed! Jake gasped. We weren't expecting to come face to face with a chaotic pile of . . . of . . . dead insects? Oh, wait. Something was moving. Several furry, multi-legged inhabitants ascended to the top of the morbid pile and scurried away. Tarantulas, I think.

"Okay," said Jake, throwing kindling, sticks, and logs on the remains of the others. "Let's get this fire blazing!"

"What? Just like that, we're going to carry on as if nothing strange had happened?"

"Yes. That's exactly what we're going to do. This could just be a Halloween prank."

That's what Jake said, but his actions suggested something far more ominous. As soon as the kindling set the twigs to burning, and the flames from those twigs lit the logs, and the fire roared, he darted toward the RV. He quickly returned, though, with his gun in one hand and a crowbar in the other.

"Just a few precautions. I always wanted to be a boy scout when I was a kid. I took the motto *Be Prepared* to heart, and I am prepared to bash bugs!"

He'd put on a happy face for my benefit. He was a good man. But both of my appetites were now absent. We cooked, we pretended to eat, then, inside, we fell asleep watching a DVD of *Kindergarten Cop*. Things would feel different, less creepy-crawly, in the light of day.

FORTY-FOUR

Jake

Before heading out to the Rusty Roof Ranch to drop Lindsey off, Wendell and I took a little walk. Actually, he took me. His nose was still on duty so he followed his nose and I followed him. First, he revisited the fire ring, circling it several times before walking rapidly toward the opposite end of the campground's loop. He stopped abruptly and sat, as if to say, this is the spot.

His nose knows something I don't know. Think. What is special about this spot? I made a 360-degree look around. Just the same two RVs that had been here all along. No new arrivals. But . . . something was different. Think. Ah, of course. The truck. There had been a truck parked somewhere in this vicinity, but no truck today. When did it leave? I could not recall.

Wendell had led me from the fire ring to this very spot. Could the truck have been parked right here? Could the owner of that truck have hidden insects under a box in our fire ring? That is too crazy. Crazy, stupid. Who does stuff like that?

"Jake, come on. We've got to go."

"Be right there."

Staring down at the hard packed dirt under my feet, three cigarette butts came into view. Hmm. I didn't have gloves, but I did have a Ziploc bag in my pocket, so I scooped them up with care using that bag and hurried back to the RV.

Our personal mysteries took cuts, or as Lindsey would say, 'shorty-cuts' and rearranged themselves at the forefront of my thoughts once again. The puzzling events that occurred near our RV—the broken step, the gas siphoning, the tire slashing, the blood—appeared first. Then Malcolm went missing and spiders showed up.

The biggest bombshell of all, and now a link in our little chain of mystery, was the news of having a half-brother, a half-brother that was responsible for the tire-slashing incident and, perhaps, more. Though I didn't need Lad to tell me to be careful, that was a given, I did appreciate his concern . . . and his help. Just as soon as we wrapped up our work here in Estes, finding that son of a bitch would be my number one priority. In the meantime, I'd make an extra effort to remain close to Lindsey, though there would be times—like today when I went to the post office—when I couldn't.

The line was relatively short and it kept moving. Simple transactions, mostly. Two women worked the counter. While waiting for my turn, I entertained myself by sizing up the women as to which might be the most helpful. Would it be the young, nice-looking woman, or the older, fifty-something, drop-dead gorgeous woman?

"Next, please. How can I help you today?"

I got the younger of the two. "I just have a couple of questions."

And before I'd begun to ask my first one, she flashed her saucy smile in my direction then caught me completely off guard by asking her own question. "Would you like some stamps with those answers?"

"Uh, sure. Got any with pinecones?"

"How about flags?"

"Flags? Is that all you've got?"

"Flags and old queens."

"Okay. I'll take a book of flags."

I began asking my questions as she dug in the drawer for the book of flags I would probably never use. Texts and emails were my main methods of communication. "Does every letter get a postmark?"

"Yes, sir. We have a machine that takes care of most of the postmarking. You weren't kidding about having questions. I was expecting something more like, 'Where is the nearest public restroom?' "

I knew right away, this young woman was not your typical postal worker. I continued. "Do you ever get or see mail in dark colored envelopes and is that a problem with regard to postmarks?"

"It's not a problem for us. It's just that the postmark might not be readable. You've used up your two questions. Now I get to ask another one. Why do you care about postmarks?"

"A friend of mine is getting blackmail; some black mail. Get it?"

"Yeah. Got it." The woman's tone took a dramatic turn and, suddenly, I had her undivided attention.

"She doesn't know who is sending this black mail so she's a little—"

"Intimidated? Worried? Frightened?" Her enthusiasm grew with every word spoken.

"Maybe. I'm just trying to help her figure it out."

She leaned in closer, glancing first to the left and then to the right, then whispered, "It would help if I could see a piece of the black mail."

I whispered back. "I could arrange that. Are you working this weekend?"

"No, I'm a Monday through Friday gal this week."

"Then I will see you here on Monday. Thanks for your help, Miss . . . Aggy?"

That was the name on her name badge. Unusual. She simply nodded and said, "Have a nice day."

It seemed I'd stumbled upon a fellow — make that a female — sleuth right here in a Rocky Mountain post office. I'd give Gabby a call and ask her to bring one of the notes or letters dressed in black (the mail, not Gabby) tomorrow when we met at the gift shop during one of her breaks. Wendell would expect Willy to be with Gabby; he'd be disappointed. Maybe I could set up a play date at the dog park over the weekend. *Did I really just think that?*

FORTY-FIVE

Lindsey

So much to do and so little time. That was how I felt this week. These hard-working, enthusiastic teachers wanted to learn it all, do it all, but I knew that wasn't possible. This morning we were sipping coffee, tea, or water, and creating several brainstorming charts using the carrousel method—when Brady burst into the room looking for Jake.

"Good morning, teachers. Sorry for the interruption. I'll only be a second."

No one seemed to mind; they all liked Brady. He was the *coolest* curriculum coordinator this town had ever seen . . . and he left most of the curriculum decision making up to them.

He pulled me to the side, handed me an envelope and proceeded to explain its existence and tardiness.

"Somehow, this letter found its way to the school board office. They think it arrived yesterday, but they're not really sure. Anyway, no one knew who Jake was so it sat there for a while before they brought it over to me."

"All right. Thanks. I will see that Jake gets this just as soon as he returns from his meeting."

I stared at the envelope as Brady walked away. Interesting. It was addressed simply to Jake Lee, Estes Park Schools. I don't know how it found its way to the office of the school board. Something about it nagged at me. Familiarity, perhaps? Hmm. Oh, well. The teachers and their charts awaited my perusal.

Chart 1: Writing experiences you currently offer your students.

Chart 2: Your most successful writing activity or lesson.

Chart 3: Current writing instruction challenges.

The data gathered on the charts would help me know how to proceed during the creation of their yearlong writing calendars, as well as how to best follow up later on. After discussing the teachers' notes and comments, everyone took a fresh air and bathroom break while I pulled out that envelope and gave it a second look.

Yes. There it was—the cause for my sense of familiarity. The handwriting on this envelope looked very similar to the handwriting on that love letter Jake received in Albuquerque. And I thought that was one of our tiny mysteries that had disappeared, never to return. I could be wrong. Perhaps I was reading far too much into the existence of another piece of mail.

I shouldn't open it. I should wait for Jake, but I might not see him for several hours. How would I be able to concentrate until then? *I should open it now; Jake wouldn't mind. He shared the first letter with me. So, it's now or wait impatiently until the end of the session.*

With my heart pounding, I opened it. I read it.

Dear Jake: You are the hottest, most handsome man I have ever seen in my entire life. Everything about you makes me want you—the way you walk, the way you talk, your gestures, your muscles, your skin, your eyes, your . . . E V E R Y T H I N G.

I want to be closer to you now more than ever before. That will happen soon, sooner than you think. Your hands will caress my body, every inch of my naked body, and I will return each caress with heat like you've never known. Do I have your attention? Are you already rising to the occasion? You won't regret anything I have planned, in fact, you will beg for more.

Till then,

Your Secret Admirer (Well, maybe not so secret. Think about that!)

P.S. I can't do this anymore. I have better things to do!

My hands trembled, the sheet of paper they held rattled meekly. Who would dare write this? It had to be someone that knew our itinerary. I read the words one more time. The postscript was written with a different pen. Obviously, a last minute after-thought added by the letter's author. As if trembling hands weren't enough, now my mind raced out of control, my stomach contributed a flip-flopping queasiness, and red-hot anger found its way to my skin's surface. But who was I angry with?

"Lindsey? Are you all right?" asked Lillian, one of the third grade teachers.

Shoving the words meant for Jake into my pocket, I did the best I could to put on a happy face. "Of course. I'm just doing a little daydreaming. You know how that is."

I lied. I didn't know *what* I was doing beyond feeling traumatized. It certainly wasn't daydreaming; it was more like *nightmaring*. I wanted desperately to talk with Jake.

But that was not possible right now. I'd have to push through the shock and get back to work.

FORTY-SIX

Jake

Hugs first, wine second, then Lindsey would tell me all about her day. I already suspected there'd been problems. Her silence on the drive back to the campsite was my initial clue.

"Jake, is there another woman in your life? I need to know the truth."

Whoa! Where did that come from? I anticipated hearing about a difficult teacher or a power failure or . . . anything but *that*. I could see she was distressed and on the verge of tears ... or was that a look of anger?

She handed me an envelope, which I opened and read quickly. *Aw, geez!* Would it never end? I didn't know what to make of this rather racy, seductive letter, many degrees hotter than its predecessor. Questions leaped into and then thrashed around in my brain. But first . . . I took Lindsey into my arms and held her close.

"Oh, Lindsey, sweetie, you are the one and only love of my life, my everything. You must know that. I don't know what is going on with these letters, but I will get to the bottom of it. I'd like to share the few thoughts I'm already having about this little mystery, but I don't want to upset you."

"I'm listening."

That's not good. Whenever Lindsey became a woman of few words that meant she was shutting down. Nevertheless, I kept thinking out loud. What did the letter's author want from me? She'd included no contact information, not even a return address. What action did she intend for me to take? The bigger question? Who was the author? We'd already gone over the possibilities back in Albuquerque when the first letter arrived. Our only suspect was the one flirty teacher—and that was a long shot—but after a few days, we'd ruled her out and had to admit we'd come up empty.

"Lindsey, one thing about this letter stands out as extraordinarily odd. Look. The address on the envelope and the P.S. note at the bottom of the letter are written with blue ink. The body of the letter is written in black."

"And the handwriting or at least the style used looks different," added Lindsey. "The letter is written in cursive, but the address and the P.S. resemble kindergarten block lettering."

Good. She'd begun to think and share her thoughts. I made some notes. There were inconsistencies, but were they pertinent? Didn't know. We both agreed that the letter writer, for some reason unknown to us, was probably not going to write to me again. But why write a letter to say that? Why not just throw it away or not write it at all?

"You know, Jake, she did tell you *why*. She wrote that she had better things to do."

"I suppose that's good." I secretly hoped those 'better things' had nothing to do with us. I kept staring at the envelope; it was trying to tell me something.

Neither of us was hungry nor had the strength to prepare a meal, so we popped a couple of small, frozen entrées into the microwave and called it dinner.

\\

He'd wanted to speak with her for a long time, to ask her why she'd left him. He would do that. He'd make the call right after having a smoke. With the anticipation of brilliant thoughts coming to mind and new words spilling from his lips, his body shivered with excitement. New conversations, conversations in real time would be spoken. What a welcome change that would be. No more looking to the past. Finally, he'd come to know her and he'd be happy.

"Lee residence."

"Is my mother there?"

"I'll check . . . Who is this?"

"Her son."

"Oh, sorry. You just sound different today. I'll get her."

"Hello. How good of you to call. How's that pretty gal of yours?"

"Don't have a gal. Just a mother. You're my mother and I want to see you.

"You've got the wrong number."

"But I'm giving you a chance to right all your wrongs."

She hung up on him. Maybe he had misdialed. The lady who'd answered the phone first had said 'Lee residence' and that was not the name he'd received from the Adoptee Internet Search Company, but this was definitely the phone number. No. That had to be her. Though the bitch wouldn't give him the time of day or even listen to what he had to say, he couldn't let it go, not after making such a long journey. Not when he could see the bright light at the end of the long, dark tunnel.

FORTY-SEVEN

Lindsey

This morning, the instant the participants hurried into the room, I had no doubt they were the teachers of kindergarten and first grade students. Their bubbly energy seemed to bounce off the walls like grasshoppers in a shoebox. Today, I'd set them free!

These teachers were quick to let me know that as much as they loved to celebrate Halloween with their students, they were also glad the high-octane day, and the day after, was over. I was delighted to hear a few teachers describing this workshop as a vacation day. And it didn't hurt that it was also … Friday.

Having the two previous groups' thoughts written on charts, and their writing topics already chosen, I was able to expedite today's procedures. Why reinvent the wheel? All we needed to do was a little modification.

Everyone agreed to begin the year by setting up and teaching students the procedures for a Writers' Workshop, and end the year with Student Choice and Author Study. This group wanted to work on adding detail to the four to six week slot devoted to poetry so they could begin implementation right away. It was a perfect writing plan for the period of time leading up to Thanksgiving and then the holidays near winter break.

This group of eight females and one male was on a poetry trajectory. Their comments came so rapidly, I could barely keep up.

"Teaching kids to rhyme helps them learn phonics."

"And that helps them learn to read."

"I want to read more poetry to the students and publish the poems they write."

The male member of this K-1 team, the teachers called him Mr. Paul, kept his cell phone next to his yellow notepad and glanced at it often. I didn't mind, but some of the teachers did. Others just teased him about his attachment to this inanimate object with statements like: Paul's on his phone; Phone call for Paul; even, in honor of our poetry day, gyrate to the vibrate and tailgate, home plate, blind date. The women chuckled, the phone actually vibrated, and Paul left the room.

"Was it something we said?" giggled one of the women.

Everyone shrugged and feigned innocence. Within seconds, Paul marched back into the room carrying enough pizza to feed an army. Needless to say, he was greeted with appreciative cheers.

The pizzas had been made to look like giant smiley faces thanks to Paul's request for creative pepperoni placement when he'd ordered the food. As we all filled our paper plates, Paul had another little surprise for us. A poem. He read his original pizza poem. *"Pizza for you, pizza for me, FYI, It's not fat-free!"*

He grinned and winked, knowing that a few of his teasers were on perpetual diets. In a way, he reminded me of Jake.

This male teacher would be referred to as Paul the Poet for the duration of the day. Oh, boy. He had really started something. Let's just say, it became a rhyming day, poems a plenty, more than twenty, served al dente!

Before the pizza was completely gone—yes, we ate it all—the teachers decided to have a special Pizza Poetry Day. Paul had a puzzled look on his face, though.

"What's the matter, don't you like that idea?"

"I love the idea, but there is no perfect rhyme for the word *pizza*. Believe me. I know. I checked the Internet."

He was correct about that, but his comment was the perfect segue into a discussion of non-rhyming, free verse poetry. Together we wrote a free verse pizza poem.

Pizza
Crunchy, tasty, smells so good.
Eat pizza with friends.
Gooey, cheesy, pepperoni.
Eat pizza with everyone!

\\

As much as he hated doing someone else's dirty work, he functioned more efficiently when following directions. Now, he was his own boss and found that designing the strategies, the moves, the actions was far more challenging than carrying out someone else's instructions. After rethinking his approach to Mom and what he really wanted from her, he called her back. His second real-time conversation commenced.

"Don't hang up this time. I got something to say."

"I don't know who the hell you are. So make it fast. Or I will put my husband on the line."

"Go right ahead. Make my day. Let's wait for your sugar daddy."

"You've got sixty seconds. Get on with it."

"I just want to meet you. Like I said, you're my mother."

"Bull shit!"

"I do not tell lies, but you . . . Think! What were you doing about thirty-six years ago? Do the words: sex with lots of men, unwed mother, or adoption sound familiar? Any of those ring a bell? I know all about you.

"You don't want to mess with me."

"Oh, I think I do. So Mommy dearest, invite me home. I want to come home."

"Bull shit! You have your own family. Get out of mine."

"I'm gonna make your day. Since I haven't aroused your motherly instincts, I'd be happy to disappear and never tell our story to the man of the house for . . . let's see . . . how does $250,000 sound?"

"I don't make deals with people like you."

The woman hung up again. How dare she? He'd tried to be nice but the bitch was totally uncooperative, unwilling to fulfill her mommy role, cold as ice. She talked tough but maybe she was bluffing. He was not ready to give up on collecting hush money from her. That was the least she could do. He'd call again, soon. Real soon.

He noticed, this time, that the twinges of pain that forewarned the return of a past conversation were absent. He rejoiced in that fact . . . prematurely; the headache that usually preceded the uttering of his own 'brilliant' words was as debilitating as ever.

Hearts! Hearts! Hearts for sale.
Have a heart, give a heart.
Need a heart, take a heart.

FORTY-EIGHT

Jake

Friday had been pleasant, even normal. (I knocked on some wood to make sure the universe heard and appreciated my appreciation.) No trauma, no weirdness, just a beautiful day in the chilly, mountainous neighborhood. I had high hopes for the weekend to be more of the same.

So, here we were, all five of us: Gabby, Willy, Wendell, Lindsey, and me. Six if we counted the bird waiting back in the car. Saturday, in the park. I think it was the third of the month. Yes, I was in a good mood, a great mood. Lindsey and Gabby hit it off immediately, and the dogs played as if they'd been best friends forever. We had the whole dog park to ourselves.

Greetings accomplished, we sat down and got right to business. Gabby pulled a couple of black envelopes from her coat pocket and handed them to me. She stared my way with the anticipation of a child watching Daddy peruse her less than perfect report card as I read the letters. No, I didn't have eyes in the back of my head like Lindsey did, but my peripheral vision served me well.

"Well, what do you think, Jake?"

"The postmarks are impossible to read, there's no return address, and the letters are definitely flirty. Who do *you* think is sending them? Take a wild guess."

She shook her head and shrugged her shoulders. "I have no idea. I've been guessing wildly for months already and nothing has popped up."

Lindsey jumped in and asked, "Where is home, Gabby?"

"Denver."

"Any old boyfriends or guys that might have had a crush on you back there?"

Gabby shrugged again, adding a negative shake of her head. I even asked her if Brady might have sent the letters.

"No way! Definitely not. Besides, he's a techie guy. He'd harass me with a text message should he ever be so inclined."

We wouldn't uncover any clues from invisible postmarks, and the letters contained nothing we could define as threatening, so none of my detective connections would have plausible cause to help me this time. Fortunately, this tiny mystery seemed completely harmless. Baffling, annoying, but harmless. I was out of ideas for the moment.

No food was allowed inside the dog park so Lindsey suggested we drive back to our campsite and have a picnic. The dogs could still play off-leash and we could all relax for a while longer.

\\

He was good with numbers and he knew her number by heart. Having only an old flip phone, he pressed the area code first, then the seven-digit number. After three rings, someone answered. "We're sorry. This number has been disconnected and there is no new number. Please hang up and try again." He tried again. The same stoic, female voice repeated the same infuriating message.

He growled. He wanted to scream, but he didn't dare. Too many people would hear him and they'd stare. He'd seen it before. *What's your problem?* He should have stayed in his truck. Now, with the judgmental, on-looking eyes of strangers close by, frantic anxiety limited his options. He muffled the onslaught of agonizing moans as best he could just before new words floated into his awareness.

Old Mother Hubbard
Won't go to her cupboard
To fetch her poor boy a bone.

FORTY-NINE

Lindsey

Jake got up early and cooked asparagus, spinach, and cheese omelets, mixed up a mini-fruit salad composed of bananas and blueberries, and brewed some peachy white tea. A perfect beginning for a wonderful day.

I cherished any occasion, now that I no longer had my own classroom, which included time with students. Kids really were the best teachers. I'd always learned something from them, regardless of their age or level of intelligence. Today was one of those special occasions.

The main purpose for visiting teachers in their own classrooms today was to familiarize myself with each teacher's teaching style. They understood I was not there to evaluate their lessons. I'd be happy to give feedback, if they wanted it, though.

I'd have only a few minutes in each classroom, so I brought my tablet—it was less conspicuous than the laptop—for the purpose of jotting down my notes. Without that, I'd never remember who was who or what

I'd seen. I looked forward to observing the teachers trying something brand new to them with their students. I was proud of their courage.

"I'll be here until four o'clock. Have fun at the post office." My mind was on the day ahead as I opened the car door. It seemed Jake's heart was still here, centered on me.

"Hey, girl," he said showing his captivating boyish grin just before taking me by the hand. "Since you're going to be putting in such a long workday, I'd like to give you a little something to remember me by."

Oh, my. That look. That special look in his eyes. He could be so romantic, so loving. We kissed. A real kiss. Not a hurry out the door, peck on the cheek kiss. No. It was a lingering, parting of the lips kiss that made me want to forget all about school and . . . No! I've really got to go.

\\

His whole body jerked; he sat up, awakened by . . . a sound, a dream, the damn voices in his head? The morning air was uncomfortably cold. He shivered as the cobwebs vanished gradually from his eyes. His accommodations? Far from sufficient. Pitiful, in fact. Fully awake now, the words, the words from his dreams beat like a snare drum in his head.

Badly . . . madly . . . sadly. Badly-madly-sadly.
LOUDLY, softly, slowly, quickly.
Poorly, richly, rightfully. so-ly Rightfully, richly.
Stop! Don't stop! Stop!
Maidenly, sisterly,
Smotherly, motherly . . .motherly?
Mother Lee? . . . Lee residence? . . .
I should be lookin' for Lees!

He held his head in his hands and could actually feel the throbbing, the pounding emitted through his temples. Though sometimes painful, he respected his dreams, the voices, the rhythms, the rhymes, certain they were sent to him from a higher power. Today's divine intervention had just arrived with a clue. Knowing what he had to do, he prepared himself for another day of research.

FIFTY

Lindsey

Sighing deeply after my husband's breathtaking kiss, I floated on air up the steps to the school's front entrance. Once in the hallway, heading toward the office, the electric energy of the children brought me back down to earth. Watching them hurrying down the hall, some interacting confidently with their friends, others noticing my presence and suddenly becoming shy, brought back memories. Those were the days.

Most of the fourth and fifth grade teachers were reviewing an element of fiction writing: characters, settings, plots, descriptive language, strong leads or hooks. Some teachers did all the talking as their students listened. In other classrooms more student participation was the norm. One teacher took advantage of the highly successful mini-lesson strategy where she explained briefly what would be reviewed, read an example from a published work of fiction, modeled what the students would soon write independently, then restated what had just occurred . . . and she accomplished all of that in less than eight minutes. Kudos!

Brady was right. These teachers were amazing. I learned quickly upon entering a second grade classroom that those teachers had teamed up to plan and implement their 5-Step Writing Process lesson—using only one sentence. It was a little crowded, but I could see that the students were excited to be doing something new with another class of kids and two teachers.

That left me with more time to spend with the kinder and first grade classes. The variety of materials and lessons used by those teachers was impressive. I observed them using math manipulatives, working their word walls, reading big books, reading to buddies, and creating pocket chart stories. It was all there. I saw students engaged, and teachers meeting students' needs.

The cutest little kinder girl, with big blue eyes and long, straight hair came up to me carrying a box. She had such a hopeful expression on her tiny face.

"Hi, there. What are you working on today?"

She thought for a moment and then answered, "Giving this box away."

"I see. Well, how is that going?" So far, we were on different wavelengths. I had no idea what the little girl was thinking or doing.

"If you take the box, then it's going good. But if you won't . . ."

And I thought Wendell was the master of making sad eyes to get his way. This kid had him beat by a long shot.

"Hi, Ms. Lindsey." Mrs. Rose, the teacher, joined our conversation. "I see you've met Jenny. And she would be so happy if you'd just accept the box." This teacher had some eye talent of her own. More pleading ensued.

Apparently, I had not responded to the pleas in a timely manner because now Mrs. Rose pretended to rub the side of her head, but really she was hiding her now winking eye from little Miss Jenny. So I took the box and thanked her profusely for it. Said I'd take good care of it. *I don't even know the contents of the box. Now I'm hoping it isn't a dead goldfish or worse.*

She hugged my leg and dashed happily back to the table where she was creating a . . . something colorful, with markers. I learned from the teacher that the box contained small jars of glitter, and I sighed with relief.

"She brought the glitter to school to share because her mom said it was too messy to use at home. Our custodian would throw a hissy fit if I used glitter inside the classroom. And I've got to keep him on my good side so he'll come quickly when there is a *green* clean up to do. Did you know that it's easier to rid a room of fleas than glitter?"

I didn't. Never had any 'flea' experience but, yes, glitter had a long *stick to the carpet* life. I knew that.

My day at the school had come to an end earlier that we'd planned. I waited for Jake on the bench near the entrance with my tablet, my purse, and my box, and hoped his day was as good as mine. I couldn't wait to hear about it. In the meantime, I organized my notes, and began to write the feedback I'd later email to the teachers that had taken me up on my offer.

"Hi, teacher." A tiny voice coming from a tiny child at the end of the bench caught my attention.

"Oh, hello, Jenny. Are you waiting for a ride home?"

"I get my ride out back. I was looking for you."

"Oh. Well, you found me. Won't others be looking for *you*? They might be worried."

"Mom's always late. So it will be okay."

"I'm taking good care of your box. See? It's right here beside me."

Jenny looked over her shoulder and then reached into her pocket and pulled out a small zip-topped plastic bag. Then she whispered into my ear, "It's fairy dust and has magical powers. It's for you."

I whispered back, "Don't you want you keep some of this for yourself?"

Looking pleased and delightfully impish, she answered, "I didn't bring all the fairy dust to school. I have that jar hidden at home. Nobody knows about it but me and you."

Before I could thank her, she dashed back into the school, presumably heading for the back door, where she should have gone in the first place. Securing my very own bag of shiny gold glitter—oops, I meant magical fairy dust—deeply into my front coat pocket, I went back to making notes and waiting for Jake.

FIFTY-ONE

Jake

I saw her even before I'd been able to open the door wide enough to walk through. She must have spotted me, too. Oh, man, she was excited about something, and I hadn't even shown her one of the black envelopes yet. Her overpowering exuberance caught me off guard.

"I'll bet you need another book of stamps. Am I right? You out of flags already?" Her head nodded up and down as she asked her question. She was really working me. But then she whispered, "Meet me on the park bench over there by the river in thirty minutes."

Now I was the one nodding and whispering, "Okay."

"Thanks. Have a nice day, sir." She used her normal postal worker voice for that last comment.

I had no idea what in the world was going on here, but I purchased a to-go cup of coffee at Starbuck's and went to wait on the park bench down by the river. Then I laughed recalling one of my favorite late night comedy sketches. *At least I would not be waiting in a van down by the river.*

238

The bench bowed with the additional weight of the newly arrived bench sitter, distracting my attention from checking my cell phone messages; my postal friend was early. She sat gazing straight ahead as if we were strangers with no plans of engaging in conversation. I leaned closer to hand her one of the black envelopes, which she ignored, but she began to speak softly, barely moving her lips.

"Don't look at me, but check out this photo on my phone." She held onto her phone and acted as if she were getting ready to make a call. "What do you see?"

Was she playing games? "I see a *selfie* of you and some guy." I had a nagging feeling that getting involved with this woman was a mistake, but here I was and curiosity got the better of me.

"How do I send this to you?"

"Hey, I don't want a photo of you and your boyfriend." Annoyed and feeling a little weird about this young woman and her actions, I stood up ready to flee the scene.

She grabbed my arm and pulled me back down. "Oh, yes you do. I sold this very guy a stamp on Friday."

Were my eyes rolling yet? "So?"

"Well, he needed a stamp so he could mail his BLACK envelope. Do you get my drift?"

"Got it! Definitely got it." The weirdness lifted . . . mostly.

I gave her a card containing all of my contact information including my email address so she could send the photo to my phone, and a big kiss on her cheek before dashing off. Now who was being weird?

Her last words? "Hey! You just blew my cover, but if you ever need any help—"

"I know where to find you."

\\

He'd known his biological mother's maiden name, Evelyn Scott, since he'd received the email message from the Adoptee Internet Search's website, but now, thanks to the housekeeper, he also knew her married name. He began his online search looking for an Evelyn Lee. There were many; the list was frustratingly long. And others hovered around waiting for a turn on the computer.

He felt rushed and he didn't like that. Pecking at the keys like an angry chicken, he searched frantically for the right Mrs. Lee. What he finally found excited him beyond his own tolerance and added a new dimension of tautness to his overloaded rationality. The pain began to travel up the back of his neck, over the top of his head settling in his eyes as a conversation from his recent past emerged.

"Special delivery. Get it done."

"I quit."

"Make her hate him or you won't get paid."

"I'm not workin' for you anymore."

"I'll be home for the holidays."

"Fuck you!"

"You're going down."

No I'm not. No I'm not . . .

The first pair of Lees are rich,

The boy will get his bone.

The second pair go in the ditch,

The chickens have come home.

As the pain subsided and he realized the incredible opportunity that had just surfaced, he practically danced out the door. This changed everything. He was highly motivated. Oh, yeah. Empire State Building high. The new and improved plan began to take shape. Upping the ante topped his list of tasks.

FIFTY-TWO

Jake

Where had the time gone? After the post office visit, I had made a few purchases—dog biscuits, birdseed, wine for tonight—then took a walk with Wendell. One more quick stop to see Gabby and I'd be done for the day. I'd better touch bases with Lindsey.

"Hi, Linds."

"Jake, where are you? I thought you'd be here by now. I finished up early."

"Oh, baby. I'm so sorry. I'm not quite finished. I'm running late and just now walking into the park's gift shop to show Gabby a photo. It will only take a second. Can you hang out there for a little while? I can be there in about fifteen minutes."

Of course she would, she was such a trooper, and she made it sound like the additional waiting was no big deal. Lindsey had an amazing capacity for strength and sweet understanding. Necessary traits for a woman married to me.

Gabby waved me over. I obliged. Seeing her was the only reason I was there although I could buy one of those pretty gold-dipped aspen leaf pins for Lindsey. Hmm. Yeah. I would do that.

Without saying a word, I brought up the photo of the stamp purchaser compliments of . . . Darn, I still didn't know her real name. Gabby's jaw dropped and her hands hit her cheeks like the unforgettable move made by the *Home Alone* kid.

"I take it you know him?"

Her reply was a nod and a covert point in the direction of the leather counter where belts and purses could be bought. I looked at the photo, I looked at the man. Photo, man. Man, photo. They were, indeed, one in the same. Gabby turned so that her back faced our guy and she added a few bits of information.

"This is a total surprise. We've worked here together since late spring. George is very polite and quiet and shy. This is hard for me to believe. But, Jake, now that the mystery is solved, I can handle it from here."

"Are you sure about that? It's sometimes those nice, quiet guys that do horrific things."

"I've got pepper spray and my Willy. I'll be just fine."

"Will you tell Brady about all this?" She merely shrugged her shoulders. "You two really are an item, right?"

"It's a little lopsided; all of the emotions are not mutual."

I reached out to shake her hand, but she moved in with one of her full-body hugs. I could see how a guy could get confused, though in the moment, he'd love it. She thanked me, she really did, and I let her know how to stay in touch, and made her promise to call if anything got weird.

"I'm just going to see if your buddy can help me with a quick jewelry purchase," I said, waving as I walked away.

FIFTY-THREE

Lindsey

Tonight everyone would shine! Everyone would glow. Wearing my long, black, knit dress, my black boots, and the gold-dipped aspen leaf pin Jake had given to me last night, I felt happy, relaxed, and even pretty. Many of the teachers had changed from their workshop attire—mostly jeans—to . . . fancier jeans and lacy tops or sparkly sweaters.

Enlarged first drafts of the school's new nine-month Writing Calendar were pinned to a 3' x 4' corkboard in the small dining room. The participating teachers eagerly explained the documents to their significant others who had joined them for the celebratory dinner.

A waiter dressed in western wear made sure everyone had a glass of champagne or sparkling water before Brady stepped to the center of the room. I felt a toast coming on.

"If you can hear me, clap once." The unimpressive clap came right away—actually, the teachers, who are accustomed to thinking on the spot, performed the request with a bunch of high-fives. After all, who could really clap while holding a champagne glass? Chuckling, Brady added, "I promise not to do the *seal of approval* or the *round of applause*." Inside joke, teacher stuff.

"But I would like to make a toast. A toast to Lindsey Lark, the leader of our fantastic week of learning. Thank you, Lindsey. Thank you for everything."

Glasses clinked, lips sipped, all was good. Then I stepped to the center to stand by Brady because I had a few words to say, too.

"Let's all thank Brady for making this week happen . . . And I'd like to propose a toast. Here's to teachers everywhere that strive to make learning relevant, rigorous, and fun for their students. That goes double for those in this room. You're amazing. I enjoyed my time with you more than you'll ever know. Cheers!"

Later, back at the campground, snuggling in our traveling home's comfy bed, Jake and I reminisced about our time in this high mountain town and agreed that tonight's party was a perfect way to end our first self-employed road trip. Tomorrow we'd begin the drive back to Tucson; we were ready to hit the road to home.

HOMEWARD BOUND

.

FIFTY-FOUR

Jake

My eyes opened. Something had roused me from my dream. A noise? The wind? Was it morning so soon? Lindsey slept peacefully and Wendell was . . . at the door frantic to go outside. He not only stood at the door, he scratched at it with his paw. He must have had a big drink of water during the night.

"Okay, buddy. Hang on. Here we go." I pulled on a pair of jeans and topped it with a sweatshirt.

The dog practically knocked me over as his huge body pushed its way out. Surprisingly, the nearest tree was not his first stop; the back of the RV was. He leaped around between the car and the tow bar making his rare grumbling, growling sounds.

On closer examination, I suspected a problem. Obviously, Wendell did, too. He still hadn't peed.

"Hey, Lindsey? Need your help for a second."

She poked her sleepy head out the door still in her bedroom attire. Not much fabric involved there; I could tell she was cold even from where I stood.

"Sure. What?"

"Pull the RV ahead about two feet. That's all. Thanks."

Wendell and I went back to observe the tow bar as Lindsey pulled forward. Damn! Just what I'd thought. The tow bar was broken, and it was practically new. If it wasn't for the dog at my side, I might have been far more upset than I was. It was like we were two ordinary guys talking auto shop stuff except that the four-legged one was the mechanic. He knew there was a problem back here before I did.

The RV and car were not going anywhere, at least not attached to each other. After locating the owner's manual for the tow package, then waiting for the sun to come up, I began to make some local phone calls, all of which were a big disappointment. Our joyful evening, now minimized by vehicle difficulties, was a thing of the past. I knew our future would be fine, but the present proved problematic. The parts we needed would have to be shipped up the mountain and would not arrive for two days. I wondered what flavor of lemonade Lindsey would be able to make out of this bowl of lemons.

"Here," she said, suddenly at my side, handing me my lined denim jacket. "It's only thirty-two degrees out here. Aren't you cold?" I hadn't felt the cold, in fact, I felt hot . . . under the collar. If only we could go home without any more problems or delays. Was that too much to ask?

"Linds, the parts we need won't arrive until sometime on Friday. Best case—they arrive in time to be installed the same day and we can take off early Saturday morning."

"If that is the best case, I'm not sure I even want to hear about the worst case."

"Yeah, well, here it is anyway. If the parts arrive late on Friday, the RV won't be ready to tow our car down the mountain until sometime on Monday."

We could do this, I tried to convince myself; we would find a workable solution. After all, we'd been troubleshooting for the past six weeks solving other people's problems. This shouldn't be too tough; we just needed a plan.

"The car works fine, right?"

I gave an affirmative nod.

"And the RV works fine, too, yes? Jake, what are you doing?"

"Dusting for prints. Look at Wendell. Now that is a dog filled with concern and behaving like a bloodhound again. And his concern is not for this metal tow bar itself. It's something else. He knows, he smells, he senses something beyond broken metal. Don't mind me, Linds. Old habits are hard to break. But, yes, the RV functions fine." *But the tow bar did not break by itself.*

With eyes bright and sparkling, her pointer finger tapped those luscious lips of hers before she spoke. "Then I've got an idea." Brace yourself lemons; you're about to get squeezed.

She did have an idea and it was a good one. After a few more phone calls, I helped her pack up the car with just a few things: some of her presentation materials, her treasured box of glitter, a water bottle, and a mug filled with fresh coffee. She'd follow me down the mountain and over to Boulder where an RV service business awaited our arrival. They'd install the new tow package; we'd hook up the car to the RV and be on our way by midafternoon. That was one sweet swallow of lemonade.

FIFTY-FIVE

Lindsey

As much as I'd rather be riding in the RV with Jake and the guys, neither of us wanted to wait until next Monday to head home. So, here I was at the end of our two-vehicle caravan . . . feeling slightly nervous; I had no experience driving on a steep and curvy mountain road. Oh, sure. There was that time two summers ago when I drove up the steep, rutted dirt road in the Zuni Mountains, but there were no cliffs, no traffic, and I couldn't drive faster than five miles an hour if I'd wanted to.

I was surprised by a cracking, jarring noise that couldn't possibly be part of the Pachelbel CD I'd been listening to. That disturbing sound was followed by, "Hey, good-lookin'. How are you doing back there?"

Then, I saw it. The very same walkie-talkie Jake had given me the night of the terrible storm we'd experienced while camping in those mountains. He must have set it, covertly, on the front seat just before we'd left.

"Doing fine, thank you. But what happened to your *over, copy, 10-4, out,* walkie-talkie words?"

"Left them behind long ago, but I could resurrect a few, just for you. Copy?"

"Yes, but it seems we are suddenly driving through a cloud or some dense fog is rolling in. Either way, I need both hands on the wheel right now. Over."

"Copy. Over and out."

Jake slowed his driving speed, probably just for my benefit. In an attempt to de-stress myself, I switched to the radio, took a few deep breaths, and began to sing along with the tune "On the Road Again". How appropriate! We'd be down the mountain and in the foothills in about thirty minutes. Knowing that, and the fact that Jake was right there in front of me, I relaxed and began to enjoy the drive.

Then a truck flew past me in a spot where it would be impossible to see an oncoming car even on a clear day. That person was really taking a chance. I didn't appreciate that one bit. I'd hoped that truck would pass Jake, too, and get far away from us, but it didn't. Not even when a short passing lane appeared. Some people were just plain strange … and inconsiderate.

At first I'd assumed this dangerous driver was just an obnoxious, stupid jerk, but then I wondered if drugs, alcohol, or a stroke were causing the odd maneuvering of the truck. No worries. I'd try to avoid this bad driver and drive defensively, and hoped Jake would take notice and do the same.

A scenic viewpoint was not far ahead. I prayed that truck would pull over, get off the road. Ah, the power of prayer! It did pull over. Okay. I could breathe normally once again. Now all I had to contend with were all the sharp curves on this two-lane mountain road.

Oh, no. The truck was back on the road and approaching fast, way too fast. Trouble, this was . . . something bad. I let out a wordless scream when that truck slammed into my back bumper. I gripped the wheel tightly as if my life depended on it and sped forward, trading one danger for another. The truck passed me again, side-swiping my small Jeep Liberty, almost forcing me off the road. Then, it pulled directly in front of me and slowed to a crawl, quickly creating more distance between Jake and me. Actually, I'd lost visual contact with him several minutes ago.

Now, while being forced to travel slowly, I kept my eyes on the road and reached for the walkie-talkie, patting my hand all over the seat; it was gone. Must have slid off the seat and onto the floor when I maneuvered through one of those sharp curves or when the truck slammed into the bumper. One jar of glitter had spilled open, too. What a mess! *Okay, I've got to think. Think!*

With the offending truck still in front of me, I slammed on the brake hoping to put plenty of distance between the truck and my car. But my plan backfired. The truck's driver floored it, laying rubber all the way as it screeched backwards up the hill. I had no choice but to swerve around the truck and move forward again. Fast, really fast.

My only hope was to catch up with Jake. He couldn't be too far ahead of me. Calling him was not an option, so I blasted the horn. Even that was difficult because it took all my strength with both hands on the wheel to avoid this assaulting truck and, at the same time, keep from crashing. Needless to say, I was driving at an unsafe speed. Everything was unsafe right now.

The RV came back into view for a few seconds. Thank God! I could see its brake lights going on and off. Jake was turning around—a challenging task on a narrow, curvy mountain road. Thank goodness he knew there was a problem and he was going to fix it. Oh! Oh, no! I gasped as the RV skidded sideways. With the menacing truck behind me once again and Jake in front of me having trouble turning the RV around, another car came speeding up the mountain road and around the curve. They honked, tires screeched, but they managed to zip around the sideways RV thanks to Jake's quick thinking and selfless move to swerve out of their way.

I wasn't prepared for what came next. It happened so fast and yet it seemed to occur in slow motion. I tried to scream. No sound. I tried to breathe. No air. My Jake had avoided the impending crash with the on-coming car, thank goodness for that, but now the RV was spinning like a windmill blade and, at the same time, sliding downhill.

"Jake! Oh, Jake. Hold on!"

I'm sure he tried to correct and straighten the RV's spin, but the adjustment was too late, the momentum too strong. I watched it all. Shaking, crying, feeling totally helpless. I could do nothing. It was inevitable that he would crash into something—a boulder, a guardrail, whatever was around the next bend. It wouldn't be me, he and the RV slipped farther downhill and away from my car, though not from my sight.

The bad quickly turned to worse, the worse to the unthinkable. The RV slammed into a large, steadfast cluster of boulders not far from the edge of the road, causing the metallic rectangle, our home-on-wheels, to crash through the guardrail, skidding and flipping until it was out of sight, gone. The noises—metal scraping on tree trunks and bushes; glass smashing against boulders; the hissing of engine fluids assaulted my sense of hearing— then . . . the silence. The horrible silence. *Oh, my God! Jake! Jake!*

All I could think about was Jake. I had to get to him. Thoughts of the truck and its erratic driver were long gone. I must have been in shock because I didn't remember stopping my car or getting out. My focus, my mission was to save Jake. Running toward the mangled guardrail, new sounds took over: the deafening pulse of my own blood surging through my head and my hyperventilating gasps as my lungs struggled for air.

"Jake? Jake!" I didn't really expect an answer . . .

Then I heard a voice.

"Damn! Old man Murphy is alive and well today. Double damn! I guess you'll have to do."

The man had a firm hold of my arm as he guided me back to my car. There I could make a 911 call. He sat me in the passenger seat with the glitter box at my feet. Then he got in, put it in drive, and headed uphill toward Estes.

"We need to call for help! Now!"

"I've got everything under control."

That was good because I certainly didn't. We'd gone maybe one hundred yards or so when he stopped and told me to get out and walk to the top of the hill and wait by the speed limit sign. He had one more detail to take care of. I thought he was going to steal my car. Could this day get any worse?

"Don't turn around and don't look back. I'll be along in a minute."

Under normal circumstances I would not have complied with illogical directions, but today was anything but normal. I had a funny feeling about this guy who I'd assumed at first was going to help me, but those thoughts were diverted when I heard a car approaching. *Think! Make a plan.* I'd flag them down by waving my arms wildly. I hoped they would stop.

I must have been mistaken. No vehicle of any kind drove by. Now I ran for *my* life as well as Jake's. The man caught up with me before I reached the sign. He wasn't pleased. Well, neither was I.

My body trembled with fear and shivered from the cold. As thankful as I was to be wearing my coat, I'd gladly have traded it for the pepper spray that was tucked away in my purse right now. I went with this man—he gave me no choice—but not without a fight. I kicked. I screamed. I cussed. Then I saw the truck, the truck that tried to run me off the road just moments ago. This was his truck? Oh, crap.

First, he tied my hands, then placed a blindfold over my eyes and sat me in the front seat. What was this all about? Who was this man? Confusion combined with shock rendered me clueless, but I was certain of one thing. Jake still needed my help. I had to get back to him . . . and the boys. Oh, my God! Wendell and Malcolm were in the RV, too, when it crashed over the guardrail.

"Calm down, Lindsey. Don't you worry your—"

"You know my name?" Shock, shock, and more shock. I needed to wake up from this nightmare. NOW!

"Yep, and like I was saying, don't you worry. I'm going to take real good care of you. Nothing else matters today."

"You're wrong about that. Very wrong."

The fury inside me grew until I exploded with more kicking and screaming. I threw my body against the door, then against my captor over and over. That's when he slammed on the brake, put it in park, tied my feet, gagged my mouth and shoved me into the small back seat of the truck. Gross. It smelled like rotten food and dirty socks.

\\

He should have strategized the snatching of his captive more thoroughly. He hadn't. He'd run full-steam ahead with his initial idea for Plan B with no consideration for the possibility of hornet's nests, cans of worms, or catch 22s. Oh, well. It was what it was, and now he had a feisty young woman to deal with. The plan still carried potential for success if he was able to cope with the changes, roll with the punches. That was a big *if*.

So far, he was on top of the world, almost home. After all, he'd made his own damn day with nobody's help. Now, on his way to deliver some well-deserved payback and gain a fortune, he was unstoppable. But the all too familiar pain began to hammer within his skull, more excruciating than ever. He experienced his own version of shock because this had never happened to him while driving in his truck. Panic surged through his body. What should he do? Would he be able keep driving or would he need to pull over?

We have super colliders and sexy joy riders,
Many misguiders and hairy black spiders.
I know something you don't know.
So take the keys and lock her up, lock her up, lock her up.
Take the keys and lock her up.
My fair lady.

No conversations today, just his own brilliant words. Short and sweet, they came quickly from his lips and then disappeared. With the pain subsiding, he marveled at his cleverness.

FIFTY-SIX

Lindsey

*P*lease, please wake up, I urged myself. This had to be a bad dream. Things like this didn't happen in real life, maybe in the movies, but not in real life. Not in *my* life.

Until I saw the light of day, and hopefully I would, eventually, I'd keep my body still, my voice quiet and try to regain my strength. And, I would listen with the ears of an elephant for clues about where we might be going . . . if only he would just shut up. His insane rambling intensified my fear.

I was fairly certain we were still headed back into the town of Estes Park. Though we were now standing still, he hadn't turned off the highway yet. That was encouraging. There would be people around, people that could help me. Then the shrill sound of a siren and the loud rumble of a large vehicle whizzed by us. A few seconds later, another siren. Hope. Glimmers of hope touched my heart. Maybe they were going to help Jake.

The noise distracted my captor from his nonsensical mumbling.

"They're wastin' their time. Nothin' left for them to rescue. Jake's long gone. Such a shame."

I attempted to speak in spite of the gag in my mouth. "You know Jake, too?" was what I said, but now I was the one sounding nonsensical. I was just more noise. Funny, though, he seemed to understand me.

"Oh, yeah. When I looked over the edge and down that steep, rocky hill, all I saw was a pile of twisted tin. No one could've survived that. Too bad. I had plans for Jake, but, like I said, you'll have to do."

The shock, the fear, took over, and sadness surrounded me, encased me like the contents of a chrysalis; a chrysalis that would never become a butterfly. Shallow breathing and praying for the strength to free myself and find Jake, were my last conscious recollections.

I must have fallen into a deep sleep. I didn't remember driving through the town or stopping at stop lights or signs, but now with the bumping and jolting motion of the truck, I was wide awake and thinking again.

I'd driven on a rough, rocky and rutted dirt road before, and this was far worse. Guessing we were not on a road at all, unless it was one of those rugged jeep trails, I figured we were making our own trail, timber bashing. Tree or bush branches brushed the sides of the truck as we tipped from one side to the other, navigating obstacles in the way.

The man must have had tools in his truck because I heard clanking and rattling, and sometimes felt an unidentifiable item graze my body. Grateful for the padding my coat provided, I braced my legs firmly against one side of the tiny backseat to minimize injury from all the bouncing and the assault of flying objects, and . . . I kept on thinking. Still unable to see, or talk, or use my hands or feet, I put my other senses to work. Escape was at the top of my current To Do list.

We were definitely in a wooded area. (I could imagine Jake, with his boyish grin, saying, 'brilliant deduction, Linds.') I felt my cheeks give in to a hint of a smile; a smile accompanied by a few more tears. The man must have opened his window because other scents drifted in to join the rotten food, dirty socks odor. Pine trees and pine needles was the strongest scent at first, but then I got a brief whiff of . . . what? Hmm. Horses, I think.

The only sounds available to my ears beyond the thrashing of the truck came from squawking birds and screeching squirrels unhappy with our trespassing.

The truck backed up and stopped, but I heard sounds like tree branches brushing, scraping against it as if we were still moving. Sounds that sent chills up my spine the same way the sounds of fingernails on a chalkboard did—only ten thousand times worse.

"We're almost home," he said, taking my arm and guiding me from the truck.

First he untied my feet, then removed the blindfold. As my eyes grew accustomed to the light I was able take a good, close-up look at my captor. I made a mental note of his appearance. There stood a slim man of average height with long, light brown hair tied back in a ponytail. He wore faded jeans, a black T-shirt, and an olive green corduroy jacket. He had no unusual markings that I could see and his face . . . deadpan, expressionless. Someday, when Jake would ask for a description of the kidnapper, I'd have one. My Sherlock would be proud of me.

I made two additional and quick observations before we began to walk. First, he'd covered the truck with more branches. It still looked like a truck, but I supposed that from a distance it might go unnoticed. Second, we were in the middle of a pine forest with no discernible trail or signs of human existence.

"Follow me," he instructed.

My nose began to drip more than just sniffling could handle. I could've let the nasal mucus drip down my face, the man wouldn't care, but I did. With the gag still in my mouth, I couldn't ask him for a tissue. He probably wouldn't have one anyway. Then I remembered there were several in my coat pocket. I should be able to get to it even with my hands tied together. Yes! I could do that.

I found a tissue; a tissue and the plastic bag of gold glitter. Little Jenny's magic dust. Little . . . Jenny's . . . magic . . . dust! A ray of sunshine, a bit of hope returned. The glitter would become my trail of breadcrumbs, but better than Hansel and Gretel's. The woodland creatures would not eat my golden glitter. I scattered the specks of gold with care. Someday they would lead me away from this place.

About ten minutes into our little trek, he removed my gag.

"Scream if you want to. But no one's gonna hear ya."

He was probably right about that. I saved my strength as we walked deeper into the forest, over rocky and overgrown terrain. Eventually, we came upon something resembling a trail—albeit a seldom-used game trail—which took us both uphill and downhill; sometimes it was steep, other times it rolled gently. Every now and then we'd trek through a clearing where I could see rugged mountain peaks in the distance. Without being able to use my arms for balance and with the dry dirt, small rocks, roots and sticks under my feet, I lost my footing several times. Each time I fell, my captor pulled me up, but I could see his patience dwindle with each successive tumble.

After many minutes of gloomy grumbling, he looked me directly in the eye and spoke. "You're sure blowing your nose a lot. You sick?"

"Allergies, that's all." Some exaggerated sniffling followed my lie. I really did feel sick, however, the ill feeling had nothing to do with my nose.

Fight or flight? I could do neither. Whether it was the altitude, my anxiety, the adrenaline, or all of the above sending jolts through my body, I found it difficult to breathe. It seemed I could not take in enough oxygen to fend off the light-headed dizziness I experienced. How much farther could it be?

"Almost home. I've got the place all ready for you, Lindsey."

"What do you want from me?" He stopped and stared as if I'd said something surprising or out of line.

"Not a thing. I don't want anything from you."

"Then why am I here?" I asked, shrugging my shoulders and looking from left to right.

"You're not even supposed to be here. It should have been Jake. And it would have been Jake, if he hadn't tried to turn the damn vehicle around. He almost ruined everything. So now, I'm gonna trade *you* . . . for dough, cash, greenbacks."

"Oh, yeah? Well, that's called kidnapping and it's a federal offense. You're looking at some serious prison time." Though I said that using the toughest, meanest tone I could muster, he found it funny. He laughed out loud.

The math was coming together for me, you know, the two plus two equals four? He planned to kidnap Jake and collect a ransom from his wealthy family. But how did I fit into the plot, his road to riches? I didn't. I didn't fit into his plan, that's probably why he tried to run me off the road.

"You were trying to kill me, weren't you?"

"Nope. I just wanted you and your car to go over the guardrail and down the cliff. I only kill chipmunks."

If I'd had a gun, I'd have shot him on the spot. Instead, I lunged at him and pounded on his chest with my tied-up hands. What was I thinking?

"Look who just got feisty and I don't like feisty. Hey, I'm tryin' to be nice, but you're starting to get on my nerves. As long as I get my money, you'll get your perfect little life back. Well, some of it."

He was right. Suddenly, I was feeling feisty. And, just like a runner, my second wind had kicked in. I needed to win this race. Win it or . . . I couldn't think about what losing might mean. At least I had the strength to keep walking and the focus to study my surroundings. That's when it hit me. I stopped dead in my tracks. No. Wait. Poor word choice. I stopped suddenly, turned, and faced this son of a bitch.

"You're the half-brother, aren't you?"

His expressionless face morphed into that of a scowling madman.

"You watch your tone with me, little lady. I don't take kindly to cold, unfriendly women." No other words were spoken for the duration of our walk, but he hummed "The Itsy Bitsy Spider" until we stood at the threshold of a run-down old shack.

Before entering, he removed my shoes and slipped my bare feet into a pair of ill-fitting flip-flops that was ready and waiting for me just inside the door. He did the same for himself.

"You will never wear your outside shoes, inside. Understand?"

I nodded, though I didn't understand. That made no sense to me. He wasn't what you'd call a clean freak—a freak, maybe, but not a clean one, at least not if the state of his truck's interior was part of the equation.

Inside the small rustic structure, I saw very little because there was very little to see. Just an old metal bed that looked like it belonged in a 1950s psychiatric ward, an aluminum beach chair, and some blankets. A poorly constructed countertop ran the entire length of the wall just under the shack's only light source: three small windows. It did seem unusually clean for an abandoned old shack. And the floor was . . . exceptionally clean.

"What do you think?"

"It's cleaner than I expected."

"Don't you listen? I told you I got it all ready for you."

"That's a lie. You're a liar. You got this ready for Jake, not me, and though it kind of makes sense that you might clean up the place for a female captive, you wouldn't do that for a guy. So, you're lying. What's the real reason you got so tidy all of a sudden? Especially with the floor, and the shoe thing? What is that all about?"

"Shut up! I'm not a liar. And I don't have to explain anything to you. I have to think . . . about the money."

"I don't have any money."

"My mother does . . . and she'll pay dearly to get Jake back."

"But you don't have Jake. You have me."

"Yeah, but she don't know that."

My hands still tied, I sat cross-legged on the bed, watching him carry a crate of glass jars in from somewhere outside. In the dim light, they appeared to be canning jars, and after giving each one a gentle, meticulous dusting, he lined them up on the counter, smallest to largest, just below the windows. Then he adjusted them so that there was one finger-space between each jar. That was weird, but then everything was weird. He went about his business as if he'd forgotten I was there. That was fine with me . . . until he began singing to himself, showing little concern or ability for pitch.

The bloomin' bloody spider went up the spider web.
The bloomin' bloody cold set in, was my spider dead?
No! No! No! My spider was alive.
The bloomin' bloody spider had narrowly survived.
We're in the money. Almost in the . . . the . . . Oh, my
head, my head.

In an instant, the man stopped his creepy-though-happy singing and his jar dusting to hold his head in his hands as he moaned. Pain. Once again, he felt pain. Pain that rendered him oblivious to the reality at hand. I, however, anticipated the fate of one of his treasured jars now rolling toward the edge of the countertop and worried about the man's reaction when the inevitable occurred. Should I keep his jar from crashing to the floor? I could do that. Yes! I jumped up and reached toward the jar with my tied-up hands . . . a second too late. Crash! The jar shattered when it hit the floor.

"What the hell?" he shouted, looking dazed at the broken jar before his eyes darted all around the room.

"It's all right. Untie my hands and I'll sweep that glass up for you. The floor will be clean in no time." I thought that might be a win-win situation. His floor would be clean again and my hands would be free of these ropes.

He kept his eyes on the floor and instructed me to get back onto the bed and be very, very quiet. I could do that. And I did it well until I saw the furry black thing limping toward me. I didn't scream but the man noticed the whimpering sound coming from my throat.

He put a finger to his lips signaling for continued silence, retrieved another jar, and scooped up the wounded tarantula that was but a few inches from my thigh. Recent memories of Halloween and the pile of spiders that turned up in our fire ring flashed like a neon sign making me dizzy again. I needed Jake with his gun and his crowbar. Now!

Setting the captured, five-legged creature right next to me, he took on the task of sweeping up the glass. I expected an unprecedented outburst of anger, even rage, but it never came.

"Have to go now. Need to have a chat with Mommy. So, for your own safety, I'm gonna tie you up and cover you up, 'cause it's going to get real cold."

"How long will you be gone?"

"As long as it takes. Two hours, two days. I don't know."

"I have to use the bathroom." I really did. "I can't wait any longer."

I didn't like the truth of my situation any more than he did. But then, by the hint of a smirk and the beginnings of a chuckle I surmised that he'd suddenly found my desperate request amusing.

"There's no bathroom here. What you see is what you get—a bed and a roof over your head. Women!" He shook his head. "I guess you'll need to visit the nearest tree before I take off. Come on."

He proceeded to put my shoes on again, his too. Nothing amused him now. Frustration and agitation had replaced the chuckles.

"You really don't need to do that. If you'd just untie my hands I could change the shoes myself."

"Shut up!"

Untying my hands was not going to happen.

"Okay, but I could just keep wearing the flip-flops and then you wouldn't need to keep switching my—"

Too late. The frustrating task was already accomplished and we were headed toward the nearest tree worthy of my deposit about ten steps from the shack's door. He refused to untie my hands, which made pulling down my snug jeans nearly impossible. His agitation continued as he stood a few paces from me and the tree, impatiently shifting his weight from one foot to the other. That lasted for maybe a minute.

The next thing I knew he was so close I could feel his breath on my neck as he unsuccessfully tugged at my jeans. I tried to help, but that only made things worse. He lifted my tied hands up to my face.

"Put your thumbs in your mouth. Do it."

He was in no mood to hear anything I might say. Or had he wanted to muffle any cries for help? Reasoning with the unreasonable was a waste of time. He slid his hands under the waistband of my jeans to speed up the progress of my bothersome need to pee and to get his show on the road. Then, out of the blue, he'd suddenly managed to acquire some patience. He lowered my jeans to the ground very slowly, sliding his hands down the side of my hips and the full length of my legs. He was far too close, too close to … everything. He stepped back a few feet, but never took his eyes from my naked, vulnerable bottom half. Now I was scared. Really scared.

FIFTY-SEVEN

Jake

There were so many muffled sounds. Beeping, pulsing, clicking, and . . . guitar music. Guitar music? *That must have been some party. Got one hell of a hangover.* I couldn't think, I couldn't talk—*am I talking? I can't even figure that out.* Every inch of me hurt, but I'd better get up anyway. Wendell will need to go out.

"Hello there. I wondered how long it would take you to wake up. How do you feel?"

Okay. I get it now. I'm in the middle of some weird little dream. I went ahead and answered the pretty dream-girl.

"Terrible. I feel terrible. And, where am I?"

"At the Estes Park Medical Center. Hang on; I was supposed to get somebody the minute you woke up. Be right back."

What was this girl doing here in my dream? Why was I in this unfamiliar bed? Why couldn't I remember anything?

"The doctor is headed this way. Let's see. Where were we? Oh, yes. You feel terrible. Well, that's to be expected. You were in an awful accident, and now what you need most is a lot of rest. I heard one of the doctors say that."

She sat down, picked up her guitar and began to play and sing softly. The music was nice, relaxing, and I drifted back into a musical, pain-escaping sleep with one fleeting thought. *I know this girl.*

Awake now and feeling less groggy, I think I mumbled, "You're still here?" The more pressing question, however, was what happened that caused me to be here lying in this bed. My brain was broken, out of order for the moment. I dozed off again.

"Mr. Lee? Mr. Lee." The voice seemed so far away. My eyes opened slowly. "Do you think you can swallow?" What kind of a question was that? Then, I wondered and had some doubt. So, before answering, I tried it. I did it. I could swallow. Big deal.

"Sure." The woman put a bending straw to my lips and I took a sip of something cold. Then she left, leaving the cup and straw within reach. Looking around at my immediate environment I came to the realization that I was in a hospital and the guitar-playing girl was a real, live person. A familiar person.

I recalled making this young woman's acquaintance the day Lindsey and I visited Santa Fe, New Mexico. That, however, did not explain what she was doing here, in a hospital room, with me. I asked her to shed a little light on this situation and her presence here in Estes Park. The wheels in my brain were turning once again, just barely though, and in dire need of some grease.

"I work here at the library from December through May every year. I like to arrive a month early so I can do some hiking before the winter hits hard and lots of the trails are inaccessible, not to mention the roads. The rest of the year I hang out in Santa Fe and live off my music."

"Okay. That explains why you're in Estes, but it doesn't make sense that you are here with me."

"Sure it does. We saw a whole shit-load of skid marks, thrashed and broken bushes and trees, and one very crunched guardrail."

"We?"

"My ride. I hitched a ride up the mountain. Anyway, when we saw all that, we turned around to check it out. Called 9-1-1. The rest is history."

"Not to me. I'm a little foggy right now."

Tiny snapshots of information flashed in and out of my mind: a honking horn, the RV swerving, an oncoming car. That's all I had. And that did not explain much. Now I was here with . . . I couldn't remember her name. Oh, geez. My head hurt, everything hurt; *I think I'm going to vomit.* I held on tightly to the bed rails.

"Oh, man. This room is spinning Do you feel that?"

She shook her head indicating that I was the sole proprietor of this unpleasant phenomenon and pressed the call button to summon a nurse. Pretty sure my pain meds or sleeping medications were increased because the next thing I knew, I was waking up again.

"I heard the doctors talking about the miracle."

My guitar-playing angel was still watching over me.

"What miracle?"

My brain was . . . slow. As slow as a snail venturing out on a chilly day. Lindsey would like that I'd said that. Thinking of her brought on a feeling of peace.

"To begin with, that you survived. Your motor home was totaled. They said it was actually a good thing that you were thrown from the vehicle before it reached the bottom of the cliff. Otherwise, there'd have been no survivors."

"Survivors? Plural? We all survived? Thank God. I was just remembering and worrying about Wendell and Malcolm."

"There were two other people in your motor home?"

"No, not people. Our dog, Wendell and our bird, Malcolm."

"I knew you had pets; I remember your wonderful dog. Just didn't remember his name. Don't think I knew about the bird."

I wondered what Lindsey was doing with them, where she was keeping them with the RV no longer available. A man, probably one of the doctors, entered the room and disturbed my struggling train of thought.

"Mrs. Lee, I'm afraid you'll need to leave in a few minutes. Jake needs some tests."

"Oh, uh, my name is Bethany Michaels. I'm a friend of Jake's. I was the one that made the 9-1-1 call."

"Then I'm afraid you shouldn't be here. Only family members right now."

Bethany and I watched the doctor walk away.

"I'm glad that you're here, Bethany. I'll talk to him. Rules were made to be broken, right?"

"You bet. I'll see what I can find out, Jake." She took my hand in hers and gave it a gentle kiss. A sisterly kiss, I'd hoped. "But I haven't heard anything about your pets. I haven't seen Lindsey and I've been here with you for almost twenty-four hours straight."

What? Was she kidding? Where was Lindsey? She should be here. She *would* be here, if she could be. What's wrong with this picture? Bethany tried to comfort me by saying that something must have occurred that caused her absence. It was probably just my state of amnesia that kept me from knowing the details. She shrugged her shoulders and offered a caring expression before leaving the room.

A new notion ascended slowly to the top of my malfunctioning thought pile.

"Hey, wait! Have you been writing letters to me?"

She rolled her eyes. "I don't even write letters to my mother." Then her tone softened. "I'd text her every day, if she and her phone were . . . smart."

Now my profound inclination toward detective work wanted desperately to rev up its engines. Damn the pain, the nausea, the dizziness. I had to find my wife. I attempted to recreate the scene of the accident from the mere fragments lodged in my clouded memory. Lindsey had been following me down the mountain road. That was a fact. The car Bethany rode in was likely the car I tried to avoid hitting, but maybe not. That was not yet a fact.

If other cars were involved in the accident, where were they? I would check that out. Maybe they caused the accident. There was another car. No, it was a truck. What was the make of that truck? I could not even recall the truck's color. My uncooperative brain, unwilling to provide aid with my recall efforts, lay semi-dormant. What should I do?

"Hey doc. I really need to make a call."

"Right after your CT scan."

"It can't wait. My wife is missing!"

FIFTY-EIGHT

Lad

When we found Jake's room, it was unoccupied. I could see from one glance at Julie's face that we shared the same horrible thought. We were too late. Jake must have succumbed to his injuries. We thanked God when we saw the bed roll around the corner and into his room a few seconds later. We learned he'd just had an EEG.

"Hi Lad, Julie. Thanks for getting here so fast. But, are you okay? You guys look like you saw a ghost."

"Yeah, well, we thought we did."

"Huh?"

"Never mind. Our main concern is finding Lindsey."

Jake filled me in on the location of the crash. He did not remember many details beyond that. Julie gave her brother a hug and told him we'd be back after investigating the crash site.

Knowing Julie, she was attempting to stay positive when she said, "Other than his memory issues and the pain from his cuts and bruises, he seemed all right to me."

Still, I thought her comment was a lot like the ones made at a funeral when someone staring into a coffin says, "He looks good, don't you think?" But I kept my grisly comparison to myself. If the accident was as horrific as we'd been led to believe, he was lucky to be alive. And it could take days or even weeks before additional internal injuries might become evident. But now I was more concerned for Lindsey's safety. Time was of the essence. At this point I didn't have a plan beyond searching for clues at the crash site.

"Look, Lad. There's the demolished guardrail . . . and plenty of skid marks. That's got to be where the RV went over," Julie said.

I parked the 4WD, 4-door Tundra truck that we'd rented at the Denver International Airport, grabbed my Secret Service-issued phone that had a built-in camera and voice recorder, (I remembered thinking how special it was, but nowadays, that's the norm on most people's cell phones.) and then we headed down the hill.

I recorded every single thought that came to my mind or to Julie's. We didn't want to miss a thing.

"Lad, this spot looks so trampled."

She was right. I concluded that the first responders doing the work of finding, stabilizing, and securing Jake for transport, caused the mangled plant life. I should have brought more bags with me. There were items scattered around that should have been gathered by the local authorities: a shoe, a camera, sunglasses, even a patch of hair and splatters of blood. The first responders missed a lot.

The vehicle had made at least two full turns as it rolled down the hill creating its own mangled plant life and beaten path. Then it slid another 100 feet or so where the pile of mutilated metal finally stopped and was wedged between several boulders and a cluster of three old pines. I looked inside as best I could. I saw the twisted remnants of Malcolm's cage. Pretty sure he wasn't in it. Most likely he was thrown from it and lay dead somewhere inside this mess. I took photos. No sign of the dog; I figured he was crushed somewhere beneath the rubble. I didn't look forward to sharing those thoughts with Jake or Lindsey.

"Over here," Julie shouted from the other side of the wreckage.

She had discovered numerous dark, reddish- brown drops and smears on the exterior side of what used to be the kitchen area. Not surprising. Jake had lots of cuts and abrasions. Then she reminded me that Jake had been unconscious and thrown from the vehicle. He'd never reached the RV's final resting place.

Upon closer inspection, we located a trail —a trail of blood heading west. Son of a gun. Was there a victim we didn't know about? If not Jake, then who? A predator? A deer? A hitchhiker? We followed for at least half a mile, though distance was hard to determine on this steep, rocky, bush-filled hill. The blood trail thinned, and we were about to give up when I spotted Lindsey's car. At least what was left of it.

"Oh, my God. NO!"

We ran toward it. We wanted to find her, but not like this, not here.

Julie saw the still, tan, bloody fur before I did. Wendell. It was Wendell. That poor dog must have hobbled all the way over here to look for Lindsey.

She petted his big head, with a river of tears running down her face. I'd never seen Julie this upset about anything in our year together. I knew he was great dog, though. Everyone loved Wendell.

She let out a weak, mournful sigh. No, wait. That sigh didn't come from Julie; it came from Wendell.

"He's alive!!! He opened his eyes."

Julie kept petting him, talking to him as I offered the dog some water from my water bottle. He managed to take in some of the liquid. He was obviously dehydrated, disoriented, and injured.

I looked up the hill toward the road to get my bearings. I now had a plan.

"Julie, keep him calm and try to get him to drink more water. I'm going to move the truck so we won't have to carry him quite so far."

Returning with a blanket from the back seat, and carefully sliding it under the dog, we headed up the hill.

"Are you sure you want to attempt this maneuver? Even though he has lost weight from his ordeal, he's still really heavy."

"I can do this, Lad. Besides, you've got the heaviest end of the blanket. Just ignore my huffing and puffing, and moaning and groaning. I might need to rest every few feet. I think the altitude is adding to my shortness of breath."

"I love your toughness, you know that, but don't hurt yourself." Yeah, that's what I said to my girlfriend, but I knew I was just as likely to be the one hurting.

We took turns talking to Wendell, hoping friendly, encouraging words would keep him alive until he received medical attention from an experienced veterinarian.

"Wendell keeps turning his neck looking back down the hill toward the car, Lad. It is as if he doesn't want to leave that spot. Odd, huh?"

"Can't really see him from my end, and if I turn around to look at the dog looking down the hill, I'll end up falling on my face. I can hear the strange sound that he's making, though. Not a bark, not a whine, not even a moan, but a combo of all three. He doesn't sound good."

"I agree, but maybe he's trying to tell us something. Maybe Lindsey is down there."

Finally, we made it to the truck and carefully loaded the dog into the backseat. I told Julie to set the phone to hands-free and listen for my call. I'd find the nearest vet, let them know the dog was on his way, and then call her with the driving directions.

Julie threw her arms around me and I held her close before whispering in her ear, "Hurry. Get Wendell to the vet and come right back." Then, a quick kiss on the lips, and she climbed into the truck. "And be careful while you're at it. Go! Go!"

If I were a gambling man, I'd bet Lindsey was no longer here, but I had to be absolutely positive about that before leaving the area. She could have been thrown from her vehicle as Jake was thrown from his. I traipsed all around the car, and checked the area between the road and the car, as well as the terrain stretching out a good hundred yards to either side. Nothing. My only discovery? The car's interior was strewn with school supplies, including an abundance of confetti and glitter, which I presumed wasn't so strange, knowing that Lindsey was an elementary teacher.

Convinced that she was not here, I snapped photos and climbed up the hill to wait for my ride. *I'm getting too old for this kind of work.*

Julie and I headed over to the sheriff's office to see their reports and gather additional information. A friendly woman at the front desk provided us with our first fact, a problematic fact. Apparently, the Sheriff was in Denver undergoing knee surgery and his main deputy was out for a few days with some kind of violent vomiting problem. *Oh, great. Who's minding the store?*

She made a call announcing our presence and within minutes two deputies walked through the door. One looked like a rookie, the other, a retiree. I tried not to be judgmental, but failed.

The rookie, with a report in his hand, did most of the talking.

"Pretty standard stuff. The driver lost control, went over the side, and rolled. Someone had called for an ambulance. It was already there, along with a fire truck loading the guy in as we pulled up."

I inquired as to whom he meant by 'we' and was informed that Deputy O'Connor, standing to his right, and himself, Deputy Trundle, were the two at the scene. After telling me that accidents happen on that road though more frequently during the winter months when the roads are snow packed or icy, the young deputy added that since there were no fatalities, the case was closed.

"Can I assume that you have photos from the scene?"

"Right here." The rookie handed me four photos: two depicting skid marks and two of the guardrail.

"That's it? No shots of the RV itself? Or the path left by its crashing, rolling journey down the hill?"

"The ambulance personnel assured us that there were no other victims down there."

Talk about clueless. Foul play hadn't even crossed their minds. It was almost as if they weren't open to the possibility. The rookie did confess that they didn't usually work calls like this one. So, I informed them of the fact that the wife of the RV driver was missing.

My cell phone vibrated with an incoming text message from my FBI buddies. WE THINK THIS IS THE GUY. PHOTO ATTACHED.

"We've got a lead. Can your office make a few copies of a photo that's on my phone?"

The deputies glanced at each other with baffled looks. Fortunately, the woman at the front desk smiled and said, "Follow me, sir. I can do that for you."

Skepticism exuded from the two men as they stood, arms crossed against their chests. "How do you know this man has any connection to the crash?"

"That's a very long story and I don't have time to tell it. But we need to find this guy. He has the missing woman." I didn't know that for a fact, but it was the most logical deduction. I held up one of the photos. "Time is of the essence. Her survival clock is ticking."

"Well, you'll need to fill out a missing person form and—"

I didn't like having to pull rank, but Lindsey's life was in the balance. I introduced myself as Agent Donovan and flashed my retired-Secret Service badge.

"Send someone to get a statement from the crash victim at the medical center. There is plenty of foul play going on here. This is not an ordinary auto accident."

We'd already passed the time frame for a positive outcome with regard to finding Lindsey alive and well. I couldn't recall feeling this much anger and frustration inside of me, ever.

Turning I added, "Where will the RV be taken, and when? I need to check it out more thoroughly. Oh, and you need to retrieve the missing woman's car. It's about a half mile north west of where the RV went off the road. FYI—It's steep right there. You'll need to dust for prints. I'm willing to bet you find a match for this guy," I said, holding up the photo again.

"There is a car, too?"

"Oh, for Pete's sake."

I headed out to parts unknown; Julie agreed to remain in town and show that photo around.

FIFTY-NINE

Jake

My sister Julie had returned to the medical center and was now at my side looking worried. Was there something about my medical condition that I should know? Something the doctors were not telling me? I wondered.

While staring intently at my sister's worried face and listening for an explanation that did not come, Miss Bethany Michaels bounced into the room. Julie looked from me to this young cutie and back again. I might have enjoyed the perplexed look on her face, if it weren't for the fact that my wife was missing. At least for the moment, worry had been replaced by curiosity.

"Sorry, Jake. There is no word or sign of your pets."

Now, another layer of sadness could be added to the growing, unbearable stack of sorrow. As if things weren't bad enough, now my dog was gone, and, probably the bird, too. That's when Julie jumped in and began to speak.

"Oh, Jake. I am so, so sorry. Lad and I found Wendell. He was still at the crash site by Lindsey's car. We think he's going to be all right. I'll fill you in on that a little later when we know more."

"Lindsey's car crashed, too? Where is she? How is she?"

Comprehending Julie's hole-ridden explanation was beyond me; I was too filled with grief and horror. Though never the crying type, here I lay, sobbing uncontrollably. My reaction to the news of her demolished car must have done a number on my vital signs. The machine keeping tabs on me made sounds I hadn't heard before and several medical professionals came running in. My heart broken, my thinking on hiatus, I heard the last few words exchanged between Julie and Bethany—

Bethany, glancing at the photo, cocking her head said, "That's a good picture of him. He didn't look that good the last time I saw him."

"WHAT? You know him? When was the last time you saw him?"

"Oh, I don't know him but I saw him about thirty minutes ago. I saw him yesterday, too. His computer must have crashed or something because he was using the one in the library."

Julie picked up her phone. "Lad. Get over here."

My sis has such a way with words . . . then, everything faded to black.

\\

The $250,000 hush money he had wanted Evelyn to pay him to merely keep quiet about his existence had been changed to a $500,000 ransom for the safe return of Jake. The only glitch now? Her disconnected telephone. Agitated. He was severely agitated, which made formulating a new plan to tell Evelyn of Jake's kidnapping almost impossible.

Tonight the twinges in his head had returned. The shack wasn't far but the darkness and the pain, the pain he knew would soon become intolerable, made it difficult to move through the forest. He knelt down, holding his head, and waited for the inevitable.

"You lied to me?"

"We thought you'd be happier that way."

"But you know how much I hate lies. How could you keep this from me?"

"You never coped well with reality. We did whatever it took to keep you happy."

"Well, I am not happy. You both lied, lied, lied."

"We tried."

"I'm leaving and I'm never coming back. Never, never, NEVER!"

In the beginning God created . . . me!
Me to be happy and free.
Let there be light even at night.
Let the birds fly and the spiders crawl
And he who crosses me? ... will fall.

SIXTY

Lindsey

I heard voices. Voices? That was good, I told myself. This man didn't seem to have any friends or accomplices so, if more than one person was heading this way they could be coming to rescue me. Then, just the other side of the wooden door, I heard a shuffling sound and knew that street shoes were being exchanged for indoor footwear, and my hopeful thoughts dissolved.

He'd brought food; he usually did. This one meal a day, if I was lucky, consisted of cold, fast food. Had I eaten yesterday? I could not remember. The time passed so slowly. So strangely.

So far, he hadn't physically hurt me, though the restraints rubbed my wrists raw and the lack of mobility added an uncomfortable stiffness. I felt my strength and my sanity slipping away. All I wanted to think about was my lovable Jake and our adorable pets. Where were they? How were they? I saw the RV go over the side and I couldn't seem to get that picture out of my head. If they were gone, then nothing mattered. But if they were alive, I had to get out of here. Find them, be with them. That was the scenario I chose to hold in my heart and my in head.

"You seem really upset tonight. Is there anything I can do to help you?"

I know that sounded crazy, it was crazy, but I was stuck smack dab in the middle of crazy. I had to make him like me, care about me; pretending to care about him, I continued. Besides, my situation couldn't get much worse than it was . . . I took that back. It could get a heck of a lot worse. To my surprise, though, he sat down on the folding beach chair and told me about his troubling predicament.

"I've got to get a message to my mom, but her phone is disconnected."

"You could write her a letter."

"Too slow. I need the money on Monday. Tuesday at the latest."

Think. Think. What would Jake do? . . . He'd get this guy out of the shack and back into town. He'd find a way to set him up to be caught, captured, arrested. It was difficult for me to think wisely. I felt so nauseated, stiff, and scared. On the other hand, I was highly motivated to get away from this deranged man.

"How about sending an email to her?"

"Already tried that. All I could find was a mailing address for her husband's office and mail is too slow. Don't you listen?"

"I am listening. There's another way. Write your letter; make it very short and to the point. Address it and take it to the post office first thing tomorrow. Tell them to send it by Instant Mail. They have ways to do that now. I'd take at least twenty dollars. That special service isn't cheap."

A pleased expression spread across his face. It seemed like a good time to ask for the favor of visiting the tree outside. Being somewhat malnourished and dehydrated, my jeans that I'd been wearing for several days slipped down without any assistance from my captor. As I squatted close to the ground, I thought, *I'd better find a way to escape before he returns from the post office tomorrow. He will be angry when he discovers that my save-the-day plan for him is bogus.*

SIXTY-ONE

Jake

A nurse hurried into my room, plugged in a phone, handed me the receiver and said, "It's for you." And dashed out into the hallway.

The voice on the phone started rattling off words a mile a minute. Not a hello or how are you feeling or even hi, this is . . . "Who is this?"

"Jake, it's me, Aggy. They told me to hurry, so I am."

"If you want me to comprehend anything that you are saying, you're going to have slow down. I am not yet up to my normal speed."

"Oh. Sorry."

"People in town are talking about the horrible accident. Next to beauty salons, the post office is the best place to hear the good gossip. You know me. I just put two and two together and realized you might be the man that crashed through the guardrail and over the edge."

"Aggy, bottom line. Please make your point." I should have added, *in twenty-five words or less.*

She explained that a guy had come by the post office earlier that day wanting to send an 'instant mail' message. He was adamant about it. The USPS had no such option for him but that she'd played along with his impossible request. She had a funny feeling about the guy and suspected there might be a connection to the accident or at least to some dastardly deed. She told him to check back for a reply in a day or two, and just ask any postal worker at the desk for his General Delivery mail.

"You'll never guess what he said his name was." She didn't wait for my 'guess', not that I would have tried. "Alvin Lee. The same last name as yours. Weird, huh? I think he fell for all that 'instant mail' stuff, though I don't know where he came up with such a wacky idea. He'll be back. What do you think?"

"I . . . I don't know yet. You might be on to something, Miss Aggy. That's short for Maggie, right?" She hung up. Was she playing games with me? Or was she suddenly in a hurry? She was an unusual woman, that much I knew for sure.

I shared this up-to-the-minute information with Lad. Today, we had the equivalent of a real lead, and until conflicting facts turned up, Alvin was our prime suspect. All we had to do now was figure out where the guy was staying. We ran with the assumption that Lindsey was with him and still alive.

Lad passed along everything he knew to the local deputies. It wasn't much. But now, they, too, knew that the suspect was in town and even frequented the local library. The name Alvin might be his real first name, but Lee? No way.

Julie came by bearing gifts. One white paper bag contained two deli style Tuscan turkey sandwiches. How did she know I'd finally be hungry? My appetite had returned, my stomach growling, no, roaring. In the other bag, the one with handles, were three paperback books: *The Memoirs of Sherlock Holmes* by Conan Doyle, *Partners in Crime* by Agatha Christie, and *Cooking Up Love* by Amylynn Bright.

"Thanks, sis. But this third book? Sounds like a romance." Did she really think I would want to read that?

"Brilliant deduction, Sherlock. I thought you might need a break from all the detective stuff whether in fiction or real life. I already read the Kindle version and the hero reminded me of you a little. Spoiler alert! Brother dear. It might make you hungry in more ways than one. Besides, Lindsey will like it. She can read it when we get her back."

Lindsey. My Lindsey had been missing now for almost four days. Each passing day lessened the chance of her survival, and of ever being found. We all knew the missing person stats when foul play was involved. The odds were not in her favor. That truth weighed heavy on my heart.

"Julie, has there been any news on Jimmy's prints or DNA? I'd forgotten all about him until just now."

"Sorry, Jake. Thought you knew. Come to think of it, you may have slept through that part of the conversation. You were still on large doses of pain meds that day. Jimmy doesn't seem to be involved in any of this."

Julie produced a computer printout of a photo from her shoulder bag. I must have slept through *that*, too. I'd vaguely remembered a discussion of a photo, but I don't recall seeing it.

"This is the guy that matches the DNA and print evidence. He's the one they are searching for."

"I'd rather it *had* been Jimmy. Lindsey could control him. I'm not so sure about the guy in this photo. I just can't believe the fact that we share the same mother with him."

"Yeah, that adds a creepy aspect to this whole horrific situation. I've been thinking about that a lot. He must be older than me by at least a year; you are younger than me. Do you know what that means?"

"Sure don't, but I bet you're going to tell me."

"It means that instead of being the oldest child in the family, I am the middle child. No wonder I have issues. But … if I didn't know I was a middle child, and my father didn't know, and my baby brother didn't know, how likely would it be for me to have some of those middle child traits? Hmm."

"What traits?"

"This is Psychology 101 stuff, Jake. You should know this."

"Refresh my memory."

"A middle child feels the need to be competitive and even secretive. That's me all right. So, yes to both of those traits. A middle child is often the family mediator. No, didn't do that. But then how could I? There would have to be a family that interacted with each other to need and participate in mediation.

"A middle child would have the fewest photos in family album. Well, there would have to be a family album. No, several expensive family portraits mounted on the wall were all we had. And, a middle child might not feel special like the oldest or youngest. That trait assumes you or I ever felt special. I know I didn't."

"Me neither." Julie spoke the truth, but I wondered if she actually cared about this middle child stuff. My gut told me that she used this discussion as a diversionary tactic to get my mind off the larger issues at hand.

Barely taking a breath she continued. "Enough of this foolish talk. Besides, the traits of a first-born suit me fine.

I want respect, I like to be in authority, and I find it difficult to delegate. And, oh yes, everyone is a little brother or sister to me."

"You know I will always be your little brother and you have my respect."

We finished our lunch and discussed the facts of the accident and the disappearance of Lindsey. We had little to go on, so far, and time was of the essence.

"I think it's time we made the call to Texas." Julie simply nodded and handed me her cell phone.

Swiping my finger across the screen, I located our parents' home phone number and tapped on it. It rang four times then the standard disconnection message played.

"What's the matter, Jake?"

"Their phone has been disconnected and there is no new number. Odd. I'll try Mother's private cell phone number."

My mother, Evelyn, answered. "Jake, how good of you to call."

I stated that there had been an accident and the guy we thought was responsible claimed to be her son.

"Nonsense!" That was her reply. I filled in with a few more details before she cut me off. Her interrupting words were in the form of a question. "Where are you?"

"I'm at the Estes Park Medical Center and Lindsey is . . ." She'd hung up before I'd finished. I handed the phone back to Julie.

"See if you have better luck with our father."

Julie called his home office number and tapped on her phone's speaker function. He said very little. He did listen, though, and Julie was able to inform him of the accident, Jake's admittance to the town's medical center, and that Lindsey was missing. She was able to add that Lad was here with her and evidence pointed to the fact that she and I have a half-brother who is likely a key player in all of this.

Father's reply was short. "Take care of yourself and Jake. I will speak with your mother."

I was pretty sure he wouldn't. He wasn't a boat rocker when it came to family. Business — well, that was another matter. He could be ferocious in that area. He was a highly respected, powerful man. At home, he was a teddy bear catering to mother's wishes. They were both talented when it came to creating a façade of perfection.

I was also pretty sure he didn't need to talk with her. Mother was shrewd and liked to know about his every move whether it was business or personal. She listened in on his calls. At least she used to.

I asked Julie to go check on Wendell and buy me a cell phone. *I need to get out of here.*

SIXTY-TWO

Lindsey

I was shocked and relieved at the same time. When the man had returned from town yesterday, far sooner than I'd expected, he was in a very good mood. Apparently, his 'instant mail' had some measure of success, or so he thought. He'd brought food for both of us. My meal consisted of a roast beef sandwich and a bottle of soda. That was a pleasant surprise; so much better than cold, stale fast food or no food at all. He ate a turkey sandwich and drank a beer.

We'd eaten together in the dim light of dusk and then he'd escorted me outside to use the ladies' *tree* before I'd had to beg him for that rare opportunity. I hadn't needed the ladies *trench* the past couple of days. With consuming so little food, and even less liquid, my digestive track was shutting down. Under these circumstances, that had its pros and cons.

I took advantage of his high spirits and continued with my attempts to build a positive, though fake, relationship with this man. I knew he'd be less likely to harm me if he liked me. So I asked him his name.

"They named me Al."

Wanting to show him that I cared and to keep the conversation going, I responded. "Is Al short for Allen or Alvin?"

He'd scowled and gritted his teeth. *What brought that on?* His reply began with a kick to the wall, which obviously hurt his semi-bare foot, then, "I hate that name." *Which name?* "Don't you ever call me that." He snarled and shook his finger at me as he spoke, then sank down into his beach chair and was snoring loudly within minutes.

Today, with the prospect of going to town, his excitement, his joy, was what I'd describe as manic. He had the mistaken idea that he could pick up a reply from "Mommy" at the post office today. According to him, all her message needed to say was that she agreed to his terms and she would meet him with the money on Monday. He'd given her the option of Tuesday, just in case she couldn't get here by Monday. See how reasonable he was? Yeah. He might be crazy but he was also clever, clever enough to omit the location of their rendezvous in our brief discussion before he left.

It was Sunday. Even if the post office managed to deliver his message, which was impossible, a reply could not be picked up today. Would he be sad? Give up? Take it out on me? I didn't know. He could be so volatile. I needed to be gone before he returned without his longed-for reply.

He'd retied me that morning with a newer, stronger rope. *Ouch!* That hurt. I spent the day chewing at the ropes like a wild animal in a trap, and I'd made some progress . . . when I heard gunshots.

My heart raced, panic set in as the sound echoed and bounced off the surrounding hills and mountains. The source of the ping-ponging pops seemed to be close, but I knew that noises in a mountainous forest could be deceiving. Perhaps it was a hunter. That would be a good thing, a great thing. It was fall. Isn't that when hunters hunted? I wasn't sure. Still tied to the bed, I couldn't get to a window to look for the shooter, so I used the only option available to me.

"Help! Please help me! I'm trapped! Help! Help!"

Someone burst through the door. I froze. Damn. Al was back.

"Don't you ever listen? I told you no one could hear you from here."

"I heard gunshots. That scared me."

"Damn chipmunks crossed my path."

"You carry a gun with you?"

"I do now."

Apparently, killing chipmunks was the only release of emotion he needed to perform for the moment. Not sure how I felt about that other than . . . better them than me. However, he was still upset, agitated and disappointed that another day had gone by without securing his money from 'Mommy.' I tried to comfort him by saying that most post offices are not open on Sunday. Surely he'd have his answer and maybe even his money by tomorrow.

"Did you bring some food? Some water? Anything?"

"I had other stuff on my mind."

He fed his tarantulas from the jars that contained other insects, which I now understood were in captivity for the purpose of being 'food' for his eight-legged pets. He happily whistled the "The Itsy Bitsy Spider" tune while he worked.

"You know, these guys don't eat solid food."

"I didn't know that."

He shifted around, his expression cynically gleeful, and looked me right in the eye. "Well, you do now. They paralyze their prey with their venom. That turns the captive's insides to a liquid perfect for any spider's dinner, and then sucks it out like a bowl of soup. Mmm. Yum!"

He didn't stay. He rarely stayed very long, and that was fine with me. Apparently, the only reason he'd come by just now was to check on me and to feed his pet spiders.

I listened as the sound of his footsteps faded away. He did not return. I assumed he'd either slept in his truck or gone back into town. Now, all I had to do was free my hands so I could untie the additional rope that tethered me tightly to the bed, and get out of here. I had a long night of rope chewing ahead of me. Frantic in the process of freeing myself, I scraped my chin on the gold-dipped aspen leaf pin that Jake had given me. *Ooo!* That was one sharp pin. A few drops of blood dripped from my chin to my hands.

I'd completely forgotten it was still attached to the collar of my shirt because my coat covered it up most of the time. Could I use this sharp pin for something? A vision of a chipmunk holding a tiny spear came and went. *That was the kindergarten teacher talking.* If only this situation were a cartoon. Of course, it wasn't. But maybe . . .

The pin did help. Not that it worked any better than my chewing routine, but when my teeth and jaw needed a break, the pin filled in. I could keep scraping away, wearing down the threads of the rope with this needle-like pin. Tired, hungry, dehydrated, and now my neck aches from the position it held hour after hour as I worked to demolish the ties that bound me. Sometime, well before dawn, I'd created a narrow, weakened spot in the rope. It was now or never. If I was still here when he came back and discovered what I'd been doing, he might use the gun on me.

On your mark . . . get set . . . pull!! I groaned from the pain as if giving birth. The rope snapped. My hands were free to untie myself from the bed. With just the coat on my back, I dashed out the door into the dark, moonless night, not knowing which way to go. But I would GO! Any place was better than here in this prison with a psychotic warden. Damn! I'd forgotten my shoes.

SIXTY-THREE

Jake

Julie had purchased a new cell phone for me and was able to have my original phone number linked to it. Ah, one tiny step toward normalcy. I was fooling around with it, checking out some of the features that were new to me, when it rang—a metallic, screechy sound. I would change the ringtone first chance I got.

It was Aggy. "I had the day off since I worked on Saturday, so I did my own little stake out. He came driving up in a grayish silver truck with lots of dents in it. He went in, then came out holding *my* envelope that *my* buddy had given to him. He left. Couldn't tell if he was happy or angry. But he was definitely in a hurry. I'm following him right now. Think he's headed in the direction of The Conference Center out on Tunnel Road."

"We'll be right there. Do not do anything. Do not make contact, but keep him in sight if you can do that safely. Got it?"

Now I had an important call to make; it was the first call on my new phone. "Lad, Julie, come pick me up, bring me some clothes, and be ready to rescue Linds and, oh yeah, make an arrest. HURRY!"

They arrived quickly. I replaced my hospital gown with some of Lad's clothes even quicker. We were heading down the hall when the nurse on duty caught up with us. She was not happy with me since I hadn't been released yet. Too bad. This might be our only chance to find Lindsey. Nothing would stop me. With the most charming smile I could muster, I told her I'd be back in a couple of hours, and to please save my place.

I shared what I knew with my sister and her semi-retired, Secret Service boyfriend, Lad. Julie used the GPS to get driving directions. *We should be there in about six minutes.* We headed out. *We* included Wendell. I kept petting and rubbing his ears. Yes, he was here by my side once again. My partner in solving crime. The vet had released him late yesterday. Said he'd be okay with his medications and a couple weeks of rest. I doubted he'd be willing to rest today. He'd want to save Lindsey as much as anyone.

More screeching announcing another incoming cell phone call demanded our attention. It was Aggy again, so I tapped the speaker icon.

"Okay, here's the deal. He drove up the hill into The Conference Center, circled around the large, paved central loop, went up and down a few dirt roads, then I lost him. I'm pretty sure I know where he is going to end up, but he might not know the best way to get there. More in a minute."

Lad immediately notified the sheriff's office to block the two roads going in and out of the property. "We're looking for a gray or silver dinged-up pickup truck. You've got the photo, apprehend if you see him. Assume he's armed, we know he's dangerous."

We were almost there. We had two able humans, one not so able, a beat up dog and only one vehicle. So we couldn't really split up. This was a huge place. Lad posted Julie outside of the Registration Building. It had a good view of the land and lots of foot traffic all around. She'd ask if anyone had seen the man or a truck fitting the description we'd received from Aggy. Hmm. Speaking of Aggy, where was she? She had a vehicle.

"Lad, just got word from a guest that the truck was spotted yesterday heading toward the horse corral. So far, nothing about seeing it today, though. Copy?"

"Thanks, Julie. We're headed toward the horses. Call if you see anything. Over."

"You guys do that too?" I asked Lad.

"Do what?"

"The copy, over thing."

"Oh, yeah. You know, old habits."

From the looks of the corral, stables, and livery area, the place could easily host a hundred horses. Today we saw a mere two-dozen animals contentedly eating from buckets—some kind of grains, I guessed—in the large corral. No cowboys in sight. No boys of any kind seemed to be around right now. We presumed this was the off-season for the horses, the stables, guided trail rides, the little buckaroos—all that kind of stuff.

We drove to the far side of the corral where the dirt road abruptly ended, got out and looked around. Wendell jumped down, too. Thought he might pick up a scent or something, but all he did was pee on a fence post.

"Jake, look at this. A vehicle has driven into the woods from this point right here."

We walked twenty paces and noticed the same, barely visible tire tracks over the dried ground covered mostly with pine needles and a few saplings. We found at least four locations with similar tire tracks.

"What do you make of this, Lad?"

"I'd say someone has been driving in and out of this wooded area recently and that someone took great care to avoid creating a worn path that someone else might notice."

"I bet they all lead to the same place." I added my two cents to Lad's observations. My wheels were spinning at top speed now.

"My thoughts exactly. But this middle track looks fresher than the others and the ground appears to be more disturbed. Hmm. The driver wasn't as careful on that trip to . . . wherever he was going."

At this point all the windows were open, allowing Wendell's nose access to any scent of Lindsey, and our ears to any cries for help. But before long even the vague tire trail ended. Completely. Our setback was short-lived and replaced by an interesting discovery—a trampled-down patch of ground and a pile of tree and bush branches. Lad and I couldn't have been any more excited than if we'd found the pot of gold at the end of the rainbow.

Suddenly, Wendell took charge of the search and rescue. He began to sniff around as if his life depended on it. This was a good sign.

It seemed we'd walked about half a mile following the dog, listening for sounds. Lad looked ahead and to the left, I looked to the right. That's when Wendell sat down and pawed at the dirt. The poor dog, still recovering from the accident, the trauma, and here I'd dragged him along on this mission not knowing what hazards lay ahead.

"It's okay, Wendell. You're a good boy." Lad handed me a water bottle he'd brought along for Lindsey. I bent to give him a drink and a pat on the head and noticed something sparkling on the ground among the dirt and dead leaves. Something gold. I picked up some golden particles. Had we struck it rich? Real gold? No, of course not. We'd found something even better. Gold glitter! Only Lindsey would have glitter out in the forest. Eureka!

Wendell smiled. Yes, our dog could smile. And his reason for suddenly sitting became evident as Lad and I took a quick but thorough look around. There was a trail of glitter. Had we glanced down at our feet or the ground, we'd have seen it much sooner. On closer inspection, we noticed a fork in the glitter trail right where the dog had pawed the ground. One trail was very fine, more like a trickle of glitter; the other consisted of gumball-sized piles of the gold spaced about ten feet apart.

"Might be time to split up. You want to flip for it?" Lad posed the question.

"Let's see if Wendell has anything more to show us."

We stood around, watching the dog. He finally got up and began to sniff around some more and seemed to favor the piles over the trickles. Perhaps that trail was fresher, stronger. We'd see. "Guess you've got the trickles, Lad. We'll take the piles. Shouldn't we be calling out her name?"

"No. Not yet. If the guy's got Lindsey with him, and he hears us, that might make matters worse than they already are. Just call me when you do find her, or need my help. I will do the same."

Wendell enjoyed his lead-dog role. With his nose to the ground, he kept moving forward. I kept watch for the piles of gold. About ten minutes into our search efforts, the piles disappeared, but Wendell kept going. In fact, he'd increased his speed. *Think positive. Hang on, Lindsey. We will find you.*

The stench that suddenly permeated the air stopped both Wendell and me in our tracks. A gagging, horrible odor is not what any detective wants to come upon when searching for another human. Attempting to regain my composure, I lifted the hem of my shirt and covered my nose and mouth with it. I had to push ahead. I had to find her . . . one way or another.

SIXTY-FOUR

Jake

Without a whine or a whimper, Wendell's stride changed. He trotted, then he galloped, disappearing around an outcrop of moss-covered boulders. I ran as fast as I could, but it was rough going with all the rocks and exposed tree roots that managed to trip me up several times. With sweat dripping down my face and my breathing labored, I pushed on hoping I was headed in the right direction.

I stopped for a brief second to listen, but I heard nothing. Wendell was either far away by now or he was no longer on the move. Which way should I go? The answer came in the form of one, lone *woof*, and my crashing through the woods continued. I'd finally caught up and found him in a dark, shady area just a few feet from a tiny stream; he stood strangely still as I approached.

I did not want to believe what I saw. Lindsey and . . . a deer. Both bloody and lying motionless. Oh, God. No! No! I knelt down beside her, blinded by a wall of my tears. Why? She was the kindest, gentlest person on the planet.

If only we'd waited for that tow bar to be delivered to Estes Park, we would have been in the RV together, and none of this would have happened. If only I hadn't tried to turn around on the narrow, curvy mountain road. If only . . . Wendell started to lick some of the blood from her face. He loved her, too.

"Wendell?"

That word did not come from my mouth.

"Lindsey? Honey? We're here. We found you. You're going to be all right."

Afraid to move her, uncertain of her injuries, I held her—just held her and prayed that she really was okay.

Then, I called Lad.

He must have run all the way because he'd joined up with us in less than ten minutes, gasping for air and dripping with sweat on this crisp, cool day.

"You will not believe what I found at the end of the trickle trail." Taking one look at Lindsey he added, "I'll tell you later."

We carefully moved Lindsey, putting a little distance between us and the sickening smell of the deer carcass.

The next call was to the deputy.

"We found her. She's sick. Send an ambulance about one and a half miles northwest of the horse corral. FYI— not much of a road once they pass the stables. Rough going. We'll listen for them and signal somehow. Tell them to follow the freshest tire tracks they can find and then look for the glitter." I ended the call before they could comment, but wished I could have seen the deputy's face when I'd mentioned the glitter.

We made her as comfortable as possible. When Lad noticed that she was shivering, trembling, he laid his jacket on top of her blood-soaked, vomit-splattered coat.

We both hoped help would arrive soon. She did manage to swallow a few sips of fresh water from one of our bottles. When we asked her what happened all she wanted to talk about was the deer.

"The gold's gone . . . Got lost ... so dark . . . then the sound, the cry ... Poor deer . . . shot. The water . . . bubbling ... so many trips. Got sick ... Had to keep it warm."

Sitting on the ground, leaning up against a tree, I held Lindsey close to me as she closed her eyes. She was not out of the woods yet, neither figuratively nor literally. Lad had double backed to show the paramedics the way. They'd be on foot carrying a portable gurney the last quarter mile.

Only a few minutes had passed when a call came in on my cell.

"Good news over here, too. We got him. Actually, one local gal and one old woman got him. OW!" Then he whispered, "She's got a big purse and sharp shoes. Our perp didn't stand a chance, especially with her sidekick here to help out."

An old woman? A sidekick? Now *that* I had to see.

Settled in the ambulance, Lindsey was transported to the medical center with Julie at her side. I assured her that I'd see her very soon. Then Lad, Wendell and I drove over to the crime scene down behind the old Cook Out Inn where *things were happening*. We came upon six vehicles—the gray truck, two sheriff's department SUVs, and three cars. I assumed one of them belonged to Aggy. Didn't know about the others.

Alvin stood cuffed and leaning against one of the SUVs as an officer asked him questions. The other was taping off the area with the ever popular and well known—thanks to TV cop shows—yellow crime tape.

Lad asked his first question. "You read him his rights, correct?"

"Yes, sir. First thing."

I nodded at Aggy who was standing off to the side with . . . Oh, my God!

"Mother? What are you doing here?"

"Oh, Jake. You're all right." She ran to me barefooted, and hugged me.

"No shoes?"

"Oh." She spoke nonchalantly, waving toward one of the SUVs. "The cop has them in a bag." Then she took on a proud and pleased expression as she added, "They are 'evidence' now. Evidence and assault weapons."

Her words took me by surprise and for a moment, just one moment, I was speechless.

"How did you know to come to The Conference Center?"

"I didn't, really. All I knew was that you and Lindsey were somewhere in Estes Park and that big trouble was brewing. I was driving into town when I heard some breaking news on the local radio station. It said there had been a possible kidnapping and the vehicle used was a gray, dented pickup truck. And *voilà*! A truck matching that description had just flown by me. I figured it was worth a shot. It could have been the guy everyone was looking for. So I took a chance and followed. What a wild goose chase. I lost him near some horses. The road just ended. So I waited there for a while hoping the truck would come into view again. I liked watching the horses. And, eventually, that truck came roaring out of nowhere, past me again, and I followed it, again."

I listened with total amazement. Who was this woman? I was seeing a side of Mother that I'd never seen before.

"But then he stopped right here. As soon as he saw me drive up in the rented Lincoln Town Car, he got out of his truck, all happy with open arms expecting a hug as if this were a joyful family reunion or something—a hug before demanding $500,000 from me. Good grief. What woman would ever carry that kind of cash in her purse? Certainly not me. I had no intention of giving him any money—not a dime!

"He threw a fit, a raging fit, and grabbed me by the arm and was about to shove me into his nasty truck when this wonderful young woman drove up, skidded and screeched, and leaped from her car looking a little crazed. I kicked one of my shoes toward her during my struggle. I think she drew blood with her first blow to his back. Yes. Look over there. He's bleeding. Anyway, enough about that. We got him and you found Lindsey alive. That's all that matters right now."

My mother's story created a new dizziness for my brain to cope with, but there was more work to be done. While Lad attended to the law enforcement matters, I decided to have a little chat with Miss Aggy. Parts of her story did not add up.

"So, you stated that you were pretty sure where he was going, and just how did you get that information?"

"I couldn't really send that 'instant message' he wanted me to send, and he wasn't going to get a reply so . . ." She hesitated to tell the rest of her story. I convinced her to go on.

"After he left the post office on Saturday I opened his message, a ransom note really, demanding $500,000 for the safe return of you. Yes, you. He wanted your mother to bring the money to the old Cook Out Inn on either Monday or Tuesday at noon or she'd never see you again.

"I knew she would never get his message so I wrote a reply as if it had come from her. *I'll be there Monday. I will have the money. You'd better have Jake with you.* Of course, his 'mommy with the money' was not going to show up. I was."

"I'm going to pretend I didn't hear any of that."

"Gotcha. Good plan. I will pretend I didn't do any of that."

"But then she *did* show up. Well, I didn't know who she was, but it seemed like she was following that gray truck, too. And she was ahead of me."

"Thank you, Aggy. I owe you a lot. But one other thing doesn't make sense to me. If you knew where the drop was to take place, how did you lose him?"

"Yeah. I may have wiggled the truth around just a bit. I didn't actually lose him. Obviously, he hadn't kidnapped you, but I told myself that he must have kidnapped someone. So, it made sense to me that he'd retrieve his prisoner on his way to collect the money. You know, for the exchange. So, I parked, watched and waited knowing I'd have backup by the time it all went down. Since we had over thirty minutes before the drop was to occur, I kind of slipped into the café for a milkshake. They make the best ones ever! I think you know the rest."

"Interesting. I need the whole truth, nothing but the truth, Miss Aggy. There are still a few inconsistencies in your story."

Using the often-used questioning strategy of repetition, I interjected a few of my questions multiple times throughout the conversation. My goal: To confirm Aggy's original statements and hope that new details would arise.

"Right. Okay, just for the sake of clarification, I was involved in two separate stakeouts today. One at the post office, the other almost on the boundary line of the Rocky Mountain National Park and The Conference Center. Let me back up. I had Monday off, 'cause I worked Saturday. I told you that, didn't I? So, I went in early with the 'reply' I had created, gave it to my co-worker, informed her that the guy whose name was on the envelope would be stopping in this morning to pick it up. I thought I told you that, too. Anyway, you're going to like this part: I also let her know that it was a personal message, not official post office business. See? No federal mail tampering charges will come up."

"Well, that's debatable."

Something about her story still nagged at me. Not that I suspected any wrong doing on her part, but something was off. Then it hit me. Her timeline.

"Miss Aggy? You want to know my theory about your involvement?" A shoulder shrug was her only response. "I think you were already on your milkshake stakeout by the time you made that second call to me pretending you were still following him as he headed out of town."

"Everything happened so fast, Jake. I could be a little confused about some of the details."

She was good. I'd give her that. I continued with my reasoning. "And, though you did want substantial backup, it was your intention to arrive first and apprehend the kidnapping suspect all by yourself."

"Okay. You got me there. But I was prepared. I had my pepper spray . . ." *What's with these women and their pepper spray?* " . . . some rope, a few plastic zip-tie restraints and a baseball bat. Now I think I'll add a couple of spiked heels to my self-defense bag."

"Agent Donovan? I think our perp needs medical attention. That hole in his back won't stop bleeding." It was good to see the locals finally giving Lad the respect he deserved.

We caravanned to the medical center to be with Lindsey and to patch up Al's wound so he could be properly questioned. And, yes, I'd check myself back in . . . eventually. Now that the numerous adrenaline rushes I'd experienced since heading out to find Lindsey had leveled off, my own aches and pains were my new worst enemy. I was forced to admit that I needed to lie down, and soon.

Will wonders never cease? There in the waiting area of the emergency room, I found my mother—the wealthy socialite who rarely lifted a well-manicured finger, but who had recently become a crime investigator/Agent Carter/an angry mother bear all wrapped into one—holding hands with my father.

After a quick hello, a guy wearing navy blue scrubs set me down and wheeled me back to my room. I didn't object, but asked if we could swing by to see Lindsey. He agreed to do that but a doctor was with her conducting an initial evaluation so I couldn't actually go in. Wendell, however, was lying on the floor just a few feet from her bed. Out-ranked by the dog. Oh, well, I'd check back in a while. At least I was no longer considered a hospital runaway.

SIXTY-FIVE

Lad

Alvin's physical injury, a deep puncture wound caused by the sharp heel of a stiletto at the hand of our over-zealous, wanna-be cop friend, was cleaned up, stitched up within an hour. Now, one of the local deputies, a regional detective, and I stood outside the small interrogation room observing Alvin through the window before going in.

"We'll take it from here, Agent Donovan. We'll keep you informed, if you'd like."

The detective wanted this one. That was obvious. Alvin's arrest, investigation, and probable conviction contained all the ingredients he needed for a promotion and also a future political bid. Ambition beyond law enforcement; it wasn't that uncommon.

Quickly, before any other egos jumped into the fray, I reminded them that our kidnapped victim had been held captive on federal lands.

"The shack's location is within the Rocky Mountain National Park. That alone gives us feds jurisdiction. But please do stay. I welcome your input. There is a great deal of crossover in this multifaceted case. Shall we begin?

"State your full name, please." Thought I'd ask him an easy question first.

"Alvin Lee." His expression vacillated between blank and smug.

"I don't think so. Try again."

The guy would not speak except for a few incorrect, almost taunting, nonsensical words.

"Where is home? Where do you live?"

"Nowhere. Somewhere. In a desert web."

We were all 'nowhere' at this point. Glancing at my colleagues, they subtly shrugged their shoulders. I'd ask one more question and then we'd call it a night.

"Al, you are obviously a smart guy. You pulled off a complex and nearly successful kidnapping. Did you have help?"

That flipped his talking switch ON. Once he began to tell his story, there was no stopping him. I pressed RECORD and away we went.

"I did the kidnapping all by myself. That was my own brilliant idea. No help from him at all. I didn't even tell him about it."

"Why didn't you tell him?" I asked, hoping to keep Al talking about a possible accomplice.

"I'd had it with him. No more, no way. That high and mighty doctor, kept me busy doing his dirty work. He paid me just enough to survive, and he promised to find my mother for me. But he lied, and just told me to go look on the Internet."

"Yeah, I hate that kind of guy. What did you say his name was?"

"Anthony. Dr. Anthony."

It was all I could do to disguise my own surprise. My wheels were supercharged now. That name always sent a chill up my spine.

"Oh, yeah. That's right. So he's a real jerk, huh?"

"Yep. His true colors began to show after that guy died—that was shocking enough—but he got even weirder after he went to jail."

Feeling a few shockwaves of my own, I wondered if his Anthony was our Dr. Anthony Sommerfield. Could Al's connection, his accomplice, be Lindsey's former husband and my estranged fraternal twin? The same man that faked his own funeral and tried to kill Jake, Lindsey, and Julie last year? The same man that was soon to be paroled from prison?

Though exhausted and needing sleep, I kept going. As long as Al kept talking, we'd keep asking questions and listening to his replies . . . even if it took all night.

It took almost all night.

Al was a strange one. One minute he was giddy about his accomplishments and the next, gloomy about his failures. All of which were illegal. However, he seemed to find some therapeutic relief by telling his pathetic story. Neither myself nor the two deputies present could recall an interrogation such as this. So many crimes had occurred at the hands of the Anthony-Alvin partnership, ranging from mail fraud to murder and everything in between.

"How did you meet Anthony?"

"I made one of those 'will work for food' signs. He stopped and asked me to hop in his car. So I did."

"What kind of work did you do for him?"

"Easy stuff. Piece of cake stuff, at first. I just followed Lindsey around and reported back to the bone doctor what she was doing and who she was doing it with."

Now there was not a shred of doubt in my mind that *our* Anthony was Al's employer. Al told us about following one of Lindsey's boyfriends around and how that man ended up dead. He'd helped Anthony move the body. After listening to a few more details about that phase of Al's work, I needed to excuse myself for a brief moment. A critical phone call had to be made.

"Sorry, man. I know it's the middle of the night but this could not wait. You can't let Dr. Anthony Sommerfield out of prison. Put a hold on the parole hearing. Find a way to stall. I've got proof he's involved in a homicide, maybe even first-degree murder . . . No, this is not the attempted murder of Jake, Julie, and Lindsey last year that we all know occurred but haven't been able to prove yet . . . This is something else and I've got an eyewitness. More later . . . Thanks."

Al admitted that he loved the thrill of traveling on the dark side of the road. That these odd jobs made him feel like he was a guy in an exciting, thriller-type movie. And it was still easy money.

"Some of your work for Anthony sounds fascinating. When did you stop enjoying your work?"

"Anthony changed that summer after breaking up with his girlfriend, Shawna, and started plotting his fake funeral. I was still okay with most of that. I made some arrangements for him, mailed some mail, and eventually did a little damage to Jake's motor home."

"Seems like you are a man of many talents." I wanted to encourage him to keep talking so I repeated part of my question. "And what made you stop enjoying your work?"

"I didn't like hiding that stupid piggy bank, but I think it really began with those sick love letters. That just wasn't right. I didn't want any part of that. Besides, it was getting harder and harder to keep my spiders happy and healthy with all the travel involved."

Love letters? I hadn't heard about those. I'd ask Jake later. *Spiders?* Ah, yes. The jars back at the shack. Eventually there would be many more interviews, questions, interrogations before this complex web of events was completely understood.

"I got really good at searching on the Internet. And when some information popped up on the Adoptee Internet Search site I had registered with, I didn't need Anthony any more. I'd quit being his damn puppet, just as soon as I earned my bonus."

"A bonus? For doing what?"

"Gettin' Lindsey to leave Jake. I really thought stealing the bird would do the trick, but it kind of backfired. The park entrance fee took the last bit of my cash, too."

Al went on and on, telling one unbelievable tale after another.

"How long have you known about the possible family tie to Jake?"

"Not sure. Less than two weeks, when I was trying to find my real mother. I found her and did some research to learn more about her. Then the voices told me to be looking for the Lees."

My mind was blown for the second, no, third—actually, I'd lost count—time in the past few hours. Al said that he knew that Anthony's Lindsey was the woman with Jake, but he didn't know that Jake was his biological mother's son, his half-brother.

He took great pride in explaining the kidnapping and how clever he was at modifying his plan as problems arose.

Our perpetrator was getting tired. Well, we all were. But his thoughts, his facts, took a turn toward fantasy and his speech slowed. Yes. We needed to wrap it up soon. Get a fresh start tomorrow.

I was surprised, even disturbed, by Al's total lack of remorse; he didn't seem to think anything he had done was wrong. We were all pushing our chairs back getting ready to stand when Al grabbed his own head, exhibiting symptoms of pain, but began to speak again. He sounded different, stranger than before. Almost otherworldly. And his bizarre, one-man-show unfolded before us . . .

Just when I thought his psychodrama was coming to a close, it morphed into a rhyme.

"Wish upon a star, Spiders in the jar.

Body's in the box, Deep beneath the rocks."

We stared in disbelief. The guy's a poet? An evil, insane poet? He and Edgar Allan Poe would've made quite a pair.

"Make my day with overtime pay.

Pay me now and pay me later.

Tick tock . . ."

"We're done. Get him out of here."

Everyone present was exhausted when I hit STOP for the final time. Alvin was escorted to a holding cell until he could be transported to an appropriate facility that included mental health evaluations, treatment, and armed guards. Without a doubt, Alvin was a disturbed and dangerous man. He'd most likely be going to Denver in a day or two. By then we'd have a transcript of his statements including his confession of the attempted murder on the highway as well as the kidnapping.

SIXTY-SIX

Jake

With Lindsey safe in a room just down the hall, I was able to get a good night's sleep and was no longer in such a hurry to leave this place. In fact, now I wanted to stick around. Shortly after breakfast, my room filled up with visitors: Lad, Julie, Edward and Evelyn. I could tell by Lad's expression that this was not a social visit. It was business, serious business.

"Before I play a few minutes of this initial interrogation tape, I'd like you to know that the tape contains many hours of Q and A with our suspect, Alvin. I shouldn't be letting any of you hear the contents of this tape, but there is one portion that I feel you need to be aware of."

"Shouldn't Lindsey hear it, too?" I asked.

My mother, who'd been quiet so far this morning, entered the conversation. "She's been through so much, Jake, and she not only has physical injuries, she must also have emotional, psychological injuries. We should spare her from any additional trauma right now."

Amazing! My mother was acting motherly.

"She's right, Jake. Besides, I have a hunch that Lindsey has already experienced, up close and personal, the likes of what is on this tape."

An ominous serving of trepidation with a side of curiosity lodged in my throat just before Lad pressed PLAY and we listened.

"He don't look so good."

"Yeah, well, he's dead."

"You killed him?"

"He fought me. I was just defending myself."

"So what now?"

"You still got connections to that funeral home you used to work at?"

"Nope. The owners won't give me the time of day. Kind of burned my bridges there."

"Build them back up."

"I don't know about that."

"You're an accomplice to a homicide. I strongly suggest you put forth a little more effort."

"Well, I know one guy that's probably still working there, but all he knows how to do is burn the bodies."

"That's all we need. Let's go find him."

Lad stopped the tape there. This morning's creepy entertainment was over. We were all stunned and confused.

I had to ask the obvious question. "Who else was there, Lad? Who's the other guy talking with Al?"

"The conversation you just heard was all Al, one hundred percent. Several times during the interrogation he took on different voices. He reenacted complete scenes from his life and he played all the parts."

I'd never seen so many jaws drop at the same time. Just hearing this small slice of the recording was difficult to comprehend; I couldn't imagine deciphering hour upon hour of such strangely delivered information.

The delivery alone was strange enough, but then I got to thinking about the content. If there was any truth to Al's statement, his odd ranting, then someone died. Who? And who did the killing? I had to ask and hoped that Lad felt at liberty to answer.

He hesitated, but then complied. "That was a reenactment of a past conversation between Al and . . . Dr. Anthony Sommerfield." Some brows furrowed, others rose, but everyone gasped. "The dead guy was none other than Emmett, Lindsey's first boyfriend after Anthony divorced her. You know, the guy that conned her out of $8,000?" We were shocked into a stupefying silence, and I wondered how Lindsey would react when she heard this horrifying news.

That pretty much wrapped up Lad's sharing of information for today, but talking among us continued. Everyone in the room suspected that Alvin had serious emotional and abandonment issues, even autism came up in the conversation. Julie mentioned the possibility of a brain tumor after Lad had updated her about the man's headaches. This brought tears to my mother's eyes. This woman of steel actually cried in the presence of us all.

Dabbing at her eyes and then her nose, she spoke through the sobs. "I am responsible for Al's problems and for the trauma he inflicted upon Jake and Lindsey. Oh, hell. I'm responsible for a lot more than that." My father, Edward, put his arm around her shoulders and gave a small squeeze of support.

A distorted vision of this entire group skipping down a yellow brick road came to mind. Yes, I knew that was silly, even inappropriate; so much worry, lack of sleep, and my pain medication might have played a role there. Nevertheless, Julie was the kind girl who just wanted to go home to Kansas; Lad was the lion looking for courage; I was the scarecrow in desperate need of a brain; and mother . . . she was the tin man hoping for a heart. Some of that made sense, but where did Edward fit into my imaginative vision? Perhaps he was the man behind the curtain. All I knew for sure was that my mother, finally, had a caring, beating heart.

SIXTY-SEVEN

Jake

Once Lindsey and I were released from the medical center, we rented a cabin at the Rusty Roof Ranch for a few days, and tried to unwind from our ordeal, our separation, our fearful days and nights. The owner was a kind, understanding man and had made an exception to his usual No Dogs Allowed rule. Wendell, however, wasn't quite his old self yet, and, in addition to a slight limp and slow movement, he'd taken on a new, unique behavior. Whenever he saw a bird, he barked, and there were dozens of birds around. Fortunately, it was not a loud, disturbing bark. It was more like a sad woof. Poor guy. He'd been through a lot, too.

Lindsey didn't say much. For now she seemed content just to walk slowly with Wendell and me around the guest ranch; her feet were still sore with bruises from her barefooted dash through the forest. Her favorite activity was to stand near the horses, and to pet them. She told me that being near them calmed her.

We decided to have a family and friends gathering before everyone departed and went on with their lives. The owner of the ranch gifted the use of one of the private dining areas. Julie made all the other arrangements; my only job was to invite the guests.

The guest list wasn't long but everyone on it had played a significant role in our lives, especially here in Estes Park. There was Lad and Julie, Edward and Evelyn, and Lindsey and me, of course. Aggy, Bethany, Gabby and Brady were invited, too. No celebration would be complete without our lovable pets, Wendell and Mal . . . I couldn't get used to the fact that he was gone. I told myself that he was just a bird . . . but he wasn't just a bird. He was unbelievably special. So was the relationship between him and the dog.

"Jake, what's wrong?" Lindsey knew me well, and I had to admit that I wasn't quite my usual self, either. Pretty sure none of us were.

"I'm okay. Just some stuff bouncing around in my head that I don't want to think about right now."

"Yes. I know the feeling. There will likely be a lot of that for a while."

I breathed in deeply and let out a long, slow sigh. "It's almost like our own tiny versions of PTSD without the guns or any shooting."

"There was a gun; there was shooting."

"Oh. That's right. Al, the squirrel killer."

"No, it was Alvin the chipmunk killer. There is a difference."

In spite of all we'd been through, Lindsey and I were still in tune with each other. Our thoughts quickly shifted to those old, silly songs sung by . . . chipmunks. Lindsey smiled for the first time since her rescue. Her smile was filled with mischief; pretty sure mine was, too.

She spoke the word using little volume but firm emphasis. "A L V I N!"

I replied using my best chipmunk impression, "OKAY!"

At least we hadn't lost our sense of humor, though seconds after our little chipmunk chuckle it no longer seemed funny.

With Lindsey at my side, I introduced Bethany to the others. Next, we'd make the rounds with Aggy. But I wanted Lindsey to be the first one to meet our unofficial, assistant detective. Aggy extended her hand toward Lindsey and said, "I'm so pleased to meet you Lindsey and I'm glad . . . things turned out okay."

"It's a pleasure to meet you, Aggy."

A smirky, mischievous look spread across her face and I wondered what that was all about. "Oh. Actually, it's Agatha. Agatha Grafton."

Eyebrows rose up as Lindsey and I exchanged looks of surprise. Then, lips turned up as knowing smiles spread across all three of our faces.

Lindsey, curious and inquisitive once again, asked, "Any famous relatives in your family?"

"No, I just read a lot. So did my mom." Did I detect a wink with her answer?

There was definitely one with my reply. "The name suits you."

"It sure does!" Lindsey and Aggy, arm in arm, headed toward the table filled with pre-dinner snacks. I would have followed but a nearby conversation demanded my attention.

I wasn't eavesdropping, not really, though I could have walked away. My parents just happened to be standing close enough for me to hear their words.

"My dear, Evelyn. I was a successful cattle and oil entrepreneur when I met you. I didn't rise to success by being naïve or gullible or out of touch with reality. I knew about your past, your child, your lies. I knew exactly who you were, but I loved you so deeply right from the start that I wanted you to be my wife regardless. I kept watch over the cattle, the oil, and you. Since those early days, with you by my side, I've been upgraded to cattle baron and oil tycoon. We've done all right, kid."

"Oh, Edward. At first I just wanted the lifestyle, your lifestyle, but after a few years, I wanted you. I fell in love for the first time in my life, which made the stakes even higher, the secret more imperative, and its discovery more damaging. I thought I'd lose you if you found out. Can you ever forgive me?"

"Already did, a long time ago. And, if you want, we'll find a way to get your long lost, biological son some help, my dear. It's up to you."

Unbelievable! I found the conversation both shocking and heartwarming. All these years the tension that filled the house, the eggshells we walked on so carefully, existed and lingered because of one untimely pregnancy, a secret baby, an adoption, and then the lies, or rather, the lack of truth.

Tonight, right here at the ranch in Estes Park, turned out to be far more than the celebration of lives saved and a mystery solved. Looking at Lad and Julie, I sensed they'd grown closer as a couple, a couple that now realized how precious life and time together truly was. I hardly recognized my own parents who'd been holding hands most of the evening and gazing into each other's eyes. Years of tension melted away. I guess the truth does set you free.

I learned from Lindsey that Aggy—I mean, Agatha, though certainly not lacking in confidence or personality, was short on family. Her mother disappeared when she was seventeen years old. Apparently, that mystery went unsolved. Our minstrel friend, Bethany, was on her own, too. Her mother was still living, but they rarely communicated and hadn't seen each other since she'd left home four years ago.

Ever since Lindsey's discharge from the medical center, I was at her side, day and night. This evening was no exception. I could see the tears welling up in her beautiful eyes as well as her effort to keep them from spilling out. *What frightening aspect of her ordeal is flashing through her mind?* She needed time to heal. I'd hoped time really did heal all wounds because we certainly had our share of them. *There I go again! What's with all the clichés tonight? I've really got to stop that.*

"Jake, even though we lost one family member, we gained two."

"Who did we lose?"

"Malcolm." I squeezed her hand as my eyes stung with tears and my throat ached as I attempted to suppress the uncomfortable, sad feelings.

"And we gained . . . ?"

Bethany and Agatha. I like them and they fit right in. This dinner feels like a gathering of family. A family affair. Let's keep in contact with them, okay?"

HOMEWARD BOUND:

TAKE TWO

SIXTY-EIGHT

Jake

Lindsey sat by the window; I had the aisle so I could keep tabs on Wendell. Securing authorization and then making the arrangements for Wendell to fly in the cabin with us was no small feat. Numerous airlines had turned down my request before I finally got the 'yes' that we needed.

I'd purchased a whole row of seats—that helped get the 'yes'—two on the left and three on the right side of the plane. The dog started off on the floor in front of the three seats but once we were in the air, I pushed up the armrests, laid down one of our own blankets, and before long he ended up stretched out, sleeping comfortably on the cushions. What's that old saying? It's easier to beg for forgiveness than to ask for permission. Would they land the plane to kick off a sleeping dog that had paid for three seats? I think not.

With no mysteries to solve and no teachers to teach, we sat in silence, holding hands as the plane flew in the direction of home. Going home never sounded so good.

That is why Lindsey's statement about needing a vacation caught me off guard.

"Don't you want to stay home for a while?"

"Oh, I didn't mean right away, but definitely before we take on any more jobs."

"I guess that makes sense. How about an Alaskan cruise? That might be fun . . . and relaxing."

"What about Wendell? They don't allow dogs on cruises unless they are part of the entertainment." She must have detected my spinning wheels and was quick to add, "No way, Jake. Wendell will not be a show dog."

"Okay. Then we will charter our own boat. A boat with a crew. I just happen to know a guy who knows about things like that."

"Does he also know about smooth-riding boats and calm bodies of water?"

Most of the time I get accused of thinking too much. Today I wasn't thinking enough.

"Oh, Lindsey, baby. I am so sorry. I forgot, but only for a moment, how waves affect you."

"Jake, because of you and your love, I think I'm over the fear and sadness I'd felt for so many years whenever I found myself near rough, choppy water; water that reminded me of my parents' deaths. I am more concerned about feeling seasick."

There was that look. That coy, Lindsey look. Sometimes, I was clueless. This was another one of those times.

"Could you ask the flight attendant if she has any crackers, please?"

"Should I ask her to heat up some soup to go with those crackers?" I thought I was being cute, clever, even funny. Her serious eye-rolling told me I was none of the above.

"I'll be right back . . . with crackers."

I returned quickly with two bags of peanuts. That should curb her appetite till we landed in Tucson, but Lindsey's face displayed a look I'd have to describe as panicked with a side of anger. For her to get weird about a snack was highly uncharacteristic.

"Peanuts are way tastier than—" I felt a tapping on my arm. A woman sitting in the row right behind us motioned for me to bend down and then whispered in my ear. Now, even without a mirror, I knew my face had donned its own panicked look as I ventured down the aisle again.

"Crackers. I need some crackers. Does anyone have a package of crackers? I really, really need them . . . now!"

Wow! To my surprise dozens of women produced packages of crackers from their purses, their pockets, their carry-on bags. Since when did cracker hoarding become such a common activity?

"Thank you," was all I could say as I raced back up the aisle to Lindsey's side with a bit more knowledge and a treasure trove of crackers. "So, you're . . . so *we're* going to have a baby? "

"I think so. Give. Me. A. Cracker. NOW!"

The crackers did the trick, worked their magic; Lindsey's stomach settled down and so did she. During most of the flight we held hands and simply relaxed. Wendell had adjusted well to his comfortable seat and the friendly skies. I'd reach across the aisle to pat his head and rub his ears now and then, though he received plenty of attention from every passenger that walked past him on their way to the lavatory. Not surprising. Wendell was an irresistible dog.

The captain announced that we'd begun our descent into Tucson; we'd land in about twenty-five minutes.

"Jake, do you think we should name our baby after someone we know?"

I ran the list of names in my head: Edward, Evelyn, Laura, Lad, Julie, Shawna, Sean . . . and knew my answer to her question. "No! No way. He needs a name of his own."

"I don't agree."

"What? Our baby doesn't need of name of his own? How can you say that?"

"I think that *she* needs a name of *her* own."

As delighted as I was to see Lindsey taking another step away from our recent horrific problems—I stuck to my guns regarding baby names. My mind was on a baby boy.

"How about the name Malcolm?"

"I'd love to give him that honor, but I think it would make me feel too sad every time I spoke the name."

"Then, what about Martin or Miles or Matt?"

"Hmm." Lindsey gave this more thought than I'd expected. "No. No. And maybe . . . So we're sticking with names that begin with the letter M?"

"I think we are. A subtle way to honor our dear departed bird."

"I'm good with that. So, how about Mallory? Or Mindy? Or Melissa?"

We laughed and toasted to our growing family, tapping (plastic does not clink) our champagne glasses that were filled to the brim with sparkling water. The flight attendant allowed a few more sips before hurrying away with our glasses, and we prepared for the landing.

Lindsey and I moved over to be near Wendell, got him to sit up in the middle seat, and we buckled ourselves in on either side of him. This was his first flight and, to be honest, we had no idea how he'd react to the landing. We wanted to comfort him during the sudden bump that would surely come when the plane made contact with the ground, and to keep his big, unbelted body from being flung forward into the wall in front of him when the braking portion of the landing process began. As usual, he took this new experience in stride. What a champ.

Almost home. We waited in our seats while everyone else collected their carry-on bags and headed toward the door. Wendell received dozens of good-bye pats on his head. Lindsey nibbled another cracker, and I tended to my new cell phone, taking it off airplane mode. The very second I tapped that setting, the phone began to ring.

"Hi, Jake. It's me, Bethany. Hey, I think I found your bird."

EPILOGUE

Lindsey

After an in-depth conversation with Bethany Michaels, we learned that she had returned to the crash site because she felt compelled to compose a song, a poem, something to memorialize the tragic event and hoped she'd find her muse there. Instead, she found Malcolm who had apparently remained near the RV, more aptly termed a crumpled mass of metal, which still had not yet been removed. She said he'd hopped onto her hand without the slightest hesitation, so she took him home with her. She attached a few photos to an email soon after our conversation—it was definitely Malcolm—and she agreed to keep him until we arranged for his pick-up. Neither Jake nor I was ready to return to the area. As much as we wanted to bring the bird home right away, the dreadful memories were still too raw, too painful. We vowed to have him with us before Christmas, and we looked forward to the new words and new tunes he'd bring with him.

As we suspected, Ms. Jillstrom lost her license. The license she never really had. The school district, though deeply involved in the investigation, decided not to press charges. As it turned out, they didn't need to. The state had enough evidence to assure that the woman would never be in a classroom with students again—even if she managed to finagle a real teaching certificate. She was charged with unlawful possession and use of a grenade, though. Hopefully, Ms. Jillstrom had learned her lesson, though Jake and I doubted that her odd personality—the root of all her evil—would ever change.

Marlow Mahoney and Robert Bentley were out on administrative leave while their district's legal department sorted through all of the evidence and accusations. With the convenience of the Internet and his knowledge of the legal system, Jake kept abreast of the list of alleged crimes—embezzlement, misappropriation of funds, unprofessional conduct—and reported to me that the list was lengthening.

Jan Rubio, the Director of Elementary Education in Albuquerque kept in touch by email; she proudly mentioned that she'd begun taking a night class called *Overwhelmed by Technology?* Most of her news was good. She and her job were both doing fine. It would take a while to build up and strengthen her teaching staff but everything was moving in the right direction, now that no one was blocking her way or orchestrating her demise. We loved that every communication from her contained a heartfelt thank you followed by <3.

Alvin was indicted for kidnapping, attempted murder, and vandalism, with more charges pending. His tenuous mental condition would be deeply investigated during his incarceration. Julie, being his half-sister as well as a psychiatrist, kept tabs on that. She located his adoptive parents and kept them abreast of Alvin's mental and legal issues. They were glad to know that he was alive—they hadn't heard from him in almost two years—but had no desire to communicate directly with him. Evelyn, with Edward's constant support and assistance, kept her eyes on every aspect of Al's psychological needs, too, as well as his lengthy legal journey. Only time would tell how all of that might play out.

And then there was Anthony, my troubled ex-husband. Due to Al's kidnapping failure, Anthony's deeds had been discovered, which in turn foiled the last chapter of his own scheme. Apparently, the main purpose of Al's most recent assignments from Anthony was to fill me with hate for Jake. To expose him as an incompetent husband and protector, and to make me think that he was fooling around with another woman—thus, the love letters. That way when Anthony was paroled, he could step right back into my life and be my husband, my hero once again. *Oh, what a wicked web we weave when ...*

Anthony would be transported back to Tucson any day now, where he would stand trial for the murder of Emmett as well as other charges related to his mastermind role in Al's criminal activity. We understood there could be years of additional investigations and trials and, at times, we'd be called on to testify.

Poor Emmett. Though a lying, conniving conman, he didn't deserve death, a little jail time maybe, but not death. Jake arranged to have his ashes moved from Anthony's fake gravesite and a new grave marker made. We never did find his family or were sure of his real name. We used the only name we knew: Emmett Anton.

333

Julie cautiously shared some of the facts surrounding the deeds of Al and Anthony with her client, Sean, but not all of them. Due to his relationship with Anthony and his visits to the prison, authorities would eventually question him, too. Perhaps additional information would be unveiled that could shed even more light on this whole bizarre, twisted series of events. Also, Sean would soon receive several apologies from those of us, especially Jake, who had accused him of co-conspiracy. We thought he was Anthony's partner in crime. No one knew of Al's existence back then.

Jake and Lad connected on FaceTime often, helping authorities sort out all that had transpired beginning with the day Anthony had hired Al a couple of years ago all the way through to Al's apprehension and arrest.

Jake rekindled his interest in writing, but came to the conclusion that fiction wasn't his thing. Reality suited him much better. His first project? A short, non-fiction story for *Real Crimes* magazine.

And me? I was content living in the moment, experiencing pregnancy, and learning about childbirth and infant care. Jake and I began to search for a new, larger house; one with space for an office for Jake, an office for me, a backyard with shade for Wendell and Malcolm, and of course, a nursery for our baby.

Right now I had no desire to engage in any work that required traveling beyond the city limits of Tucson, Arizona, our hometown. I thought I might try writing a few children's books or a book of my songs and poems. Lad's mother, Elisabeth, always welcomed new additions to my Art Journaling Teachers' Guide that she'd published last year. So I had options.

Our first road trip was over, but it would never be forgotten.

Cricket Rohman earned her MA in Literature and Philosophy from California State University. She authored picture books and big book songbooks used by teachers before making the longed-for leap to writing adult fiction. She finds inspiration and joy splitting her time between the Arizona desert and the Colorado mountains. *Hit The Road, Jake!* is Book 3 in The Lindsey Lark series.

Cricket loves to hear from readers; connect with her online.

Email: cricketrohman@gmail.com

Website: www.cricketrohman.org

Facebook: https://www.facebook.com/CricketRohman Author/

Dear Readers:

One last thing . . .

I am honored that you took the time to read my novel, ***Hit the Road, Jake!*** Book 3 in The Lindsey Lark Series. Thank you. The main characters, Jake and Lindsey, live in my head every day as I contemplate their future adventures. The dog, Wendell, is not only in my head, he's in my heart. And I must admit that I had a dog just like him years ago.

If you enjoyed this book, I would be forever grateful if you would post a review on your favorite bookseller site, Goodreads, or your own blog. And, I'd love it if you'd drop by my Facebook author page, click on the red tab "Read My Book" and join my email list. It's true. I really do love to hear from readers.

In case you missed them . . .

Book 1 *Wanted: An Honest Man*

Book 2 *Letters, Lovers, & Lies*

Brief descriptions are located on the following pages.

All my best,

Cricket Rohman

WANTED: AN HONEST MAN
Book 1 in The Lindsey Lark Series

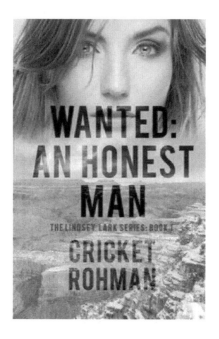

With a little mystery, a little romance, and shocking twists and turns, WANTED: AN HONEST MAN captures the bittersweet growth of a young woman trying to make sense of her turbulent life.

Lindsey Lark, a beautiful, talented teacher is a fighter and a positive thinker, but after the man of her dreams betrays her, then steals her beloved dog, she struggles, and is not yet aware there is far more to her heartbreaking situation than meets the eye.

Strange, threatening phone calls begin to haunt her. A stalker, perhaps? Though she doesn't want to be alone, she isn't ready to go looking for new love, but men find her anyway.

A handsome college student involved in some tricky human research gets into trouble in more ways than one. His inherent propensity to play detective, though helpful at times, seems to attract Murphy and his darned Law far too often ... and now his eyes are on Lindsey. Will his heart follow?

"Charming ... unexpected ... emotionally charged!"
--Amylynn Bright, author of Finish What We Started

"Ms. Rohman's entertaining novel, WANTED: AN HONEST MAN, has all the hallmarks of a bestseller including a cast of inspired characters that bring real world authenticity to her tale."
--BookViral

Buy now: https://amzn.com/B01FG5R2P4

LETTERS, LOVERS, & LIES
Book 2 in The Lindsey Lark Series

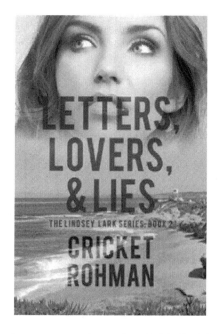

Mysterious, romantic, and sprinkled with a few
heartwarming students and a delightful dog, LETTERS,
LOVERS, & LIES captures the importance of persistence
and the power of love.

Lindsey Lark, keynote speaker, goes on tour while her boyfriend, Jake, writes a detective novel. Sounds simple enough, but a mystery soon dominates their lives when bizarre notices of her ex-husband's funeral arrive. Foul play is suspected and murder is on someone's mind.

Lad, a retired Secret Service agent, is Lindsey's right-hand man for the duration of the tour. He's handsome, he's a man of few words, and, as the list of threats lengthens, he takes on the role of bodyguard, much to Jake's dismay.

Jake and Lindsey are in love, but so much stands in their way. Letters from a dead man. Unwanted advances from a transgender acquaintance. Separation and jealousy. A few things in the couple's favor? They are smart, multi-talented, and they love to laugh.

"Cozy mystery lovers and romantic drama buffs will enjoy the twists and turns as Jake and Lindsey rush to solve their personal whodunit before it's too late."
---John Reinhard Dizon, author of The Nightcrawler Series

Buy now: https://amzn.com/B01FIE9BZC

69556564R00195

Made in the USA
San Bernardino, CA
17 February 2018